NOT

DEAD

Other Titles by Award-Winning Author Anita Dickason

Au79

"I wasn't quite ready for the dizzying speed when the storyline took off and the action didn't stop. I loved it!" *Amazon top 500 Reviewer*

"Riveting action thriller. Terrific dialogue, amazing intrigue and intense action keep you turning pages." *Readers' Favorite*

GOING GONE!

"Excels at ratcheting up the tension and developing well-nuanced characters." *Book Viral*

"If you like action-thrillers, this one has murders, covert agents at risk, car chases, explosions, ex-special forces good and bad guys, paramilitary action, gun battles, etc." *Amazon top 500 Reviewer*

SENTINELS of the NIGHT

"Will have serial killer mystery fans and paranormal urban fantasy junkies alike getting excited over a new series which has something for just about everyone. A compelling debut novel." *Readers' Favorite*

"A riveting high stake read—*Sentinels of the Night* proves an edgy and notable debut for Dickason with the promise of more to come." *Book Viral*

www.anitadickason.com

NOT DEAD

Anita Dickason

Mystic Circle Books

Publisher: Mystic Circle Books
Cover Design: Mystic Circle Books & Designs, LLC

ISBN: 978-0-9968385-9-7: Paperback
978-1-7340821-0-4: Hardback
978-1-7340821-1-1: eBook

Library of Congress Control Number: 2019914753

Acknowledgments

To my Family:

thank you for your love

and support.

To Pat Pratt:

my heartfelt thanks.

Cast of Characters

Arnie Williams	Atlanta Detective
Ashley Logan	Mandy's Aunt & Tribune Editor
Betsy	Doll
Boomer (Leslie Hill)	Meridian Officer
Chad Bishop	Meridian Police Chief
Dale Kennedy	Meridian Detective
Doyle Neville	Bad Guy
Edith Monroe	Cousin to Nora, Thrift Shop Owner
Fran Coleman	Wife of Bait Shop Owner
Frank Evans	Atlanta Officer
Gwen Shelton	Second Chance Owner
Hattie Griffin	Resident-Mobile Home Park
Henry Smythe	Tribune Reporter
Irvin Neal	Bank President
Jim Hayden	Bosque County Sheriff
Kathy Norton	Mandy's Mother
Ken Larkin	Deputy Sheriff
Lew Walker	Bad Guy
Lydia Powell	Secretary, Meridian PD
Mandy Norton	Missing Child
Mark Johnson	Meridian Officer
Nancy Sullivan	Red Rooster Waitress
Nick Olson	Water Park Employee
Nora Graham	Owner-Thrift Store
Peggy Jenkins	Deli Owner
Peter Norton	Mandy's Father
Ray Hart	Atlanta Officer

Rick Coleman	Bait Shop Owner
River Paxton	County Canine Officer
Sgt. Anderson	Atlanta Officer
Sharon Ward	Coordinator-Explorer Troop
Susan Eberly	Kidnapped Child in Atlanta
Tania Carr	Meridian Officer
Todd Holcomb	Deputy Sheriff
Vance Griffin	Resident-Mobile Home Park
Vicky Milford	Atlanta Detective
Wendy Allen	Employee-Thrift Store

The past is written

It cannot be altered

It is the future you seek

To find the lost

A gift is given

But beware

To hear, you must listen

Chapter One

❧

In a small, musty thrift shop, a barrel-chested man meandered along a narrow aisle. Amidst the clutter of clothing, knickknacks, kitchen utensils, dishes, jewelry, and other junk piled on the tables, he searched for his bait. Tucked under his arm were two he'd already found.

Working his way to the back of the store, he rounded the end of an aisle and walked into an unexpected blast of freezing air. Startled, he stopped. While the goosebumps still lingered, the cold air was gone. With a shake of his shoulders, he chalked it up to problems with the old building and turned his attention back to the tables in front of him. Hell, nothing but baby clothes, not a single doll among them, he thought, before turning to head to the checkout counter

A flash of light on a table pushed into the corner caught his eye. Curious, he stepped toward it and spotted a small doll propped against a stack of baby clothes. How had he missed seeing it?

The doll was old, maybe too old for what he needed. The face was dirty, and the dress tattered and stained. Long pigtails hung over the doll's shoulders. About to pass it up, he changed his mind when he saw the price on the tag tied around the wrist. For twenty-five cents, he'd find a use for it.

At the front counter, he laid the dolls next to the cash register.

"Someone is in for a nice surprise," the clerk said.

The man mumbled, "Yeah, got granddaughters." The lie, one he'd used before, easily rolled off his tongue.

The clerk rang up the first two dolls, then picked up the old one. With a puzzled look, she asked, "Where did you find this one?"

"At a table in the back."

She turned it over, then fingered the price tag.

Impatient to get out of the store, he asked, "Is there a problem?"

"Uh ... no. I just don't remember this doll, or pricing one this low." With a shrug, she rang it up.

As he hurried out the door, swinging the plastic bag filled with dolls, she watched with a baffled expression. Then another customer stepped up to the register, and she forgot about the odd sale.

A few days later

His body hummed with anticipation as he gazed at the deserted street. Since he'd taken the time to study the small, residential neighborhood, he didn't expect any screwups. He knew who came and went—and when. During one of his nightly visits, he'd even timed a dry run. Before anyone noticed, he'd be long gone. Still, he played it safe and circled the block one more time before backing into the driveway of a vacant house. After opening the passenger door, he made sure his thickset body blocked the view of anyone driving by.

From a plastic bag lying on the front seat, he removed a bottle and rag. Unscrewing the cap, he ignored the sweet odor that floated in the air as he quickly doused the rag with the colorless liquid and shoved it into his jacket pocket.

After recapping the bottle, he wiped his wet hand across his thigh, then picked up a second bag. Upending it, a doll dropped onto the seat. As he reached for it, the sound of a child's laughter echoed. As he stepped back to look toward the sound, an unexpected sense of danger sparked a prickle of chills. He glanced along the street and houses. Even though he was unable to account for the odd feeling, it tugged at him. When he shifted his gaze to the girl in the backyard, he dismissed it as nothing more than his anxiety over grabbing a kid this close to home. Despite his protests, he had to admit finding her was a stroke of luck.

Her arms filled with dolls, the pink bows tied to her shoes, and nut-brown curls bounced in rhythm as she trotted across the yard.

Oblivious to the man who watched, she laid the dolls on the small table near the patio. In a high-pitched voice, she said, "Betsy, you get to sit across from me," and propped a doll on the chair. With the second one in her hands, she studied the remaining chairs, then said, "Emily, you sit here." Picking up the last one, she ran her hand over the doll's hair with a soothing motion. "Daisy, are you feeling better?" she asked before setting the doll on the chair.

Still talking, she reached into the box next to the table and grabbed a plate and cup. After placing a set in front of each doll, she said, "I'll be right back. Sarah wants her ride." Hopping out of the chair, she ran toward a tricycle where another doll sat in the small basket hooked to the handlebar.

Hell, what was he doing, just standing here? If the kid followed her normal routine, she'd only make a couple of turns in the yard. If he didn't get to the gate on the other side of the house in time, he was screwed and would have to try another day.

He reached inside the truck, grabbed the doll, and stuffed it under his coat. As he hurried along the sidewalk, he kept an eye on her. After adjusting the doll in the basket, she straddled the tricycle and began to pedal. He didn't have a choice. He ran. By the time he reached the gate, his lungs heaved, and sweat beaded on his forehead.

With the back of his hand, he pushed up the latch, then shoved the gate open. Reaching under his coat, his hand fisted around the doll's soft body. As she came around the corner of the house, he held it up. In a hushed tone, he said, "Mandy. Look at what I found."

The pedals stopped. With a wide-eyed stare, the child studied him before gazing at the doll.

"Is this pretty doll yours?" He waved it in front of him. His other hand clenched the rag inside his pocket.

Curls jiggled as she shook her head no.

"Would you like to hold her?"

Her face lit up. She slid off the tricycle. "Sarah, you wait here. I'll be right back." After a quick pat on the doll's head, Mandy took a few steps toward him, then stopped.

He shook the doll again. The long pigtails brushed his hand. "She's so lonely and needs a friend."

Her eyes narrowed in disapproval. "You let her get dirty."

"Oh, no, I didn't. Someone else did. That's why I want to give her to you. I bet you would take really good care of her."

She wasn't coming any closer. Had he made a mistake in using the old doll? Kids these days only wanted new stuff. The beads of sweat trickled down the side of his face. The time was passing; too much time. Since she'd seen him, he couldn't stop now.

As he took a step toward her, she walked up and extended her arms to reach for the doll. He dropped it and grabbed her. Before she could cry out, he slapped the rag over her mouth and nose. Mandy's hands beat against his, then slowly weakened as the drug took effect.

He stuck the rag in his pocket. With an arm wrapped around her limp body, he picked up the doll, gathered the child in his arms, and ran to his truck. When he threw her on the backseat, he realized the doll was gone.

After tossing a blanket over Mandy's body, he stepped around the front of the truck, looking back along the street. "Hell! Where is it?" he muttered. It was probably lying by the gate or in front of the house. Should he go back?

The fearful cries of a woman decided the matter. He had to leave. Even though he was irked about losing it, he wasn't overly concerned as he slid behind the wheel. After all, the damn thing only cost him a quarter. Since no one could link the doll to him, it wasn't important. Besides, he had other dolls.

The truck rolled out of the driveway, and he slowly drove away.

Chad walked into the station and greeted the woman seated behind a desk. "Lydia, it's going to be another gorgeous fall day. I sure hate to spend it inside."

His secretary scoffed. "Oh, no. You don't get to play hooky today. I've already got a stack of letters and reports for you to sign, and you have a meeting with the mayor this afternoon."

"Slave driver," he quipped. Her chuckles followed him into his office. As the new police chief in Meridian, a small community in Central Texas, Chad Bishop still hadn't adjusted to the administrative demands of the job.

Halfway through the reports, he paused when the police radio on the corner of his desk squawked. The dispatcher in the sheriff's call center sent two of his officers on a four-year-old missing person call. Chad choked. Not again, he thought, before logic took over. Even in a small town, a child could disappear. He dismissed the momentary burst of fear as nothing more than a knee jerk reaction.

With a quick tap on his speed dial, he called Mark Johnson, one of the two officers dispatched to the call.

"Chief, did you hear the call?" Mark asked when he answered.

"Yes. I'm on my way. Make sure you search every place a child can hide in the house and any outbuildings." He'd once found a toddler asleep on a chair under a dining room table. No one had thought to look there.

"Will do," Mark said and disconnected.

Grabbing a portable radio, he walked out of his office. Her brow raised in a questioning expression Lydia looked at him.

"A kid's missing."

"Who is it?" Her tone held a note of anxiety.

"The dispatcher said a Kathy Norton called."

"Oh, no, that's Mandy! How could it happen? Kathy watches her like a hawk. What can I do?"

"I'll let you know after I get there."

During the drive, he thought about the search procedures he'd need to coordinate if they didn't find the girl. Chad's department had four officers and a secretary. Meridian didn't have a high crime rate. Most incidents involved an occasional drunk, family disturbance, theft, or a car crash. If he had to conduct an extensive search, he didn't have anywhere near enough officers.

Chad pulled behind Mark's squad car. After exiting, he paused. His gaze scrutinized the street and houses. Shadows cast by large trees dappled the yards and pavement as the morning sunlight streamed through the thick limbs. The only sounds were the occasional rustling of dried leaves from a light breeze and in the distance, the rumble of a lawnmower. Most of the neighbors were probably at work, and it was a school day. That was a problem, fewer eyes to notice anything unusual.

Shifting his focus, he studied the Norton house. The single-story, brick and frame home sat on a corner lot. Chad strolled along the sidewalk, examining the house from both sides. Large windows flanked the front door. The shrubs in front were low to the ground. If the drapes were open, anyone inside could see a pedestrian or vehicle that passed. They were closed, another problem. A wrought iron fence enclosed the backyard. The gate was open.

A voice called out. "Chief Bishop."

His officer, Leslie Hill, nicknamed Boomer, stood in the open doorway. Attired in a neatly pressed uniform, not a single scratch or smudge marred his wide leather gun belt and attached accessories. Boots gleamed from a high gloss polish. Boomer had recently graduated from the regional police academy. This was his first week on the job. Chad had yet to learn how his new rookie came by his nickname.

One of Chad's changes to the department was the six-week field training program for new recruits. He'd assigned his new officer to Mark, who was the department's most experienced patrol officer.

When Boomer stepped away from the doorway, Chad could almost hear heels click as his body stiffened to attention.

"Chief, the girl's not in the house or garage. We've searched every room, closet, even under the beds."

Suppressed fervor sparked in Boomer's eyes. His voice had a slight tremble, which wasn't surprising. He'd turned twenty-one in the academy. Chad figured the kid was probably thinking—don't let me screw up. Like most officers, he'd felt the same anxiety in his rookie days on the job.

Chad asked, "Who's in the house?"

"The mother, Kathy Norton. She's talking to Mark. He's still trying to get her information. She wasn't here when we arrived. We finally found her in the woods."

In the kitchen, Mark stood next to a counter with a small notebook and pen in his hands. Seated at a table, a dark-haired woman stared at the officer. Tears trailed over her cheeks. "Mark, I can't stay here. I've *got* to go find my daughter. Don't you understand?"

At the sound of Chad's footsteps, her head turned toward him.

Hope shone in her eyes until her gaze met his, then they darkened with fear.

"I'm Chief Chad Bishop."

Choking back the tears, her hand brushed her cheeks. "Chief Bishop, we can't stay here. Mandy has to be wandering around in those woods, or on a street."

"We're going to search." He looked at Mark. "Did you get a photograph?"

"Not yet," he replied.

Kathy said, "There are several on the mantel in the family room. The one with the doll is the latest. Her father took it a few weeks ago." Her voice broke, and she paused before saying, "The doll is her favorite."

"I'll be right back." Chad nodded to both officers to follow him as he walked out of the kitchen. In the family room, he looked at Mark. "What have you found out?"

"Not a lot. After her husband left for work, she let Mandy go into the backyard to play. She thinks it was a few minutes after eight. Kathy came inside, loaded the dishwasher, then made the beds. About twenty minutes later, she came back to the kitchen, looked out the window, and didn't see Mandy. After checking the backyard, she ran into the street, then headed into the woods."

Chad stepped toward the mantel and studied Mandy's pictures. Her short brown hair was a mass of curls. Above rosy, plump cheeks, her dark eyes glinted with mischief. The slight smirk on her lips clutched at his heart.

In one of them, she cradled a doll in her arms. He removed the picture from the frame and slid it into his pocket. "Mark, did you get a clothing description?"

He flipped open his notebook. "Dark blue leggings with a matching green and blue hoodie over a white and blue t-shirt. Oh, and white tennis shoes tied with a pink bow. Height is about three foot and around thirty to thirty-five pounds."

Chad said, "You and Boomer check the woods. Let's make sure she's not there. I'll stay here."

They headed toward the front door, and Chad walked back to the kitchen.

"Ma'am, I'm taking the picture with the doll. My officers are leaving to search the woods. I want to walk through the house and backyard."

While he didn't doubt Mark had done a thorough search, Chad felt the need to reassure himself. He didn't linger in any of the rooms until he reached Mandy's bedroom.

Astonished, he stood in the doorway. Dolls were everywhere. They were lined up on shelves mounted low on the wall where small hands could reach them. One was on the desk, another on the dresser, and two were on the bed. There had to be over a dozen.

At the sight, Chad's nerves twitched, triggering deep-seated and unwanted memories. Nonsense, he told himself. Of course, a little girl would have dolls. There was no reason to be unduly concerned.

He walked into the room. Snugged against a wall, the bed was covered with a pink and white bedspread. The two dolls leaned against a stack of pillows; their arms bent upward as if to reach for something.

When he turned, a flicker of light sent him spinning back toward the source, the dolls on the bed. Their eyes glittered. His earlier reaction shifted to a sense of foreboding as he stepped toward the bed. Bent over, he studied them, then grunted with annoyance. The gleam was nothing more than a reflection of the light shining through the window.

Still irritated, he turned to walk to the closet. Inside, two storage boxes and several pairs of shoes sat on the floor. Clothes hung from tiny hangers, a frightening reminder Mandy was a small and defenseless little girl. After a quick glance over his shoulder at the dolls on the bed, he left to search the garage.

Other than one car parked inside, there wasn't anywhere a child could hide. Before walking out the door that led to the backyard, he checked inside the vehicle, even opening the trunk, just to be sure.

Outside, he paused to stare at the house next door. The neighbor's yard didn't have a fence. A child could easily get into the woods at the back of the property. If Mandy had wandered off, the only way she could get out of the yard was by the gate or through the fence. He quickly eliminated the fence as a possibility. It was in good condition. There were no holes or gaps a child could crawl through.

A small swing set was in the middle of the yard. Tiny dishes sat on a table near the back porch. After seeing the numerous dolls in Mandy's bedroom, he wasn't surprised to see more propped in the chairs around the table. With one last glance around the yard, he strode to the side of the house.

When he spotted the tricycle, with another doll sitting in the basket, he stopped. After staring at it for a few seconds, he turned his gaze to the gate that stood open. The latch was simple, lift the bar to open it.

A good investigator collected details … details that could have meaning, and then again, could be so much useless trivia.

A shout broke into his thoughts. Outside the fence, Mark and Boomer trotted toward him.

Mark said, "We checked all the way to the back where another street cuts through. She's not there."

After another glance at the gate, Chad said, "Let's go back inside."

Kathy stood in front of the kitchen window, which overlooked the backyard. When the three men entered, she turned, and her shoulders slumped. "You didn't find her." It wasn't a question.

"Do you know if the gate was open when you found Mandy gone?" Chad asked.

"Why … yes. It was."

"Are you sure?"

She nodded. "I remember I didn't have to open it when I ran to the street."

"Do you leave it open?"

"Oh, no. It should have been closed." Puzzled, she hesitated. "I checked the gate when I took Mandy's tricycle outside. We've always been so careful to make sure she couldn't get out of the backyard and wander into the street."

Chad thought for a moment, then asked, "Could Mandy open the gate?"

Kathy's body swayed, and her face turned pasty white. Chad grabbed her and eased her onto a chair. He didn't need to hear her shocked whisper to tell him the case had gone from bad to worse.

Chapter Two

~⁊~

*P*anic-stricken eyes stared at him. "No! She couldn't. Dear God, please don't let this be true."

In a heartbeat, Mandy's disappearance shifted from a child wandering off, to an abduction.

"How often does Mandy play outside?" Chad asked.

With her hands tightly clasped to stop the trembling, she said, "When the weather is nice, almost every morning. Once my husband leaves for work, we pick out the toys she wants to take outside." She stopped to take a deep breath, then added, "She has a tricycle she loves to ride. Even her dolls get to go along. There's always one in the basket."

"How long does she stay outside?"

"If I let her, she'd be out there all day. But it's usually an hour or so, two at the most."

A shout came from the front of the house. "Kathy!"

She shouted back. "In the kitchen," then jumped up.

A man rushed in. His glance took in the three officers clustered around the table before looking at his wife.

She flung herself at him, crying, "Mandy's been kidnapped. Oh, god, Peter! Someone took her."

With Kathy crushed against his chest, his face paled as he looked at the officers, before locking eyes with Chad. "What are you doing to find her?"

Chad hadn't realized he knew Kathy's husband until he walked into the room. Not long after he arrived in Meridian, he'd met Peter at a Chamber of Commerce meeting.

"Peter, we've only started our investigation and are getting information about your daughter. Have either of you seen anyone suspicious in the last few days, in a vehicle or walking?"

Peter answered, "I haven't. Kathy?"

She lifted her head. "No. What are we going to do?"

Chad answered, "We need a list of your activities for the last month. As many details as you can recall. Where have you shopped or visited? Who's been to your house … friends, relatives, repairmen?"

He explained about the Amber Alert and the search procedures he'd implement, then added, "Please don't touch anything in the backyard or the gate. I want to get pictures. What type of phone service do you have, a landline, or just cell phones?"

Peter said, "We've got both. Since I'm a realtor, I work at home a lot and need a fax machine."

"What are the numbers?" Chad jotted them down, then asked, "Do you have an answering machine with caller-ID for the landline?"

"Yes," Peter said.

"I don't want you to answer the phones unless you know the person, or until I can get a trace set up."

Kathy gasped. "The kidnapper. You think someone might …" She stopped and pressed her face against her husband's chest.

"At this point, I can't tell you what will happen, but I want to make sure we've got all the bases covered. In the meantime, let any unknown calls roll to your voice mail." Chad paused. This next topic was always difficult—the reward money. "I'll contact the county crime stoppers association. They'll put up a reward."

Peter said, "We'll add to it."

Chad laid his business card on the table. "My cell phone number is on the back. I'm available, no matter what time of day or night. As soon as I have more information, I'll be back." He tipped his head toward Mark and Boomer. "My officers will start a search of the neighborhood."

He motioned for the two men to follow him. Outside, he said, "I don't like the set routine. Dad leaves, Mandy goes outside to play. The backyard is visible to anyone driving past the house. It wouldn't take long for someone to pick up on the pattern of activity, unless this was a random drive-by, see a little girl, and grab her out of the backyard."

"I thought she'd wandered off until you brought up the gate question. Someone else opened the gate," Mark said. "Do you want me to get the information to Lydia for the Amber Alert?"

"No. I'll take care of it. Give me what you have, then string crime scene tape across the gate. I don't want anyone back there until Dale gets here."

He looked at his rookie. "Boomer, this is how it works. Mark will take one side of the street. You take the other. Knock on every door. If no one answers, note the time and address in your whip-out book. If you get a response, get their name and contact information. Ask if they've been home all morning. Find out if they saw or heard anything. I'm talking about the sound of an engine, maybe being revved or the squeal of tires. Find out if they've seen anyone or any vehicles that seemed out of place in the last few days. Write down every answer. Make sure you note the time you talked to them. Any questions?"

Boomer gulped. "Uh … no, sir."

Chad took a last look at the open gate before walking to his car. The jolt of fear he'd experienced all too often rushed over him as he slid behind the wheel. Deep in his gut, he knew it wasn't going away any time soon.

When he walked into the police station, Lydia stopped typing. Her voice tense, she asked, "Did you find her?"

"No. I'm certain she's been kidnapped."

"Oh, my god, no." Thoughts of her three grandchildren fluttered in her mind. "How are Kathy and Peter doing?"

"Barely hanging in there." He dropped the page from Mark's notebook with Mandy's description on her desk, along with the picture. "Get the Amber Alert typed up and over to dispatch. Then set up a flyer with the picture and hotline number."

"What about the reward?"

"I don't know yet. I have to call Irvin Neal at the bank, then contact Peter. Is Dale back from the wrecking yard?" Earlier, his detective had left to take pictures of the cars involved in an accident the previous day.

"He walked in a few minutes ago," she told him.

Chad nodded and turned toward the hallway. The station wasn't large. The reception area and his office were on one side of the building. Lydia Powell doubled as a receptionist and secretary. A hallway split the other half with two offices on one side and bathrooms, a breakroom, and a conference room on the other. He walked into one of the offices. Dale Kennedy was repacking a large case sitting on top of his desk.

Looking up, he said, "Hey, boss. Did you find Mandy?"

"No. I take it you know the Norton's?"

"It's a small town. I doubt there is anyone I don't know. Peter and I play golf together. I heard the call come out. What happened?"

Chad relayed the details and handed him the list of phone numbers. "Head out to the house. Fingerprint the gate and get pictures of the backyard."

Dale shook his head in disbelief. "I'll get started on setting up the taps. It won't take long. I don't understand how someone could grab Mandy from her home in broad daylight."

"It happens, more often than most people realize. Mark and Boomer are contacting the neighbors. I'm hoping someone saw something. Toss a few of those portable barricades in your car. The Amber Alert is going out. We might need them when the reporters show up."

"I'll do it, but uh … I'm not sure it'll be an issue."

Absorbed in his thoughts on organizing the search, he had to ask, "What won't be an issue?"

"Reporters. We only have one in town."

Exasperated, Chad rubbed his neck. "Hell, you're right. It was an Atlanta reaction. Take them anyway. They might come in handy."

In his office, he hit the speed dial to call a longtime friend. Jim Hayden was the county sheriff. They'd been roommates in college and had kept up their friendship, even though Jim stayed in Texas, and Chad headed to Georgia. The bond would come in handy as he was about to requisition the fancy new motorhome Jim had acquired.

When Jim answered, Chad said, "I've got a bad one. A four-year-old is missing. Odds are, someone kidnapped her. I need to borrow your new RV."

Jim didn't hesitate. "Where do you need it?"

"Delilah Lane."

"I'll have it there in about thirty minutes. We can use it as a staging area and coordinate the search from there. Who's missing?"

"Peter and Kathy Norton's daughter."

"Good lord. I had lunch with Peter last week. What else do you need?"

"Manpower, as many officers as you can spare. Mark and Boomer have started contacting the neighbors. Even though they've already checked the woods behind the Norton's place, I want to get River's dog in there."

"She's off duty, but I'll call her. We'll need something Mandy has worn. How soon before you're back at the location?"

"I'm getting ready to leave my office. If River gets there before I do, tell her to contact the family for a piece of clothing."

A sense of relief flashed through him as he hung up the phone. His personnel problem had been solved for the immediate future. The next call was to the president of the local bank, who was also the director for the crime stoppers group. Irvin was in a meeting. He left word for him to call.

He was reaching for the keys he'd dropped on his desk when the slam of the front door echoed, followed by an angry voice demanding to speak to the police chief.

Lydia said, "He's in his office. Hey! Wait a minute! You can't just …"

A woman marched through the open doorway, followed by his secretary.

Lydia said, "I'm sorry …"

Chad raised his hand as he interrupted, "It's okay. I'll handle it."

Despite the woman's bristling antagonism, he couldn't stop a spark of interest when his gaze swept over her. A face, framed by short dark hair, could have graced the cover of any fashion magazine. Delicate brows swept across a high forehead. While her eyes were narrowed, it didn't detract from the contrast of the porcelain tone of skin to the brilliance of dark eyes. Her curvaceous body was attired in a tight skirt, which stopped at the top of her knees, and a frilly red jacket over a white sweater. He hadn't missed the long legs that ended in killer-style stiletto heels when she stomped into his office.

She stopped in front of his desk with her fisted hands on her hips. "Since you're seated behind this desk, I assume you're Chief Bishop."

"That would be an astute observation." He leaned back in the chair. "And … you are?"

"Ashley Logan. What are you doing to find Mandy Norton?"

Logan. The name jingled a memory, but he couldn't place where he'd heard it. "I can't discuss the case, but it's being investigated."

Placing her hands on his desk, she leaned forward. Her eyes flashed with contempt. "A child's been abducted. You're just *sitting* there, and all you can say is … it's being investigated. My god, what kind of second-rate department are you running?"

His temper climbed, but his tone was mild as he said, "I don't make it a practice to reveal details of a case to just anyone who walks in."

"Chief Bishop, I'm not *just* anyone. Mandy is my niece. My sister and brother-in-law are devastated. They couldn't tell me much of anything other than three officers showed up, wrote down some information, did a quick search, and then left. Aren't you aware the first few hours a child goes missing are the most critical?"

There's a detail most people don't know. "I can assure you we're doing everything possible at this point. Officers have searched the woods and are now canvassing the neighborhood."

Lydia stepped into the doorway. "Irvin is on the phone."

Chad nodded and motioned toward a chair. "Please sit down. I have to take this call."

He picked up the phone. "Irvin, thanks for the quick response. Peter Norton's daughter is missing. What can you put up for a reward?" He jotted a note as he listened, then said, "The family will add to it. As soon as Lydia has the flyers, I'll get a batch to you." He listened for another few seconds, then said, "I'll call if there's anything else you can do."

As he hung up the phone, Ashley asked, "What's the reward?"

Chad looked at her. She still stood in front of his desk, her body rigid with anger. "A thousand to start. Irvin's going to make a few calls, see if he can get some donations. Peter said he'd add to it as well."

"No! I'll take care of it. Make it twenty-five thousand. If we need to go higher, I'll provide it."

He shouted, "Lydia, make the reward twenty-five thousand dollars."

"Why hasn't an Amber Alert been sent out?"

This was the second comment about a procedure in a kidnapping investigation. Why couldn't he remember where he'd heard her name? "Do you live in Meridian?"

"I don't know why it would make a damn bit of difference, but yes, I live here. I'm the new editor of the Tribune. What about the Amber Alert?"

Chad choked back a groan. A couple of weeks ago, he had breakfast with the mayor. Charlie mentioned the Tribune had hired a hot-shot reporter from a Baltimore newspaper. Not only was she the girl's aunt, but a damn reporter to boot. Christ, this was a complication he didn't need. It should have killed his quick thrust of attraction, but somehow it didn't.

"Ms. Logan, the Amber Alert is being prepared. As more details become available, I will contact Mandy's parents."

"That's not good enough. I demand to know what steps you are taking, not only as a family member but also as a reporter. Either way, I'm entitled to the information."

His voice tight with suppressed irritation, he snapped back. "As a family member, I suggest you go back to the Norton house and help them. As a reporter, you'll receive a news release as soon as it's available. Now, if you'll excuse me, I have to leave."

He stood at the door, and once she exited, he followed and pulled it shut.

"Lydia, I'm meeting Sheriff Hayden."

She motioned toward a box sitting on the corner of her desk. "First box of flyers. More are printing. I'll send them with Dale."

His phone chimed. Pulling it from his pocket, he glanced at the screen, then turned it. He held it in front of the woman who angrily tapped her foot. "The Amber Alert." Repocketing it, he picked up a flyer from the box and handed it to her. "If you want to help, hand them out." With the box in hand, he turned and walked out of the office.

Chapter Three

***

Shocked by the man's arrogance and nonchalant attitude, Ashley watched him walk out the door. It wasn't what she expected.

Before accepting the position at the Tribune, she'd researched the key players in town. Chad Bishop had worked for the Atlanta Police Department for eleven years. Then he just up and quit. About six months ago, when the Meridian police chief retired, Bishop applied for the position. None of her research explained why he'd left the department. At the time, she didn't have a reason to dig deeper. Now, she did. A child's life was at stake, and she wouldn't accept a half-assed, shoddy investigation.

Ashley turned to Lydia, who watched her with a guarded expression. "Do you know where he's meeting the sheriff?"

Lydia's lips thinned in disapproval before saying, "No, I don't. If there isn't anything else, I have work to do." She turned to her keyboard.

Well, so much for trying to pump his secretary. Ashley studied the flyer as she walked to her car. Grief welled inside her at the sight of Mandy's picture. One reason she moved to Meridian was to be closer to Kathy and her family. Now, this. How could it have happened? A gritty resolve deepened inside her. She wouldn't leave the investigation in the hands of someone who didn't have a vested interest.

Before she started the car, Ashley considered her next step. First, she'd stop by her office. Then, she had every intention of becoming Chad Bishop's worst nightmare come true.

The Tribune, a bi-weekly paper, had a far wider circulation than most city newspapers. Besides the city residents, it included most of the people who lived in the county. When she walked into her new office, the contrast to the noisy, cluttered newsroom of the Baltimore Sun still hit her like a slap in the face.

This was her second week on the job, and Ashley wasn't entirely convinced it had been the right move. Even her boss at the Sun had questioned her motivation. She'd built a reputation as a hard-hitting but fair investigative journalist. Oh, she'd done it for the right reasons, or so she thought. If a drunk driver hadn't killed her fiancée, Ashley doubted she would have ever had the urge to return to the area where she grew up.

Seated at his desk, her one full-time reporter pounded away on his keyboard. Her lips twitched upward at the look of determination on his face. Henry Smythe disliked computers and growled whenever the system even hiccupped. He claimed an old-fashioned typewriter was better any day of the week than a fancy computer with all the time-saving gimmicks, which never seemed to work.

He stopped. Seemingly frustrated, he ran a hand through the white hair that curled over his collar. With a round face, wide cheekbones, and a button nose, Ashley had no difficulty imagining him in a red suit. Suspenders held his pants in place over his large belly, and along with the twinkle in his eyes, added to the illusion. Born and raised in Meridian, he knew everyone.

Henry looked up at the sound of her footsteps. A sympathetic look settled over his face. "I heard the news. How are Kathy and Peter doing?"

Since Henry was her conduit to the rumor mill, which ran amuck in the small community, Ashley wasn't surprised he already knew. She tossed the flyer on his desk. "As well as can be expected."

"And you?"

"Same."

"I uploaded a story about Mandy's kidnapping on our website."

"Where did you get the details?"

"Lydia called me."

Why did his answer not surprise her?

He picked up the flyer and studied Mandy's picture. "She's a sweetheart. I remember her whispering in my ear last year at the Christmas parade that all she wanted was a doll. She had all the details to make sure I'd know which one."

A weak chuckle erupted as Ashley dropped into the chair next to his desk. "You're ... the town's Santa Claus?" Guess her image wasn't so far off after all.

"I've been doing it for the last twenty or so years. I took over when my daddy passed on." His eyes scanned the details on the flyer. He snorted before saying, "Twenty-five thousand. Damn, that's a big chunk of change." With a suspicious expression, he glanced at her. "It didn't come from the crime stoppers group."

"The family added to it. As soon as you can, print off copies of the flyer. Plus, I want to put out a special edition of the paper with the flyer on the front page."

Henry looked at the wall clock. "It shouldn't take long. I'll get started on it."

She nodded. "Before you do, what can you tell me about the police chief?"

"Do you have a reason for asking?"

"Two … hardheaded and doesn't like reporters."

"I'm not surprised you picked up on it. I've talked to Chad several times since he landed in town. The man's always cordial, but not overly cooperative. After he was hired, I interviewed him. Some of his answers were vague. I sensed there were issues he didn't want to discuss. I didn't push. If it doesn't affect his job here, I figured it was his business."

His chair creaked as he settled back, shifting into his gossip mode. His hands rested on his belly. "He's a Texas boy. His family lives up around College Station. Chad graduated from Texas A&M. It's where he met his wife. She was from Atlanta and didn't want to stay in Texas. They moved, and he went to work for the Atlanta Police Department."

"He's married?" A flicker of disappointment shot through her. She hadn't seen a wedding ring, but nowadays the lack of one wasn't much of an indicator.

"Nope. They're divorced."

The twinge of relief was disregarded as nothing more than satisfying her innate curiosity. "Why'd he move back to Texas and take a job in Meridian of all places?"

"I asked him. He just said he was ready for a change, and the sheriff recommended the job."

"Jim Hayden? What'd he have to do with it?"

"They were roommates at Texas A&M."

"Ah." She was familiar with the lifelong ties of loyalty that developed between students. Her dad had been a graduate. When she was growing up, her mom always joked about the A&M bond. She claimed her dad had the nose of a bloodhound when it came to finding out if someone he'd met had also graduated from the university.

"Is he any good?" The question had hovered in the back of her mind ever since she got the call from Kathy.

His lips pursed as Henry hesitated. He understood only too well why Ashley had asked. He'd be asking the same question if it was his child. "Yes, I think he is. Despite his reticence, when I talked to him, I got a sense he knew what he was doing. And, if Jim Hayden recommends him, it's good enough for me. Since being elected sheriff, the changes Jim's made have proved to be damn good."

"Do you need any help with the special edition?" Ashley asked.

"I've got it covered. What do you plan on doing?"

"What I do best … talk to people."

Driving out of the parking lot, Chad replayed his clash with the newspaper's new editor. He'd kept his temper under control, even though his past dealings with reporters had left him with an edgy dislike for the profession. Especially after that last incident, when he was still with Atlanta PD. The fact the woman was the child's aunt would make avoiding her damn near impossible. As much as Chad hated to admit it, he was stuck with her.

His phone rang. He tapped his earpiece to answer. It was Jim letting him know where he'd parked the motorhome. After disconnecting, he called Mark to tell him to meet him at the command center.

The box of flyers on his front seat prompted his next call. When a woman's voice answered, he said, "Sharon, it's Chad. We've got a missing child. I've got flyers that need to be distributed and need help from your troop."

After listening, he said, "It's Mandy Norton. Jim has his new motorhome parked a block west of the Norton house. We'll use it to coordinate the search. As soon as you get everybody rounded up, meet me there."

The troop was the local chapter of the Texas Law Enforcement

Explorers Association. Assigned to a police department, the Explorers studied and trained in law enforcement procedures. After Chad was hired, he contacted community leaders to set up a local chapter. Much to everyone's surprise, when the announcement for enrollment was broadcast at the high school, the kids stood in line to sign up. Sharon Ward was a teacher at the school and had volunteered to be the coordinator. Using the Explorers to hand out the flyers would free up his officers.

Chad pulled behind a line of sheriff's cars parked along the street near the motorhome. From the outside, it looked like an RV suitable for weekend jaunts around the countryside. That is if you ignored the large, red letters, Bosque County Sheriff's Department, on the side. As he opened the door, Chad sighed. He'd love to have a setup like this for his department but couldn't justify the cost. At least, he had access to this one, which was better than nothing.

The interior was outfitted with a communication and computer system. Deputies were already typing on keyboards in front of the two monitors. Jim sat at a large table with Mark next to him. In front of them were a city map and three boxes filled with donuts. Boomer hovered behind Mark's shoulder.

Chad dropped the box of flyers on the table and poured a cup of coffee before pulling out a chair. As he reached across the table to snag a donut, he said, "Boomer. Sit down. You're part of this investigation."

"Yes, sir!"

Munching on a sugary bite, he thought, somehow, I've got to get the kid to loosen up.

"Mark brought me up to date on the progress or lack thereof." Jim gestured toward the map. "We've just started on the search pattern. I've also got my officers checking the sex offender registry database."

Chad just nodded, chasing the donut with a mouthful of coffee.

That's what the two deputies were doing. It was a task he could check off his list.

Jim looked at the box of flyers. "We'll need to get them passed out."

"I've already got it covered," Chad said. He licked the sugar off his fingers, then added, "Sharon is getting the Explorers released from class. She's rounding up a few parents to help. They should be here within the hour."

The door opened, and another deputy walked in. Outside, the booming bark of a dog echoed. Jim's eyes darted to the open doorway.

River laughed, then said, "Don't worry. I left Rufus outside."

Chad bit back a chuckle. For some unknown reason, Rufus was enamored with Jim. If the dog weren't on a leash, he'd make a beeline toward him. More than once, he'd heard Jim mutter about the damn dog hairs and slobber on his uniform.

"Mark and Boomer have already searched the woods," Chad told her. "I'm hoping Rufus can pick up a scent."

"If you don't have a piece of clothing, I'll head over to the Norton house," she said.

"I don't, but I want to go with you."

The large bloodhound sat next to the steps. When the dog soulfully looked up at him, Chad leaned over and rubbed his head. He could have sworn Rufus sighed with pleasure. River reached down and unsnapped the leash attached to a metal bracket. As they strode toward the sidewalk, a woman came around the front of the motorhome.

Irritated, Chad said, "What are you doing here?"

"When I couldn't get any information from you, I decided to see if the sheriff was more cooperative." Ashley's eyes narrowed as she looked at Rufus. "Why the dog?"

Her curt tone did nothing to ease his annoyance. "After I get a piece of Mandy's clothing, we're going to search the woods again. Sheriff Hayden's inside. Since talking to you will slow down our search efforts, I doubt he'll be agreeable to answering your questions."

River had stopped on the sidewalk and was listening to the conversation with avid interest. When Chad stepped beside her, she leaned closer and hissed, "Who's *that*?"

He grunted, then said, "The new editor of the Tribune, and Mandy's aunt."

River looked back over her shoulder. "Uh, oh."

Behind him, Chad heard the click of those ridiculously high heels on the concrete. Ignoring them, he said, "River, check around the gate before we leave."

Dale was in the front yard as they approached. "I'm done out here. I didn't get any usable prints off the gate."

Disappointed, Chad nodded. "Did you talk to the Norton's?"

"Yeah. I let Peter know why I was here."

Ashley had caught up and passed them. When Peter opened the door, she marched inside, followed by Chad and Dale. River stopped and ordered Rufus to stay. He dropped to the ground. His head rested on his long legs.

Inside, Kathy rushed out of the kitchen. "Ash, have they found her?"

Ashley put her arms around her sister and pulled her close. "Nothing yet, but the police chief is here to talk to you."

Kathy gulped and wiped the tears from her face. "Let's go into the family room."

Once the Norton's were seated with Ashley alongside her sister, Chad took a seat across from them and motioned toward the officers standing near the door.

"River Paxton is the sheriff's canine officer. Her dog is one of the best-trained bloodhounds in Texas. We've already searched the woods behind the house, but we're going to search it again. We need a piece of Mandy's clothing. Something that hasn't been washed since she wore it."

"Her sweater," Kathy said.

Peter stood. "I'll get it."

River stepped forward. "I'll go with you. Do you have a large plastic bag?"

At their look of surprise, River said, "I like to drop clothing into a bag to keep any conflicting scents to a minimum."

When they returned, River held a clear bag with a pink sweater inside.

Once Peter was seated on the couch, Chad picked up where he'd left off. "In addition to the search of the woods, officers will go door-to-door with a flyer with Mandy's picture. If someone isn't at home, we'll keep going back until we're able to make contact. The Amber Alert has gone out. Every law enforcement agency has been notified."

"We saw it on our phones. Dear God, I've seen one of those so many times." Peter's hand reached for Kathy's. "Now it's for … our daughter."

Leaning forward, Chad said, "I promise you; I'll do everything in my power to find her."

Kathy's red-rimmed, watery eyes stared at him. "But you can't promise you'll bring her home."

Chad sighed. Concern and sympathy radiated on his face. "No, ma'am, I can't. I wish to god I could."

Ashley looked at him in amazement. The caring and personable attitude were at odds with her previous impression. Who was the real Chad Bishop, the one she'd encountered earlier, or the one trying to bring some measure of comfort to her sister?

It suddenly dawned on her how attractive he was. Dark hair, long for a cop, brushed the collar of his shirt. His face was rugged and bronzed. Dark eyes under thick black eyebrows added a hint of mystery and danger. Muscular forearms seemed to contradict his lanky build.

A shudder of grief rocked Kathy and brought Ashley's musings to an end. It didn't make any difference what kind of man Chad Bishop was, or how good looking. All that mattered was whether he had the experience and ability to find Mandy.

Chad stood. "We've finished with the yard. If anything occurs to you, call me. You have my cellphone number. Day or night, the time doesn't matter."

Once Chad and the other officers had left, Ashley turned to her sister. "Why don't you lie down?"

"Oh, Ash. How can I sleep?" she cried. "All I can think about is Mandy. What's happening to her. Is she hurt or ... or been ...?" Another shudder rocked her body. "I can't bear the thought. How do I shut it down?"

"We can't let ourselves dwell on the what-ifs. We've got to be strong if we're going to pull through this." Peter tugged on the hand tightly clasped in his own. "How about a cup of tea?"

"No, no. Her toys are still outside. I've got to get them," Kathy said.

"I'll do it," Ashley told her. "You get the tea going. I'll join you for a cup myself. It sounds good."

A weak chuckle came from Kathy. "Who are you kidding? You hate my herbal tea."

Outside, Ashley wandered in the yard. She stopped to push on the small swing. Two days ago, Mandy had sat on the seat, squealing, "Higher, Auntie Ash. Go higher." Leaning down, she picked up a teddy bear, hugging it to her chest. Her eyes closed as grief rushed through her.

With a sigh, she tucked the bear under her arm and walked to the small table. On three of the four chairs, a doll was propped. Set in front of each and the empty chair was a cup and saucer, white with yellow daisies around the rim.

Another image flashed in her mind; Mandy on her knees in front of the Christmas tree ripping the wrapping paper off a box. Ashley could still hear her cry of delight when Mandy saw the tiny set of dishes inside. This time, she couldn't stop the trickle of tears.

Nearby was a plastic container. After wiping her face, she stacked the plates and cups, placing them in the box along with the dolls and teddy bear, then set it on the back porch. Walking to the side, she picked up the tricycle and doll. In the distance, she heard the bay of the dog. Damn, that's where she needed to be as she set the bike on the porch.

With the box cradled in her arm, she opened the patio door. The low murmur of voices echoed from the kitchen. Ashley stopped in the doorway. Peter leaned against the counter with his wife snuggled against his chest.

Her heart ached. Wishing she could do more, she said, "I'll drop this in Mandy's room. Then, I'm headed to the command center."

Kathy stepped back, wiping her cheeks with the back of her hand. "Told you she'd wiggle out of drinking the tea."

Inside Mandy's bedroom, Ashley set the box on the floor. For a moment, she stood in the center of the room, her gaze lingering on each doll. She didn't remember a time she'd seen Mandy without one in her arms or nearby.

After another bout of tears threatened, she turned to walk out. When something brushed her cheek, she gasped. Twisting, her eyes raked the room. The window was closed, and the curtains hung limp.

Blaming it on her overwrought nerves, she turned. Still, she couldn't dismiss the strange notion; it felt like a small hand patted her cheek. As she walked out, she sent a nervous glance over her shoulder.

Chapter Four

❧

As Chad approached the command center, a large group of civilians and officers milled around in front. Sharon and her troop had arrived. The teenagers, clustered on the sidewalk, chattered away as they kept a close eye on the officers. Sharon spotted him and motioned with her hand. He stopped to answer her questions, then walked inside.

Jim stood near the table. "Did you get what you needed?"

"Yes. River checked the gate, but Rufus couldn't pick up the track. How are you coming with the assignments?"

"With Mark and Boomer's help, it's done."

Chad said, "Then, let's get the briefing started."

Jim stepped out the door ahead of him. Rufus, who had been quietly sitting beside River, threw back his head and howled, then stood, straining against his leash. River ordered the dog to sit.

Despite the tense mood, several chuckles erupted. The dog's infatuation with Jim had spread like wildfire through the local agencies. A few weeks back, someone left a stuffed toy dog that was a replica of Rufus on Jim's desk. A chain with a red metal heart hung around the neck. Jim still hadn't found the culprit, though he told Chad he suspected a fireman. They were notorious for their practical jokes.

Over the rumble, Chad said, "Everyone! Listen up!" The laughter died away. "We have a missing four-year-old, Mandy Norton. She disappeared this morning around eight-thirty from the backyard of her home. Until we learn otherwise, we're treating this as a kidnapping."

He motioned to the box Jim held. "We have missing person flyers with her picture and description. Grab one. We have assigned a residential section to each officer. Check with Jim for your grid assignment and to get your log sheet. Enter the address, time, and who you talked to at each house. If no one is home, make sure you note it on your log, along with the time of the attempted contact. Ask about suspicious vehicles or persons they might have seen. If someone has information, contact Jim, and he'll arrange for an officer to take a statement. The Explorers will pass out the flyers to local stores."

Jim said, "Sharon, I've got a list of businesses. Make sure each one gets crossed off. We don't want to miss one."

"Any questions?" Chad asked. He glanced around the group and bit back a groan. With a determined stride, Ashley was headed his way.

When she looked at him, he said, "The Amber Alert has gone out, so you'll probably get questions. Don't discuss the investigation. Anyone who wants information can contact Jim or me."

Her face hardened with hostility. She'd gotten the message—stay away from the officers.

Dale pulled Chad to one side to tell him he'd received a call from the phone company. The trace was active. When Chad looked back, Ashley was gone.

River and Rufus took off for the woods. Thoughts of the provocative reporter vanished as he broke into a run to catch up.

At the edge of the thick stand of trees, River paused and unzipped the bag. She waved it in front of Rufus, letting him get a good whiff of Mandy's scent, then closed it and stuffed it in her backpack.

"Find, Rufus. Find." The dog took off at a high lope, his nose shifted from side to side along the ground. River trotted behind him, straining to hold the leash.

Several times, she glanced over her shoulder at Chad and gave a negative shake of her head. As they moved deeper into the woods, the dog crisscrossed in and around the trees. When she tugged on the leash to stop Rufus and bent over to look at the ground, Chad moved up beside her.

"Look at this." She pointed to the base of a tree. "Someone has been here recently." The ground was gouged and leaves crushed. Scrapes and cuts damaged the bark on the trunk.

Chad looked at the large branch over their heads, then turned to stare at the Norton house. "I'll be damned. If someone sat in the crook at that branch, they could see the entire backyard. It might just be kids playing around."

Squatting, he studied the ground, then looked up at the branch. "Then again, maybe not. These footprints are in the right spot where someone's feet would land when they jumped down. They look like the same shoes, but there are too many to know for certain. Judging by the number of scratches on the trunk and prints, someone climbed up there several times. I'll get Dale out here to get a few pictures."

After he finished his call, River said, "Chad, there's no point going any further. Mandy hasn't been here. Rufus would have hit on something by now. I'm sorry."

"It's what I expected. Still, the possibility had to be eliminated."

"Do you want me to return the sweater?"

"No, I'll do it."

River handed him the bag, then tugged on Rufus's leash. The two trotted back to the street.

Dale walked up, and Chad explained what they'd found. Leaving him to take the pictures, Chad strode back to the van. Chilled by the thought someone may have watched the Norton house, the abduction took on an even more ominous tone.

When he stepped inside, Jim stood in front of the computers. Turning to see who had entered, he raised his eyebrows.

Chad tossed the plastic bag on the table. "At least, we know where she hasn't been. River found signs someone could have watched the house."

Jim's face turned bleak. "Damn! If it's true, then Mandy was targeted." He sighed, then added, "We found two possibilities on the sex offender registry. Here are the addresses and their mug shots from when they were arrested." He handed a paper to Chad.

"Dale and I'll check them out."

"Do you want me to return the sweater to the Norton's?"

Chad picked up the bag. "I'll hang onto this. We might need it again."

Outside, he waited for Dale. Jim's comment was unsettling and added to his uneasiness as it dovetailed with his suspicions. This was more than see a kid and grab-type abduction.

When Dale walked up, he said, "We've got a couple of people to visit," and handed him the paper along with the keys. "You drive. I need to make a few calls."

Once they were on the road, Chad started contacting the police and fire departments in the nearby towns to ask for help. With his attention on his notepad, he didn't see the white SUV at the intersection.

Furious over the comments from the obstinate police chief, Ashley drummed her fingers on the steering wheel and waited for the light to turn green. She knew they were directed at her, a warning to back off. If the man believed his threat would work, he was in for a rude surprise. The problem, as she glanced at the flyer on the seat, was what or where to go next. This wasn't like running down leads in a big city.

A police car passed in front of her. *It's the police chief. Where are they going?* When the light turned green, Ashley punched the accelerator. Turning in front of an oncoming pickup, she ignored the driver's irritated blast of the horn. Wherever Bishop was headed, it was out of town as she passed the city limit sign. When they turned onto a remote county road, it was a certainty they'd see her if she followed. She pulled to the side and waited a few seconds.

By the time she turned, Bishop's vehicle was out of sight. Ashley hoped her strategy worked. She checked each driveway she passed. As she rounded a curve, ahead was a weather-beaten sign for a mobile home park. She spotted the back of his car in the driveway.

A surge of excitement ramped the emotional turmoil eating at her insides. Had they found a lead on Mandy? How could she find out? Driving by the entrance, she saw the police car headed to the back of the park. Damn! There was no way to get inside without them seeing her vehicle.

Ashley turned onto a road that ran alongside the park. She still couldn't see anything. Then inspiration hit. She drove just far enough, so her car was out of sight of anyone in the park.

Hopping out, she strode back until she reached the fence behind the park. From the edge of the road, she eyed the rough terrain, before she looked down at her shoes, and groaned. Maybe this wasn't such a smart idea after all. Then, she thought of Mandy and stepped into the knee-high weeds.

The stiletto heels sunk and slid as she stumbled over rocks and trash. Thorny stems gouged her legs. Grimly determined, she persevered, picking her way around the worst of the weeds until she reached the back of a mobile home near Bishop's vehicle. Peering around the corner of the building, she stared in dismay. They were already inside. She didn't even get to see who came to the damn door.

Chad slid his phone into a pocket. His gaze studied the place as Dale drove along the dirt road. Rocks and weeds covered the landscape, but most of the mobile homes were well-maintained. Wood signs marked the lot number for each resident.

"We're looking for number sixteen. There it is." Chad pointed to the farthest unit. In front was an older model truck. He typed the plate number on the computer terminal mounted on the floor between him and Dale. The return listed Doyle Neville as the registered owner, and there were no active warrants out for his arrest.

As he exited, he glanced around the seemingly deserted park before walking to the wood porch. It wobbled as he stepped up and pounded on the door. When it swung open, a burly man, dressed in grubby jeans and a dirty T-shirt, stood in the doorway.

"Neville, I've got a few questions to ask you?"

The man's eyes shifted to Dale, who stood behind Chad, then to their car.

"Cops, damn cops. I got nothing to say," he growled, then stepped back to shut the door.

Chad's shoulder slammed against it. Caught off guard, Neville stumbled backward. Chad stepped inside, followed by Dale.

Neville's hands curled into tight fists as he glared at the two officers. "You can't force your way in here. I got rights. I want to see a search warrant."

With a pointed stare at the man's hands, Chad told him, "Don't have one, but it doesn't mean we're not going to have a friendly chat."

"Get out of here then, or I'm calling my attorney."

Dale stepped into the short hallway that led to the bedrooms.

Another roar erupted. "Wait a minute! You can't go back there."

Dale snorted and ignored the man's protest.

"Go ahead. Make your call." Chad rested his hand on top of the butt of his gun. "We'll wait right here until he arrives. Until then, I want to know where you were around eight-thirty this morning?"

Dale strode back into view and shook his head no at the questioning look on Chad's face.

Hooking his thumbs over the waistband of his pants, Neville sneered at Chad. "Well, now, how about that? I just happened to be eating breakfast at the Red Rooster. You can call. That nosy bitch who works the morning shift will tell you."

Despite the man's display of bravado, Chad saw beads of sweat on Neville's forehead. He pulled his phone and tapped the speed dial for Jim. When the sheriff answered, Chad said, "Need you to check out Neville's whereabouts this morning." Keeping his eyes on the man's face, he added, "He claims he was at the Red Rooster eating breakfast." After listening for a few seconds, he disconnected.

Chad's hand motioned toward the cell phone on the kitchen counter. "If you want to call your lawyer, we've got time."

Neville's lips thinned, and his eyes gleamed with anger.

When the man didn't move, Chad said, "I thought so. Where are you working?"

The man grunted. "I'm done answering questions."

"If that's the way you want to play this, my next call is to your parole officer."

Neville's face turned sullen as he muttered, "Here and there."

"It's not good enough. I want to know where."

"Just odd jobs. A lumber company in Whitney sometimes needs an extra driver. I help a guy who mows yards."

Chad's phone rang. "Bishop." He listened, his gaze never leaving

Neville's face. The sneer was back. His every instinct tingled at Neville's smug look. The man knew something.

After disconnecting, Chad said, "Your alibi holds up ... for now. But I've got a missing child, and you're a prime suspect. Don't leave town, or I'll have your parole revoked. Your next stop will be a prison cell."

Neville chortled. "Can't blame it on me. Like you said, I got me an alibi, and there ain't nothin' you can do about it."

His voice grim, Chad said, "I wouldn't count on it." He took a step backward. Behind him, Dale opened the door. "Oh, by the way. There's a reward; twenty-five thousand for any information that leads us to the girl."

"Twenty-five big ones?"

"You heard right."

Neville's hands slid into his pockets as he rocked on his feet. His eyes gleamed with avarice.

Chapter Five

❧

What the devil was taking so long, Ashley wondered? Not knowing what was happening inside, and the throbbing pain that crawled from her feet into her legs had amped-up her frustration level. For the umpteenth time, she cursed the heels. To keep from sinking into the ground, she'd tried to push herself higher on her toes, which only intensified the stinging jabs in her calves. Then, she said to hell with it, and let them sink.

When the door opened, and the officers stepped out, she couldn't stop a groan of relief. Finally, something was happening. As she watched them walk to the car, her hopes plummeted. No one was going to jail, and she still didn't know who was inside.

Disgusted, Ashley waited for them to drive out of the park. What a waste of time. She should have expected it instead of getting her hopes up. She'd investigated far too many stories that took weeks, even months to resolve. Still, this was Mandy, and her fears were going to cloud her judgment.

Once Bishop's vehicle turned onto the roadway, she tromped to her car. As soon as her butt hit the seat, off came the damned shoes. While her hand massaged a foot, she mused over the reason for Bishop's visit. She hadn't learned a frigging thing about why the cops were even there. She should have stayed put and waited for them to leave. Eyeing the mangled heels didn't improve her disposition.

Now what? A light chuckle erupted when an idea popped into her head. Why not? At least she'd find out who the cops talked to, though it would probably piss off the police chief. She laughed to herself. *Like I really give a damn.*

From inside the glove box, she grabbed a small canister. Early in her career, she'd been assaulted during an interview. The cameraman and a passerby had helped restrain the guy, but it had been a valuable lesson. Since then, she always had a can of pepper spray handy.

With a moan, she slid her feet back into the shoes, then started the car. Inside the park, she stopped near the front porch. As she exited, her gaze scanned the pickup and license plate number.

The porch wobbled when she walked up the steps. A heel sunk between the wooden slats. Cursing, she tugged her foot free. After tapping on the door, she gingerly stepped back down to the ground.

A scruffy, overweight man opened the door. His eyes gleamed as his gaze raked her from head to toe. "Well, well. Ain't you a good lookin' one." He leaned against the doorjamb and grinned, exposing yellow, stained teeth. "Sweetheart, whatever *you're* selling, I'm buying," he said and laughed.

Her hand slid into her pocket and fingers wrapped around the can of spray. "I'm the editor of the Tribune. I'm writing a story on police procedures. Why was the police chief here?"

He straightened. An angry look crossed his face. "I don't like cops or reporters. Get back in your fancy car and get the hell out of here."

With a soothing tone, she said, "A lot of people don't like either one. Still, if you've got a problem with the local cops, a reporter can be an ally, even tell your side of the story. What's your name?"

He snarled. "I don't know what you're after, but I didn't have anything to do with that missing girl."

Excitement shot through her, though she didn't let it show. "Well, if you didn't, I can get the word out to people. Let them know you're innocent. But I need your name."

"Humph! Neville, Doyle Neville. Make sure you get it right." When she didn't move, he added, "Shouldn't you write it down?"

Ashley wasn't about to let loose of the can. "I'll remember. Why were the cops here?"

"I got a record, and whenever something happens, they come snooping around. It doesn't matter that I'm innocent."

"Do you have an alibi?"

He smirked. "You bet I do. I was at the Red Rooster eating breakfast. That smart-mouthed cop knows it."

Her heart sank. This was a dead end.

A sly look crossed his face. "Is it true there's a big reward?"

"Twenty-five thousand dollars. Do you know anything?"

"Maybe I do, and maybe I don't."

"If you do, and it leads to finding the girl, I'll make sure you get the reward."

He stepped off the porch and walked toward her. "Why don't you come inside and let's talk about it?"

Taking a step back, she glanced around the deserted park. "Not today. I have another stop to make as soon as I leave here. Call me at the Tribune if you decide you know something."

Just as she turned, he grabbed her arm. Twisting from his grasp, she yanked the door open, slid inside, and slammed it shut. Her finger jabbed the door lock button. Ashley started the engine and jammed the gear shift into reverse. Dirt and rocks flew as the back of the car spun. Neville jumped back, his hand raised in an obscene gesture. With a deft spin of the wheel, she straightened the tires and tore down the driveway.

Shaken by the encounter, Ashley didn't take a deep breath until she turned onto the highway. For what it was worth, she had a name. Did he know something? Or was it a ploy to get her inside? One thing was for sure, Doyle Neville was worth watching. But how could she do it? She pondered the question during the drive back to town.

Her first stop was home. If she was going to prowl around, in god knows where, she needed to ditch the heels and suit. After that, another visit to the command center seemed like the right place to begin.

Dale turned onto the main highway. "Neville knows something. You had him sweating."

"That concerns me. Why would he be nervous when he's got an alibi? Doesn't add up." Chad said.

"Well, you sure got his interest with the mention of a reward."

"Twenty-five thousand's a strong lure."

"How'd the reward get so big?" Dale goosed the gas to pass a slow-moving farm tractor, a familiar sight in this neck of the woods. "The most I've ever seen the crime stoppers shell out is a thousand."

"It came from the aunt."

"Was she the woman at the Norton's?"

"Yeah."

"I didn't recognize her. Who is she?"

"Ashley Logan." Bitterness tinged his voice. "The new editor of the Tribune."

Dale whistled in surprise. "Oh, hell! That's Ashley Logan! I'd heard the new editor was in town. It complicates the issue."

"We've already butted heads."

Dale chuckled. "I'd like to have seen that."

Chad grunted.

"She's a looker. Married?" Dale asked.

"I don't have a clue."

He cast a sideways glance at his boss. "If she isn't, I bet it'll add juice to some of the singles roaming around."

Catching the look, Chad exclaimed, "Don't include me in your scenario. I'm not interested. I don't like reporters, even one who is attractive."

"Hmm… so you think she's hot?"

"Dale, shut up. This isn't a topic for discussion."

"Whatever you say, boss." Another grin split his face.

When he arrived in Meridian, it hadn't taken Chad long to get indoctrinated with his new staff. Dale invited him to a weekly poker game that involved everyone who worked at the PD, the sheriff's department, and some of the firemen. Who showed up depended on who was working and who was off for the night. His secretary even sat in on occasion. Mark and Dale had promptly relieved him of all the spare cash he had in his pocket. Chad wasn't much for gambling, but it had broken the ice with his officers. Since then, he might be the boss, but he was treated as one of the troops, which meant they stuck their noses into his private life.

Chad's phone rang. Casting a look of disgust at Dale, he answered. It was Jim.

"We've expanded the search area. A group of off-duty firemen saw the Amber Alert and showed up to help."

Chad said, "We're on our way to Lew Walker's location, then we'll head back to the command center." After disconnecting, he stared out the window, though he didn't see the passing terrain.

Dale glanced at him a couple of times, wondering what had put the frown on his face.

As they pulled into the driveway of an apartment complex, Chad abruptly pulled his phone and called Jim.

When he answered, Chad told him, "We need a copy of all the security camera tapes for the service stations and convenience stores for the last month. Same for any business in town that uses cameras."

"It'll mean pulling officers off the door-to-door search."

"Can't be helped. We need to get those tapes before they can be erased or overwritten."

"I'm on it," Jim said and hung up.

Chad had been glad to leave the hectic pace of a big-city police department for the laid-back atmosphere of a small town. Now, he rued the lack of personnel.

"Dale, as soon as we get back, I want you to coordinate getting those tapes. Set up a file with dates, times, and locations for each one. I don't want to hunt through a stack of them just to find a particular tape."

As they exited, Chad turned his attention to the next suspect. Walker had been convicted for kidnapping. Someone saw the little girl get into his vehicle and followed the van until the police caught up with them. He'd copped a plea to get a reduced sentence and had been paroled about a year ago.

Outside the first-floor apartment, Chad knocked.

A voice called out. "Who is it?"

"Police! Open the door."

"What do you want?"

"Open the damn door!"

It slowly opened. A face, with heavy jowls and narrow set eyes, peered around the edge.

"You can't just barge in here," Walker growled.

"What I can do is call your parole officer and tell him you're not cooperating with an official investigation. How long do you think it'll take for you to be back in jail?"

"What the hell. I got nothing to hide," he said, swinging the door open. The nauseating odor of cigarette smoke drifted into the hallway.

Walker, a heavyset man with beefy arms and hands, shuffled into the middle of the room. A couch covered with magazines and newspapers faced the television. Empty beer cans and takeout bags littered the coffee table.

The man reached down and picked up a pack of cigarettes lying next to an ashtray filled with ashes and butts. As he clicked the lighter, his hand trembled. Drawing in a deep pull of smoke, he eyed Dale, who ambled into the bedroom.

"You seem a bit nervous," Chad remarked. "Since you said, you don't have anything to hide, I'm wondering why?"

Smoke blew out Walker's mouth as he mumbled, "Don't like cops. It's reason enough."

"Well, this cop has a couple of questions. Where were you this morning?"

"Right here. Haven't left the place since yesterday." He jerked his head in the direction of the bedroom. "What's he looking for?"

"Checking to see if you're alone. Got anybody who can confirm you've been here?"

"No." When Dale walked into the living room, Walker's eyes flicked between the two officers.

With a hard stare, Chad said, "A little girl was kidnapped this morning. Since this is right up your alley, you might want to come up with an alibi."

"Wasn't me." He looked at the tip of his cigarette, grinned, then added. "Since I don't have a car, I couldn't kidnap a dog, let alone a kid. My old lady took off with most of my stuff, including the car, when I went to jail."

"You could have borrowed one. If you did, I'll find out."

"You can look all you want." Walker sucked in another deep pull of smoke.

"Don't leave town," Chad said. "If you're clean, there's a hefty reward for information."

"How much?"

"Twenty-five thousand."

His eyes widened in surprise. "I'd like to have a go at it." He bent over and smashed the butt in the bowl. "Damn shame, I don't know anything."

Chad stepped to the door. As his hand reached for the knob, he glanced over his shoulder. His voice harsh, he said, "I meant what I said about not leaving town."

As they walked to the car, Chad asked, "What do you think? Is he involved?"

"I'm not sure. Despite his denials, Walker's interested in the reward."

"We need to interview everyone in this complex. Never know what will crawl out if we start flipping rocks."

"We're starting to be spread pretty thin," Dale commented.

"I know. Head to the station. You can pick up your vehicle, then meet me at the command center."

All the way into town, he thought about the two men and the lure of the reward.

Chapter Six

❧

Musing over the best way to approach the sheriff, Ashley strode toward the command center. As a reporter, Jim Hayden was unlikely to tell her anything. If she made a plea as the representative of the family, he might open up.

A group of firemen clustered near the motorhome, where Jim stood in front talking about search assignments. She stopped to listen. After they walked off, Jim turned and spotted her. His eyes flashed with a look of exasperation.

A grim smile crossed her face. Despite his attitude, she wasn't leaving. Footsteps sounded behind her. It was Chad. He nodded as he stepped off the curb and walked by her.

Infuriated by the brushoff, she called out, "Chief Bishop!"

With a noticeable sigh, he turned.

"I want to know what's happening with the investigation."

"Ms. Logan, I can't tell you anything other than we have search parties out, and the hotline is operational. When I have something to report, I will contact the family."

"Chief Bishop, it's not enough." Her voice vibrated with anger. "It appears your department is ill-equipped to handle an investigation of this magnitude. What are you doing to get additional help?"

His eyes narrowed.

That struck a chord.

Since he wasn't about to admit he had the same concerns, he said, "Ms. Logan, I can assure you my department is more than capable of running this investigation. I can also assure you I'll enlist the help of anyone I believe can contribute to our efforts to find Mandy. Now, if you don't mind, *I'd* like to get on with the search."

As he turned away, she asked, "What did you find out from Doyle Neville?"

Chad whipped around. "Where did you get his name?"

"I have ways." She smirked. She wasn't about to say she followed him. "What did he tell you?"

"Sticking your nose into an official police investigation won't help anyone, let alone your niece."

Her anger ratcheted at the nerve of the man. "If I knew what you were doing, I might not have to *stick* my nose in. And, as Mandy's aunt and the person who is putting up the bulk of the reward money, I've got a right to stick my nose wherever I damn well please."

"Not in my investigation, you don't." He turned to Jim, who had watched the fiery exchange with far too much interest. "Let's get inside."

Fuming, she glared at the door as it banged shut. Damn him! Since he refused to cooperate, she had no compunction in running her own investigation.

Inside, Chad jerked out a chair. "The woman is insufferable." The sharp jab of lust that struck when he saw her on the sidewalk added to his annoyance. Jeans, atop hiking boots, clung like a second skin to her long legs and tight butt. An open jacket brushed her hips and barely covered a knit top and the breasts which swelled above the low-cut neckline. The suit she'd worn earlier had concealed what turned out to be a sexy, muscular build. The lady had spent time working out.

Jim grinned at his longtime friend. "She does rub you the wrong way. I don't believe I've ever seen you this riled up over someone. Still, she has a point. She's the child's aunt and did put up the money."

"What! Don't tell me you're on her side. We don't need a damn reporter in the middle of this," he growled.

"I don't like dealing with a reporter either. I'm only saying she has a point. She might be easier to work with than against."

Chad snorted.

The door opened, and Dale walked in, followed by two deputies. At the sight of his boss's angry face, he asked, "Something happen?"

Chad said, "Our new editor found out about Neville."

"I saw her leaving. How'd she come up with his name?"

"I don't know, but I'd sure like to find out." Shaking off his irritation, he said, "Jim, I'd like for Dale to coordinate the search for the tapes. Who have you assigned?"

Jim nodded to the two deputies who leaned against the wall. "I pulled Todd and Angela off the door-to-door search. I have a list of stores." He stepped to the counter against the wall and picked up a stack of papers. He handed a set to each officer.

"If I've missed one, let me know."

Dale nodded, then looked at Todd and Angela. "I'm ready to go when you are." The deputies followed him out the door.

Jim pulled out a chair. "What happened with Neville and Walker?"

"You already know about Neville's alibi, but Dale and I got the impression he may know more than he's telling. The reward got his interest."

Chad stood and walked to the coffee pot. "Walker claims he doesn't have a vehicle. Said his wife took it when he was in jail."

He poured a cup, took a sip, then grimaced. "Damn, how long has this stuff been sitting here?" Chad took another sip. "I've got an officer headed to the apartment complex to interview his neighbors."

Jim sighed and leaned back in the chair. "Chad, I've got a bad feeling about this one. I examined what you and River found in the woods. Someone was watching the house. I don't have any doubt Mandy was targeted, but why her?"

"If we can find the answer to that question, we might have a good chance of finding her. I downloaded Neville and Walker's mugshots on my phone. Before I go back to the office, I'll stop at the Norton's. They might recognize one of them."

Ashley rang the doorbell. When her brother-in-law saw her standing on the porch, a look of hope crossed his face. As soon as she stepped inside, he asked, "Anything?'

She shook her head. Kathy stood in the hallway with the same look in her eyes. It died as she stared at her sister. Her body slumped. "Nothing?"

"I'm sorry, Kathy. There is no news."

At her cry of distress, Ashley rushed to her side. With her arm around her sister's shoulder, she led her into the family room and eased her onto the couch.

"I can't stop crying," Kathy mumbled as tears ran down her face. "I can't stand this, the not knowing. She's out there somewhere." Crossing her arms, her body rocked. "Oh, God, is she hurt or …"

Ashley said, "A lot of people are out searching, so there's hope. We're going to find her."

Peter leaned over the back of the couch and dropped a handful of tissues in Kathy's lap.

Ashley picked up one and wiped the tears from her sister's face. "Have either of you had anything to eat?"

Peter said, "We don't seem to have much of an appetite."

"I feel the same way, but we need to eat something," Ashley said. "I'll see what I can find. Peter, you stay with Kathy."

Ashley quickly assembled several sandwiches. At the sound of the doorbell, she hollered out, "I'll get it." When she looked through the peephole, she groaned. Damn. She didn't feel up to going another round with him, but she couldn't ignore him. She had to open the door.

Chad said, "I need to talk to your sister and brother-in-law."

"Is it absolutely necessary? Kathy isn't up to a whole lot of talking right now."

Despite her chilling glare, his tone was soft with concern. "I don't like disturbing her any more than you do. It's important."

Ashley sighed and stepped back to let him enter. Peter and Kathy stood in the doorway to the family room.

Chad greeted them and motioned for them to take a seat. Peter sat next to his wife. Ashley perched on the arm of a chair.

As he discussed the details of the search, his eyes flicked to her face. Her lips twisted in a sardonic smile as if to remind him of her earlier accusations. Jim was right. The woman had a way of crawling under his skin.

Ignoring her, he pulled his phone, clicked on the screen, and held it up. "Have you seen this man? Maybe in a store or on the street?"

Peter held out his hand. "May I take a closer look?"

Chad handed the phone to him. Kathy and Peter stared for several seconds at the image. Peter was the first to answer. "No, I've never seen him before. Kathy?"

She shook her head. "I haven't either."

Neville's comment about mowing yards prompted his next question. "Do you hire anyone to take care of your yard?"

"No, I do it all," Peter said.

Before he could retrieve the phone, Ashley plucked it out of

Peter's hand. Her gut twisted when she saw it was Neville. "Is he a suspect?"

Chad held out his hand. "A person of interest right now." He tapped the screen again to bring up Walker's mugshot. He handed the phone to Peter. "What about this guy?"

Peter and Kathy both shook their heads.

Ashley leaned over to study the picture. "Who is he?"

It didn't escape him that she'd asked for Walker's name but not Neville's. How did she know about Neville, he wondered, though all he said was, "Just another person of interest."

Not wanting to argue in front of Kathy and Peter, she didn't comment, though her eyes flashed with anger.

Peter passed the phone back. "Chad, what happens now?"

"We're still running down leads. The teams will be back out at daylight to continue the search."

After he left, Ashley said, "Sandwiches are on the table."

She planned on staying long enough to make sure Kathy ate, then she had her own agenda. She wasn't giving up and going home.

Kathy choked down a few bites before pushing her chair back. "I'll be in Mandy's room."

His face stark with grief, Peter watched her walk out. "I have this god-awful pain in my gut that tells me we may never know. So many children disappear, never to be heard of again."

Ashley gripped his shoulder, then picked up his plate. Peter, like Kathy, had eaten very little, but it was better than nothing.

After stashing the plates in the dishwasher, she asked, "Do you need me to stay here tonight?"

"No, we'll be fine." He sighed. "Well, as fine as can be expected under the circumstances."

A cry echoed from the hallway. Peter shot out of his chair. "Kathy!"

She stumbled into the kitchen with a doll clasped in her hands. "This isn't hers!"

"What?" Ashley exclaimed as she reached for her sister's arm.

Kathy pulled back and shook the doll in the air. Her voice edged upward with a note of hysteria. "This doll isn't hers. Don't *you* understand? This isn't Mandy's doll. Where did it come from?"

In a calm and even tone, Peter said, "There must be an explanation. Let me see it." After studying it, he handed it to Ashley. "Kathy, are you certain? She has a lot of dolls."

Her hands fluttered in the air. "You know Mandy says goodnight to every doll she's got. I'm telling you this isn't hers. She doesn't have one this old or in this condition. How'd it get into her room?"

"I can tell you," Ashley replied. "I found it in the yard when I picked up the toys."

She studied the doll, turning it over to look at the back. There was nothing unusual about it. The doll had a soft body, and the dark hair was pulled into pigtails on each side of the hard, plastic-style head. The face was smudged with dirt. A tattered and stained dress covered the arms and legs. She didn't find a manufacturing label.

"Then how did it get into the backyard?" Kathy's red-rimmed eyes darted between Ashley and Peter. "Did the kidnapper leave it?"

"Ashley, where did you find it?" Peter asked.

"Propped in one of the chairs at Mandy's little table. I dropped it in the box along with the rest of the dolls and toys."

"I don't understand." Peter stared at the doll with a confused look. "If the kidnapper left it, why would it be on a chair? It doesn't make sense. There must be another explanation."

"It has to be connected to the kidnapper," Kathy said. "I saw the dolls Mandy took outside, and this wasn't one of them. I've *never* seen this doll."

"Is it possible it was in her room, and you missed seeing it?"

Ashley asked.

Kathy hesitated before saying, "I don't see how, but maybe I did."

Ashley said, "Could she have come back inside and traded out the dolls?"

"I would've heard the door. It squeaks as it slides on the rail." Her shoulders slumped as a defeated look crossed her face. "Peter, maybe you're right. Why would the kidnapper put it on a chair? I would think he'd have taken it with him. But if it was in her room, where did Mandy get it?"

Ashley laid the doll on the table. "We may all be jumping the gun here over something that doesn't have any connection to Mandy's disappearance. I'll get it to the police chief. Even if it's not connected, he needs to know."

"I'll get you a bag," Peter said.

Her sister's insistence she'd never seen the doll had set off a familiar tingle of nerves. A strange doll suddenly appearing in the backyard was too much of a coincidence. Was it possible the doll was linked to the case? Then again, how did the doll get on the chair? Believing a kidnapper would take the time to set it there did seem to be unrealistic.

She kept her doubts to herself as she snapped several pictures of the doll before sliding it into the plastic bag Peter handed her.

"Tomorrow morning, I'll come by before I go to work." Hugging them both, she fought back the tears as she headed to the door.

In the car, Ashley pulled a tissue from the box in the console and wiped her eyes. Should she track down the police chief? Every time she encountered him, he annoyed her. Even if the doll were connected to the case, he wouldn't be able to do anything tonight. Confident she'd see him the next day, she'd wait since she had other plans.

Chapter Seven

❧

Since her encounter with Doyle Neville, thoughts about the man had rolled in the back of Ashley's mind. Deep in her gut, instincts honed by years of investigating Baltimore's criminal activity tingled. Despite his so-called alibi, she felt he was involved. Maybe he didn't kidnap Mandy, but she'd bet her last dollar he knew who did. Evidently, Chad had the same impression. He thought it important enough to show his picture to Kathy and Peter. Her innate nosiness itched to learn the identity of the other man, but for now, she'd concentrate on Neville.

What seemed like a good plan in town turned into a sea of doubt when she turned onto the lonely, dark county road. Her heart rate kicked up several notches. Picking up the cellphone from the console, she glanced at the screen. *Yes! Thank you, thank you, I've got bars.*

The sight of the bright floodlight at the entrance to the park and cars parked near the homes brought another sense of relief. Lights shone through many of the windows, including Neville's place. At least, it wasn't deserted as it had been earlier in the day.

Ashley turned onto the same side road, drove a short distance before turning around. After flipping off the headlights, she eased her vehicle to the side of the road.

Snuggled in the seat where she could keep an eye on Neville's trailer, her thoughts shifted to the second suspect. Who was he? Where did he live? Her mind devised ways to worm the information out of Chad. After rejecting several, it was obvious the tight-lipped police chief would be a waste of time. Maybe she could find out from one of the other officers. The only problem was Chad had clamped the lid down on the investigation, and there weren't many people involved she could contact. It was a frustrating difference between a small-town reporter and one in a big city. In Baltimore, there was always someone willing to talk.

Uncomfortable, she changed her position in the seat and tilted the wheel to give her more room. Her thoughts shifted to the mystery of the doll. How did it get into the backyard? Unconsciously, her fingers stroked the bag lying on the seat. Was it possible the kidnapper had left it? The picture of someone striding into the backyard, in full view of anyone inside the house, just to put a doll on the chair didn't make sense. Or had the kidnapper grabbed her from the backyard? No, that didn't jive with the tricycle near the gate. Still, Kathy's insistence she'd never seen the doll bothered her. There had to be a rational answer to the puzzle. She should have asked if any children had been to the house.

This was going nowhere fast. It was getting late, and there were fewer lights in the park. Lost in her thoughts, she hadn't noticed the fog creeping across the landscape. She straightened to stare at the strange sight. The dense mist shimmered with a green glow, something she'd never seen before. Was it some type of weather anomaly? For some reason, it raised the hackles on her neck.

Since it appeared Neville was in for the night, it was time to leave. Driving on a fog-laden road wasn't her idea of fun, which probably accounted for her odd reaction.

As her hand reached to start the car, the lights in Neville's home blinked out. He stepped out the door, hesitated as he glanced around the park, before walking to his truck.

Excitement re-energized her. The suspect was on the move. Had he waited until the other residents had gone to bed? She didn't start the engine until he'd driven out of the park.

It wasn't as difficult to follow his truck as she expected. While the fog was getting thicker, the taillights on Neville's truck were clearly visible. She backed off the accelerator to keep from getting too close and arousing his suspicions. After he turned to head toward Meridian, it was even easier. When he pulled to a stop in front of a convenience store, Ashley's enthusiasm crashed. A store! This was his nefarious trip? Disgusted, she debated whether to call it a night and go home. Since she was here, she might as well keep an eye on him. On the parking lot across the street, she backed into a spot that let her see inside the store.

Neville opened the door to a cooler, pulled out a six-pack, then ambled along the aisles. Before walking to the checkout counter, he picked up a couple of bags. He laid the items in front of the clerk, then pointed to a rack behind the man.

With the six-pack in one hand and a plastic bag in the other, he walked out and set the stuff on the passenger seat. When he drove out of the parking lot, he turned in the direction that would take him home.

Well, rats! She'd wasted several hours to watch Neville buy beer, what was probably chips, and … what was the other item? Curious, Ashley pulled across the street. Strolling into the store, she walked to the cooler and grabbed a bottle of soda. When she reached the counter, she glanced at the rack behind the clerk. Her curiosity intensified. It was a display of pre-paid cell phones. Why would Neville need a burner phone? With her thoughts focused on the reason, she paid for the soda and walked out.

Behind her, a voice growled, "What do you think you're doing?"

As her body twisted, her hands jerked upward. The bottle flew into the air and then hit the ground with a thud. In front of her, the police chief scowled at her with a hard glint in his eyes.

"Chad Bishop, don't you ever scare me like that again. What were you thinking, to creep up on a woman at night?"

"First off, I didn't creep. If you had bothered to look when you strutted out of the store, you'd have seen me. While I do hate to repeat myself, if you'd stay out of my investigation, this wouldn't have happened. What in god's name possessed you to follow Doyle Neville?"

Well, hell. There went her hope he didn't know. To give her time to think, she bent over and picked up the bottle.

Chad snickered. "I wouldn't recommend unscrewing the cap. Now answer my question."

The nerve of the man astounded her. "I don't have to answer or explain anything. I'm not one of your officers you can bully."

His eyebrows shot up. "Bully! Jesus H. Christ, have you lost all sense of reality? People like Neville can chew you up and spit you out without a second thought."

"I can take care of myself."

A look of disbelief crossed his face. "I'm not sure you could take care of a spider if it crossed your path."

Outrage flashed in her eyes. "Don't you dare demean me or my abilities. I have a stake in this investigation. I won't sit around until you deem it appropriate to tell *me* what is happening."

She turned and marched to her car.

"We're not done here," he shouted.

Her hand on the door handle, she glared at him over the top. "Oh, yes, we are. Here's something for you to think about. Why did Neville buy a pre-paid phone?"

"How do you know that?"

"How do you think? I just watched him buy it."

Ashley jerked open the door and slid behind the wheel. The bag on the seat caught her eye. She set the bottle in the cupholder. Grabbing the bag, she stepped out and hollered, "Hey," and tossed it to Chad.

He caught it in midair.

"That was in the backyard. It doesn't belong to Mandy."

She slid back inside. When she backed, gravel shot across the lot.

Anger seethed inside him as he watched her drive away. Didn't the woman have any sense? Ashley Logan was a thorn in his side, but it wasn't his only problem. God knows he didn't want to be attracted to her. The disastrous end of his marriage still rankled. He didn't have any yearning to go down that path again and wasn't interested in any kind of relationship, casual or otherwise. Chad suspected Ashley would fall into the category of otherwise. What he couldn't deny was that she stirred his blood.

"Damn, how much worse can this get?" he muttered. He looked inside the bag. An image flashed in his mind; dolls propped in chairs around a small table. This doll was one of them. What did Ashley mean when she said it didn't belong to Mandy?

Uneasiness settled in his chest. As he pulled the doll from the bag, an icy gust of wind sent a chill racing down his back. The uneasiness deepened into foreboding. No, it wasn't possible. It had taken months, but he'd convinced himself it had all been his imagination, just a hellish nightmare. Sliding the doll back into the sack, he headed to his truck, unaware of the wraithlike mist that had built, or its green-tinged tentacles crawling towards him.

During the drive home, Ashley's anger dissipated. Though she hated to admit it, fighting with Chad helped to keep the terror she felt for her niece at bay. She wondered what might have happened had she met him under different circumstances. When her fiancée was killed, something inside her died. Friends told her it took time to heal; there'd be someone down the line. Ashley hadn't believed them until she crossed paths with Chad Bishop.

While the man was undeniably attractive, she wasn't about to let him know. Although, it didn't stop her from thinking about the what-ifs. Chad was someone she didn't expect to find in Meridian. Why was he here? She'd left Baltimore to escape the memories, make a new start. Was that Chad's reason? A small-town police department was a big step down from Atlanta, not much different from her career change.

Her finger tapped the remote to open the garage door. Inside the kitchen, she dropped the large tote bag on the counter and reached for a wine glass in the cabinet. Even though she was exhausted, she didn't want to wait to dig into Chad's background.

In the spare bedroom she'd converted into an office, she switched on the table lamp and set the glass on the desk. Pulling the keyboard toward her, she typed Chad's name along with the Atlanta Police Department. A series of articles popped up. With the search option set to start with the oldest date, she read through article after article.

Amazed by what she'd discovered, Ashley reached for her glass. It was empty. Engrossed in reading, she didn't remember drinking any of it. Leaning back in the chair, she pondered the details of Chad's career.

He was a highly decorated officer. Selected as Officer of the Year was only one of many commendations, community awards, and two life-saving bars for pulling victims from a burning house.

One of his last cases received a vast amount of publicity. A child had been kidnapped, and Chad was the lead detective. After he located the girl at a house in Atlanta, the SWAT team stormed the home. One reporter stated the girl would have been dead in a few hours if she hadn't been rescued.

The circumstances of how Chad found the child had come under considerable scrutiny. The lawyer for the man arrested for the kidnapping claimed the search warrant was defective. Chad had not established reasonable cause for the search. According to the lawyer, the details of how he found the girl's location was hazy and couldn't be verified. The judge ruled against the lawyer, but it still left a stain on Chad's record.

Even though Chad saved the girl's life, he was severely chastised by several reporters. They claimed his actions could have resulted in a kidnapper being set free and painted him as a rogue cop willing to take the law into his own hands. Shortly after the damning articles, Chad resigned and ended up in Meridian.

No wonder the man didn't like reporters. She could certainly understand his animosity. They'd shredded his reputation.

Still, her instincts told her something didn't add up. Ashley had every intention of finding the reason. Police Chief Chad Bishop would just have to get over his dislike of reporters because she was in this to the end.

Chapter Eight

～～

Restless, Chad bunched his pillow to get comfortable. It was a futile effort. Instead, he stared into the darkness. The endless repetition of thoughts about the kidnapping clogged his mind. He couldn't shut them down. After another glance at the clock, he gave up. The office was where he needed to be, not in bed.

When he walked in, he was surprised to see Lydia already at her desk. "You're here early."

She sighed. "It was a short night. Doesn't look like you got much sleep, either."

"Hard to under the circumstances. Anyone else here?"

"Dale's in his office looking at the security tapes."

"How many calls have we received on the hotline?" Since each one had to be investigated, it meant another load on his woefully small department. None of them could be ignored. One might be the lead that would break the case open.

When Lydia shook her head, stunned, he stared at her. "Not a *single* one!"

"No."

Dismay moved through him. The case had no leads, nothing, except a doll and the purchase of a burner phone. Each of which probably meant diddly squat.

"What's in the bag?"

"The Norton's found this after Mandy disappeared," he told her, pulling the doll out of the bag. With three children, all girls, plus several grandchildren, he figured she'd know more about dolls than he did. "According to Ashley Logan, it doesn't belong to Mandy."

Lydia reached for it. "I haven't seen one of these in years. This was a popular style about twenty or thirty years ago, maybe older. My daughters had quite a collection."

"Where would you get a used doll?"

"I'd try the thrift stores. A lot of people donate used toys," she said, handing the doll back.

"Do me a favor and type up a list of all the thrift stores in the area. I'll be in Dale's office."

When his boss walked in, Dale stopped the video that scrolled across his monitor. He eyed the doll in Chad's hand. A broad grin crossed his face. "Might not want to let folks see you carrying a doll around. It's not good for the image of a rough and ready police chief."

Chad grinned. "Could be I want to show off my softer side."

Dale laughed. "I guess it's possible, but I'm not sure you've got one."

After laying the doll on the desk, Chad stepped to the table with the coffee pot. "But in this case, it might be evidence." He poured a cup. "Ashley Logan gave it to me." He thought it prudent not to mention she'd actually thrown it at him. "She said it was in the backyard and doesn't belong to Mandy. I'll ask the parents about it."

Dale picked it up and shot a sly look at Chad. "Hmm … when did you see Ashley?"

"Last night. The woman was following Doyle Neville. I caught her watching him at the Stay and Go convenience store."

"Good, god! I'd have thought she had more sense."

"Ashley Logan's a problem that's not going away, although she did see him buying a burner phone. Which raised an interesting question. Why would he need one when he already has a cell phone?" He took another sip of the hot brew.

After examining the doll, Dale laid it down and tapped his keyboard. "Damn good point and adds to my belief that Neville's got a finger in this particular pie." Several photos appeared on the screen. "She's right. Here are my pictures of the backyard. That doll is on one of the chairs."

Chad leaned over the desk to look at the screen. "I thought I remembered seeing it there. Maybe it belongs to a kid who was visiting."

"Want me to bag it and put it in the evidence bin?" Dale asked.

"No. I think I'll keep it."

When Dale looked askance at him, he added, "Lydia suggested checking the thrift stores. Someone might recognize it."

"Do you want me to go with you?"

"It's more important for you to stay on those tapes. Anything pop out at you yet?"

"No, but I just got started. Did Lydia mention we haven't had a single call hit the hotline?"

"She did. So far, it's not looking good."

Before leaving, Chad stepped into his office to check for messages. On his desk was a report from Tania Carr, his night shift officer. She'd canvassed the apartment complex where Walker lived. Most of the residents interviewed didn't know the man. Two women saw him walking to a grocery store located nearby. No one had seen him driving a vehicle, which sparked an idea.

Chad walked back to Dale's office. He stopped in the doorway.

"Keep an eye out for Neville's truck on those tapes. Also, dig deeper into his background."

"Will do," Dale answered.

Attired in underwear, Ashley contemplated the clothes hanging in the closet. On a normal day, she'd opt for an outfit appropriate for the office. After the events of yesterday, and the uncertainty of what might happen today, she decided not to risk another painful experience. Dressed in a pair of jeans, and a t-shirt printed with Aggies Rule, she pulled on hiking boots.

Since she planned on stopping at a bakery to pick up the bran muffins Kathy liked, she skipped her usual breakfast of cereal and yogurt.

Peter opened the door. Unshaven, his face was drawn, and his eyes red-rimmed. "Any news?" He stepped back to let her enter.

"I've heard nothing, though I'm going to stop at the command center. How's Kathy doing?"

A grimace crossed his face. "Not good. Every time she drifted off to sleep, a nightmare woke her. Neither of us got much rest. She's in Mandy's room. I can't get her to leave."

Ashley handed him the bag of muffins. "How are you holding up?"

He led the way to the kitchen. "What can I say? It's horrific. I don't know when I've ever felt so out of control, useless. The phone's been ringing off the hook. Chief Bishop said if we didn't recognize the number to let it roll to the answering machine. Same with our cell phones. The phone company has a trace set up."

He set the bag on the table. "So far, it's been friends trying to help. Several have donated money to the reward fund. Speaking of which, I found out why the reward is so large." A flush crossed his face. "I … uh …."

Ashley held up a hand. "Don't worry about it. I'm glad I can do something. I'm going to check on Kathy."

Pale and listless, her sister perched on the edge of Mandy's bed. Her eyes stared at a row of dolls. When Ashley walked in, she looked up. Pain bit deep inside Ashley at the bleak expression on her sister's face. She choked back the tears. Her grief wouldn't help Kathy.

When she sat, her sister leaned against her, saying, "I guess there's no news."

"No, there isn't."

"How do we get through another day?"

"By not giving up hope."

"This is all my fault," she cried. "I should have watched her more closely. But I thought she was safe in our backyard."

"No, don't go there. This isn't your fault."

Ashley racked her brain to think of something to divert Kathy's thoughts. As she stared around the room, the dolls gave her an idea. "I've been thinking about the doll. Have you come up with any notion on how it got into the backyard?"

Kathy straightened; her hand swiped at the tears on her face. "No, I haven't."

"Have any other children visited who might have brought a doll?"

"A few. Several friends have children about the same age as Mandy. I don't remember if any of them had one."

Ashley stood and pulled Kathy up. "Come on, let's talk to Peter. I brought muffins. Since I skipped breakfast, a cup of coffee and a warm muffin sounds good."

The microwave dinged as they walked into the kitchen. When Peter opened the door, an aroma of cinnamon rose in the air.

Once they were seated, Ashley mentioned her idea. "Kathy and I've been talking about the unknown doll. Which, by the way, I gave to the police chief." She didn't believe it was necessary to tell them she'd tossed it at the man. Instead, she added, "I'd suggest calling any friends who have visited and have kids. Ask if they're missing one."

Peter waved his fork in the air. "That's a good idea. We should have thought of it."

"I didn't realize Mandy had so many dolls." Ashley took a sip of her coffee. "Kathy, look through her room. Let's make sure there isn't anything else unusual." It was busywork, something to keep her sister occupied.

"Have you made a list of your activities for the last few weeks?" she said, before popping a bite of muffin into her mouth.

Peter motioned to a stack of papers lying on the counter. "Yes. Chad asked for one."

After swallowing, she asked, "Would you make a copy for me?"

A look of surprise crossed Peter's face. "I've already got an extra one." He picked up a stapled set and handed it to her. "Why do you want it?"

"I'm … um, I'm helping with the investigation." She wasn't going to tell them if Chad had his way, she'd never see the list.

"Ash, do you think it's a good idea? It could be dangerous," Kathy said.

"Oh, I won't get into anything that'll be a problem. Remember, I'm a reporter. I'm good at getting people to talk. That's all I'm going to do, talk to people."

She glanced at Kathy's plate, gratified by what she saw. Engrossed in the conversation, her sister probably didn't realize she'd eaten the two muffins Peter put on her plate.

In the command center, Jim was seated at the table, littered with coffee cups and file folders. Chad eyed his friend and the lines of fatigue around his deep-set, dark blue eyes. "What time did you get here?"

Jim glanced at the wall clock. "About an hour ago."

"Anything?" Chad asked as he poured a cup of coffee.

"Nada. Nothing's turned up. It's like she disappeared into thin air. I contacted dispatch and had them transfer the hotline to here. If a call comes in, we can react faster than waiting on the dispatcher to let us know."

"Good idea. I should have thought of it. Guess I'm still used to a big city department running the entire investigation."

"Small towns take some getting used to," Jim said.

"It's not all bad. How many are involved in the search?"

Jim glanced at the sheets on the table in front of him. "Over forty, which includes officers, firemen, and civilians."

Chad set his cup on the table and pulled out a chair. He picked up the sign-in log. Everyone involved in the search was required to sign-in and provide their contact information. He quickly scanned the list of names, some he recognized, some he didn't.

He glanced at Jim. "Are you running backgrounds on anyone you don't know?" It wasn't unheard of to have a criminal maneuver his way into the investigation. According to the profilers, it boosted the sick thrill they got from committing a crime.

"Yes, but so far, there's only two, a young couple who recently moved to town. With the additional exposure from the Amber Alert, I expect more volunteers will show up today. There are still a few residents who need to be crossed off the list. I'm putting officers at intersections to stop drivers and show them Mandy's picture. Once the Explorers and any other civilian volunteers finish passing out flyers in town, they'll start on the rest of the county."

"Something else happened last night." Chad told him about his encounter with Ashley at the convenience store.

"Damn! Is she working with a full deck? I know Neville. He's got a long rap sheet, assaults, drugs, thefts, in addition to the sexual offense arrest. We've had several complaints from residents."

"She's determined to get involved and definitely *isn't* backing down. Short of throwing her in a jail cell, I don't have a way of stopping her."

Jim grinned. "I'd like to see you try it."

When an image of his hands on her luscious body flooded his mind, he shot a look of irritation at his friend.

Jim smirked.

Ignoring him, Chad took a sip of his coffee before asking, "What do you know about her?"

"Not much. Most of it, I found out from Peter. We were talking about Texas A&M one day, and he mentioned Kathy's dad was a graduate. He said his sister-in-law worked for a newspaper back east. I think she and Kathy grew up somewhere around Houston."

"Seems odd she'd take a job as the editor of a small-town newspaper after working for the Baltimore Sun. How'd she end up here?"

"I'm not sure, but it's not any stranger than you up and quitting Atlanta PD and moving here."

"It was time to make a change," Chad said.

A look of curiosity crossed Jim's face. Chad had always sidestepped his questions on why he'd quit. He started to ask, then changed his mind. If Chad didn't want to talk about it, there must be a good reason. Instead, he asked, "Any thoughts on how the doll got into the backyard?"

Chad shrugged. "Not a clue. My next step is to check with the family. It may be nothing more than some kid left it there. If not, Lydia suggested I contact the thrift stores. Maybe someone will recognize it."

"Anything yet on the tapes?"

"Dale's weeding through them. I told him to look for Neville's truck, which reminds me, I got the report on the interviews where Walker lives. No one has seen him driving a vehicle." Chad tossed his cup in the trash. "I'll be in touch."

Instead of driving, he walked to the Norton house. It was a typical fall morning in Texas. The nights cooled off, and the sun had yet to warm the air, which could turn muggy as the day progressed. As he neared, his eyes scanned the parked cars looking for Ashley's vehicle. He didn't want to start his day with another confrontation.

Peter answered the door. He looked older, but grief did that to people. There was an instinctive flare of hope that changed to despair, as he said, "Come in. You just missed Ashley."

Chad hoped his face didn't reflect the surge of relief. "How are you and Kathy doing?"

"We're holding on, but sometimes I wonder how."

Chad followed him to the kitchen. Empty plates and cups littered the table. Seeing Chad in the doorway, Kathy rose, then sunk back into the chair. "Do you have any news at all?"

"Not yet, though a lot of people are searching for your daughter."

Peter motioned to a plate of muffins on the counter. "Ashley picked them up on her way over here this morning. Would you like one with a cup of coffee?"

"I appreciate the offer, but I only stopped to ask about the doll you found. Do you know who it belongs too?"

"No," Peter said. "Ashley wanted to know if someone left it here. After she left, I called two families who have been here in the last few weeks. It doesn't belong to any of their children."

So much for his hope that she'd backed off the investigation.

"Chad, is there any chance the kidnapper left it?" Peter asked.

"I don't know. I looked at the pictures my detective took of the backyard. The doll *is* sitting on one of the chairs at the table." He turned to Kathy. "After you found Mandy missing, did you pick up the doll and put it there?"

"Oh, no. I didn't even look at the dolls. Besides, Ashley is the one who picked up the dolls and toys and put them in Mandy's bedroom, which is where I found the doll."

"Are you sure it wasn't in the backyard before Mandy was abducted?"

"Didn't Ashley tell you? I've never seen it before, and I'm almost certain Mandy did not take it outside."

Chagrined, he couldn't admit her sister hadn't told him anything. Then Kathy would want to know why.

"Hmm … I just wanted to make sure," Chad said.

"Ash asked if I would go through everything in Mandy's room. She seemed to think it was important. I'm not sure why."

He suspected Ashley had come up with a reason to keep her sister occupied. If it helped, he'd play along. "Please let me know if you find anything. The most insignificant detail can sometimes become critical to a case. Are you letting your calls roll to the message machine?"

Peter said, "The only ones have been from family and friends. Does it mean there won't be a ransom demand?"

"It's possible, but you still need to take precautions."

Peter picked up a file folder and handed it to Chad. "This is the list you requested. We've tried to recreate our movements for the last month, along with who has been to the house."

"This will help."

As Chad walked back to the command center, he perused the documents Peter had given him. Most of the activities centered around work, church, grocery stores, gas stations, and other local businesses. They'd spent a day at a local water park. No repairs or deliveries. The visitors were families they knew. Nothing struck him as out of the ordinary.

When Chad stepped back into the command center, Jim was leaning over the shoulder of a deputy who held a phone to his ear. He was reading the notes the deputy jotted down. When the call was complete, Jim turned to Chad. "First call on the hotline. Someone said they spotted a car with a child who looked like Mandy. They got the license plate number."

The printer spewed out a piece of paper. "It's the vehicle registration." Jim grabbed it. "Damn! This one's not going anywhere. I know the family, and they have a girl who could be mistaken for Mandy. Still, I'll get someone to stop at the house just to be sure."

Chad stepped to the printer and ran a copy of the papers Peter had given him. He handed them to Jim. "List of activities for the last month."

"I'll go over this. Did you spot anything?"

"No, but I haven't examined them in detail. I'm headed to check out the local thrift shops."

Chad had opened the door when Jim's voice stopped him. He glanced over his shoulder.

"Almost forgot to tell you I sent a deputy to keep an eye on Neville," Jim said.

"If he moves, let me know."

Chapter Nine

❧

Seated in his truck, Chad picked up Lydia's list of stores. She'd even added locations in the surrounding towns. The first two were downtown. Might as well start there.

On the main drag, the stores were just beginning to open, and he had no difficulty finding a place to park. In the middle of the block, a weather-beaten sign for Bits & Pieces hung over the door.

As he approached, he spotted the flyer for Mandy taped to the front window. He stepped into a small room. On each side, shelves held what his mother would call knickknacks. A long counter extended along the back wall. Leaned over it, a woman talked to someone seated on the other side.

His gaze crawled over the enticing view of jeans molded to a shapely backside and long legs encased in boots. The tinkle of the overhead doorbell interrupted their conversation. The woman glanced over her shoulder. As she stared at him, Ashley Logan's eyes narrowed in disbelief.

Chad choked back a groan of dismay. Although he wondered what she was up too, he ignored her as he stepped up to the counter. Setting the sack with the doll on top, he laid his arm over it.

One of his first tasks as police chief was to meet the business owners in the small community. He'd spent several days going from store to store to introduce himself. Nora Graham's store had been one of his first stops.

"Morning, Nora. It's another beautiful day."

Eyes, in a face surprisingly smooth for a woman in her late sixties, sparked with a gleam of curiosity. They flicked between him, Ashley, and the bag. Small towns thrived on gossip. The new buzz for the morning coffee club would be his and Ashley's visit.

"Howdy, Chief." She chuckled before adding, "At my age, every day is beautiful. I don't take anything for granted."

"I'm not certain about the age thing," he said, as he leaned toward her. "I heard about the line dancing at the senior center. I doubt I could keep up with you."

She laughed again. "You come on over and try. We'll see if you can hold up." Her demeanor turned serious. "Have you any news about this awful kidnapping?"

"Nothing yet, but a lot of people are looking for Mandy."

Nora nodded. "I've heard about all the volunteers. Have you met our new editor, Ashley Logan? What am I thinking? Of course, you have, since she's Mandy's aunt."

Chad glanced at Ashley. "Ms. Logan."

Ashley ignored him as she gleefully eyed the bag. "You brought the doll. Good. All I have is a picture on my phone." She made a grab for it, but Chad pulled it out of her reach.

"I'll handle this."

She glared at him as he turned to Nora. "Do you recognize this doll?" He pulled it from the sack.

Nora reached for it, turning it over to examine the back. "No. I've never seen it. Why are both of you asking? Does it have something to do with Mandy?"

More grist for the rumor mill, but it couldn't be helped. "It may or may not. It's a lead *I'm* running down." He shot a look of irritation at Ashley, before turning back to Nora. "Do you sell used toys?"

"Oh, yes. We've got a whole section."

"Have you sold any dolls lately?"

"I haven't." She stood and stepped to the doorway that led to the interior of the store, then hollered, "Edith, get out here."

Sitting down, she looked at Ashley. "Edith Monroe's my cousin."

Another elderly woman, her face lined with wrinkles, stepped through the doorway. Wisps of white hair stuck out from under a ratty black and white ball cap. Emblazoned on the front was a small rocking chair with the words 'Old Women Rock.' A pair of glasses suspended by a cord hung around her neck.

"Stop screaming at me. I can hear you. What do you want?"

"If you'd turn up your dang hearing aid, I wouldn't have to shout. Our police chief here wants to know if we've ever seen this doll."

Chad stifled a grin as he listened to the feisty exchange.

Edith shuffled to the counter, perched the glasses atop her nose, looked at Chad, then Ashley, and finally the doll. The thick lens magnified her eyes before she pushed the glasses down to peer over the top at Chad. "Nope, never seen it. Why are you asking?"

"Edith, you know the Norton girl is missing. He's *investigating*!" Nora exclaimed.

"Of course, he's investigating. You think I didn't know that? I wanted to know what a doll has to do with it," she barked back. With another sharp look at Chad, she added, "We've never had something this bad happen here," as if it were his fault. Turning her attention to Ashley, she said, "You're the new editor."

"Yes, I'm also Kathy's sis ..."

Edith interrupted. "If that idiot of a reporter, Henry, is going to write about a missing child, he needs to learn to get his facts straight. His last article on home canning was riddled with mistakes. Anyway, what does a man know about canning? Humph! Bet he never screwed down a lid on a single jar."

Ashley said, "I'll be sure to mention it to him."

At the quiver in her voice, Chad flicked a glance her way. Her eyes glinted with humor as they met his.

"Yes, yes, Edith," Nora said. "I've heard enough about that article. It's all you've talked about since the paper came out. Don't need to rehash it again. The Chief's got more important stuff to worry about than the right way to preserve peaches. He wants to know if we've sold any dolls lately."

"If you'd check the dang sales receipts, you'd know we haven't. I keep telling you writing down all that information is a waste of time." She sniffed, turned, and shuffled toward the doorway where she stopped and glanced over her shoulder. "I expect you to find Mandy. Do you hear me, Chief Bishop?"

"Yes, ma'am. I'm going to do the very best I can."

Edith sniffed again before walking out of view.

Chad turned to Nora. "Here's my card. If you think of something, call me."

"I will."

He stuffed the doll back into the bag and followed Ashley out the door.

Outside, Ashley walked a short way along the sidewalk, then stopped. Her laughter rang out. When Chad caught up with her, she said, "What a pair. I bet it's how their entire day goes, bickering back and forth."

Chad's breath hitched. Her dark eyes gleamed with joy. What a difference from the stern disapproval he'd seen ever since she first strode into his office. He thought nothing could make her more desirable. She'd just proved how wrong he was.

He chuckled, then said, "They've probably been at it most of their lives."

Suddenly, her eyes filled with tears. "Oh, no, why are we laughing? We're not any closer to finding Mandy."

Chad understood the need for the light moments in an investigation. Sometimes, it was all that kept a person from getting mired in a pit of grief. In his case, it was usually referred to as cop humor, a way of deflecting the emotional trauma. Should he explain? Deciding he shouldn't, he said, "Every step in an investigation is one step closer. Where are you headed?"

Her body stiffened. "Why? Are you going to stop me?"

Chad took a deep breath, wondering if he was about to make the biggest mistake of his life. "I figure you're doing the same thing I am, checking thrift shops. No point in either one of us following the other. Do you want to team up?"

Her eyes widened in surprise, then narrowed as a look of suspicion settled on her face.

Chad could almost feel the wheels churning as she stared at him. As he watched the flow of emotions flickering across her face, Chad's lips tightened to stop a grin from erupting. Was she always this touchy, or did he bring out the worst in her? "Well, made up your mind yet?"

"Hmm … what's the catch?"

"Are you always this suspicious?"

"Yeah, comes with the territory."

He laughed. "No catch. I've got a list my secretary gave me. The next one is around the corner."

"I've got a list too."

"Figured you did." He looked at his watch. "Tell you what. Let's check this store, then grab a bite to eat. I missed breakfast and suspect all you had was one of those muffins I saw at your sister's house. While we eat, we can compare lists."

"You've been to see Kathy and Peter?" Without realizing it, she turned to walk alongside him.

"They said you'd just left. It seems I was one step behind you."

Another chuckle erupted. "So far, it's par for the course, my being … one step *ahead* of you," she said.

He shot a quick glance at her. She grinned.

"Don't push your luck," he quipped.

Her tone turned serious. "I got a call from Peter. He said none of their friends left the doll."

"He told me when I was there," Chad said.

She mused as they strolled along the sidewalk. "I've covered stories on missing children, but I never fully realized the depth of the fear and grief for a parent."

"It's rough."

"Are there many you've never found?"

"Yes, but even one is one too many." He heard her deep sigh.

"Never thought I'd experience it firsthand. Chad, are you going to find her?"

He wondered if she realized she'd said Chad, not Chief Bishop, with a sarcastic tone. "I wish I could say yes, but I don't know. All we can do is keep working the leads. Maybe one of them will lead us to her."

As he held open the door to Shards of History, she looked up at him. "I guess you aren't such a prick after all," she said, before strolling inside.

Chapter Ten

⁓❧⁓

Their visit didn't last long. The owner didn't recognize the
doll, and she carried very few toys.

Outside, Chad asked, "Is the deli across the street, okay?"

"Uh, oh, yes. It's fine."

"What are you thinking?"

"I'm still trying to figure out how the doll got into the backyard.
It's not Mandy's. It doesn't belong to any of their friends. Where did
it come from?"

An image flashed in his mind. No, he wasn't going to even
consider it as a possibility. "There has to be a rational answer. We
just haven't found it."

As he escorted her across the street, Chad's hand lightly wrapped
around her arm. The warmth of his touch sent a jolt of anticipation
rushing through her. The man was too damned attractive for his own
good. To stem the flood of emotions her imagination kindled, words
tumbled from her mouth. "I guess jaywalking isn't against the law in
Meridian." *Ashley, he's going to think you're an idiot, talking about
jaywalking.*

He laughed. "I don't believe the city council has enacted any new
ordinances in the last fifty years. And no, crosswalks didn't exist back
then. The last one on the books prohibits livestock on the sidewalk."

"Livestock?"

"Yep, cows, goats, horses, sheep. You know—livestock." He laughed.

"You've got to be kidding."

"Nope. Look it up."

"I will. It would make a good article for the newspaper."

Inside the small deli, Chad greeted the woman behind the counter.

"Chief, good to see you. You're early today. The usual?"

"Yep." He looked at Ashley. "Have you met Peggy Jenkins? She's the owner."

Ashley extended her hand across the counter. "Ashley Logan. I'm the new editor of the Tribune. Nice to meet you." She wondered how long it would take before she could stop saying the new editor.

Peggy shook her hand. "I know. Seen you around town. Welcome to Meridian."

Ashley glanced up at Chad. "So, what's your usual?"

"Turkey on rye."

"Good choice, but I like soups." Her gaze had scanned the menu board mounted on the wall. "I'll have a bowl of potato chowder along with a glass of iced tea."

"You got it. You folks have a seat. I'll get your tea."

Chad steered Ashley to a table by the front window. Since they were the only customers, they had their pick.

"You two know each other?" Ashley asked, wondering at their exchange of warm smiles. Peggy was an attractive, thirty-something woman. Since Chad was in his early thirties, she could understand his attraction. Her mood nose-dived.

"We met right after I got to town." Before pulling out her chair, he dropped the bag with the doll on a table next to them. "Trying to get settled in my house and a new job didn't leave much time for cooking. Peggy does takeout. Her husband is the chef."

As she sat, Ashley refused to consider the upswing in her feelings was anything but a result of Chad's old-fashioned courtesy.

When he stepped around the table, a frown settled on his face as he stared out the window. Ashley twisted to see what caught his attention. It was a truck driven by Doyle Neville.

"What do you know about him?" she asked.

For a second, he hesitated as he settled in his chair. No matter how damn attractive she was, Ashley was a reporter. Still, Jim had made a good point. She did have a stake in this. Maybe it was time to rethink his position. He glanced toward the counter to make sure Peggy was out of earshot before saying, "He's a sex offender."

"I figured as much. Otherwise, you wouldn't have contacted him as fast as you did."

He pulled his phone and tapped a number. "Jim, have you heard from your man on Neville?"

"Yes, but he hasn't located him."

"He's in his truck and headed south on Main toward Highway 22.

"Can you follow him until my deputy can catch up?"

"No. By the time I get to my truck, he'll be long gone." He listened for a few seconds, then disconnected.

"What was that all about?" Ashley asked.

Chad leaned back as Peggy approached with two mason jars filled with tea. After setting them on the table, she said, "Food will be out in a few minutes."

He nodded, picked up the glass, and took a sip. Time to get her off the subject. "How'd you find out about him?"

She shot him a sly look and unfolded her napkin. "You know a good reporter doesn't reveal sources."

"Ashley ... give it up."

She liked the way his deep voice sounded when he said her name.

Her fingertip brushed the condensation on the glass as she rested her chin in her other hand.

"Ashley." His tone was insistent.

"I ... uh ... I followed you."

"You did what! I don't believe it. I'd have seen you."

Another smug look crossed her face as her gaze met his. "Guess not, since it's what I did." She took a sip of tea. "You and your detective were inside Neville's place at that mobile home park."

"I'll be damned. Did you follow us when we left?" Chad wondered if she knew about Walker.

"No. I didn't get a chance. Couldn't get back to my car in time."

Chad had rocked back on the chair legs. The edginess in her voice told him there was more to the story. "What did you do?"

"Not much. Just stopped by to have a chat with him after you left."

The front legs of Chad's chair thumped the floor. "Not much! Holy hell!" he hissed. "I can't believe you'd take such a risk."

A mulish look settled on her face. "I've encountered Neville's type many times on assignments in Baltimore."

"Baltimore is a busy city with lots of people, and cops are only minutes away. It's not the same as a remote mobile home park in the middle of central Texas that has no one close. God-a-mighty!" His hand ran over his face as he frowned at her. "And then, you had to follow him."

"Nothing happened." She leaned forward to glare at him. "Quit getting all riled up."

"Ahem, excuse me."

Their heads jerked around.

Peggy stood next to the table with a loaded tray balanced on her arm. "If you two have finished, I'll be glad to set these dishes on the table."

Chad grinned up at her as he eased back in the chair. "A slight disagreement."

"Uh-huh, I could tell." After setting the plates and bowls on the table, she pulled the tab from her pocket and dropped it near the table's edge. "Let me know when you're ready for a refill on the tea."

She turned and strode back behind the counter.

They both reached for the bill, but Chad's hand was faster. "I've got this."

For a moment, Ashley fumed. She didn't want to be indebted to him, then realized how stupid it would be to argue over who paid. Instead, she said, "Okay, let's call a truce. What's done is done. Is Neville a suspect?"

Reluctantly, Chad said, "Not a strong one."

"What does that mean?" she asked, spooning up a bite of soup. A look of surprise passed over her face. "Wow, this is really good. I'll have to consider getting takeout myself." For several minutes, she relished the rich, creamy taste.

Watching her enjoyment, Chad munched on his sandwich and hoped she was done with the questions about Neville, which died when she dropped the spoon in the bowl.

"So, what's the deal with this guy? Why isn't he a good suspect?"

After swallowing a swig of tea, he said, "He's got an alibi."

"Yeah, I know. Neville made a point of telling me when I talked to him," Ashley said.

A spark of irritation flashed in his eyes at the reminder. Not wanting to rehash his argument, he said, "We've got nothing on him, other than I guess you'd say a cop's instinct. Jim's assigned one of his deputies to watch him."

"I'd think tailing someone in a small community would be difficult." She pushed her bowl aside and with a casual tone, asked, "Who got the assignment?" When Chad said he didn't know, she shot him a suspicious look.

With raised hands, he protested, "I really *don't* know."

Making a mental note to find out, she said, "What's the next stop on your list?"

He chewed the last bite of his sandwich as he pulled the list from his shirt pocket. Swallowing, he said, "Lydia added several that are nearby."

Ashley reached into her tote bag. Opening a notepad, she read the locations she'd found, while Chad compared them to his list.

"I don't have those last two," he said and wrote them down. "We should be able to check all of them today. Do you have anything else on your agenda?"

After swallowing the last of the tea, she absent-mindedly said, "No, I'm all yours." When she realized how her words could be misconstrued, a blush stained her cheeks. Her eyes shifted down as she refolded the napkin she'd laid in her lap. "Uh, what I meant was I … have nothing planned."

When Chad didn't respond, her gaze darted upward. Her breath caught at the back of her throat at the hot spark of desire in his eyes. The intense look vanished as if a shutter had closed. Did she imagine it? His phone chimed. Mentally, she sighed. Saved by the proverbial bell.

Another unwanted thought crossed her mind. Did she really want to be saved? Then she realized the call was from her brother-in-law. Something was wrong.

Chapter Eleven

His tone calm, Chad asked, "Peter, are you certain? Have you checked the entire house?"

Ashley wanted to ask him to put the call on the speakerphone until she glanced around. A couple stood at the counter. Scratch that idea. Frightened, her heart raced as she waited.

"I don't suppose you have a picture?" Chad asked. He listened, then said, "I'm on my way."

When he disconnected the call, Ashley couldn't contain herself. "What's going on?"

Chad looked at the couple who had sat near them. "Are you done?"

"Yes."

"Let's go." He pulled a twenty from his wallet and tossed it on the table.

Ashley shot out of the chair and headed to the door. Chad grabbed the bag, then waved goodbye to Peggy as he followed.

"What happened?" Ashley demanded to know as soon as he stepped outside.

Grabbing her elbow, he steered her along the sidewalk. "Where is your car?"

"At my office. I walked here."

"Mine's just down the street. We'll go in it."

"Dammit, Chad! I want to know why Peter called," she muttered as they passed another couple who slowed to look in the window of an antique store.

"I'll tell you in a minute."

He stopped beside a truck and opened the passenger door.

"Whose vehicle is this?"

"Mine. I didn't want to use a squad car today."

After sliding behind the wheel, he tossed the bag into the back seat, then shifted to face Ashley.

Angered by his sudden aloof attitude, she jammed the seat belt in place. A sharp click of metal echoed.

"Peter said a doll is missing."

Her head jerked up. "That's it! That's the big mystery you couldn't talk about until we got to your truck; a doll is missing?"

"According to Peter, they don't know when it disappeared."

"Okay. I still don't see how it's important."

Memories of another doll flashed in his mind. Ignoring a tingle of apprehension, he said, "It's a detail. Sometimes, the smallest detail can break open a case. As for not wanting to talk about it, I don't like someone eavesdropping on my conversations about an investigation. It's easy to blow a comment into something it's not."

He turned the key in the ignition, but not before Ashley caught the bleak look, which flashed across his face. The instinct that had led to several awards for outstanding investigative reporting kicked into high gear. Is that what happened in Atlanta, someone overheard a remark? She suspected there was more, a whole lot more, Chad wasn't saying.

As he steered into traffic, he said, "We're stopping at your sister's house before we head out of town. I have a couple of questions."

During the short drive, thoughts tumbled in her mind. How was she going to crack open the mystery Chad was hiding?

Peter opened the front door as they exited the vehicle. "Saw you pull up." His eyebrow raised in a silent question as he looked at his sister-in-law.

"We joined forces," she explained as she followed Peter into the house.

Kathy was in the doorway to the family room. "Anything, Chief Bishop?" she anxiously asked.

"No. Please call me Chad. I have a few questions about the missing doll."

After everyone was seated, he asked, "When did you find it missing?"

"Right before Peter called you. I told you Ashley asked that I check Mandy's room."

"I remember."

"I don't know why I didn't notice it before." Her hands twisted in her lap. "It's Betsy."

"Betsy?" Chad said.

A faint smile lit Kathy's face. "Mandy has a name for all of them. Betsy's her favorite and goes everywhere with her. When she goes to bed, it's in her arms, tucked tight against her."

The image of another child with a doll clutched in her arms flashed in his mind. His apprehension twisted into a surreal fear, a feeling he'd experienced before. It scared the hell out of him.

"When did you last see … um, Betsy?" He hoped no one heard the slight tremor in his voice.

A troubled look crossed Kathy's face. "That's what I don't understand. She gets to take four dolls outside. She'd take all of them if I let her. Betsy is always one of them; she takes turns with the others."

Chad asked, "You're sure Betsy was in the backyard yesterday morning?"

She hesitated as her hands continued to twist and turn. "Yes. I remember seeing it in her hands when she walked outside."

Chad looked at Ashley. "Your sister told me you picked up the dolls in the yard. How many were there?"

"Four. Three at the table and the fourth on the tricycle."

Kathy exclaimed, "I don't understand. There should have been five with the other doll. The kidnapper must have swapped them."

"Did you find a picture of Betsy?" Chad asked.

Peter shook his head. "No ..."

Kathy interrupted. "Chief, uh ... Chad, you already have it. It's the doll in the picture of Mandy you took from the mantel."

With a sheepish look, Peter said, "When we talked on the phone, I didn't realize you already had a picture. I hope we didn't bother you with something unimportant."

Chad stood. "No, you didn't cause a problem at all. I want you to call even if you think it's trivial. As I said to someone earlier, any little detail could become important."

After saying her goodbyes with a hug for each, Ashley followed him out the door. As she got into the truck, she asked, "Chad, is everything all right? You seemed troubled in there."

Her voice broke through the muddled thoughts rolling in his head. "I'm puzzled, that's all."

She had an edgy sensation that he was lying.

Before starting the engine, he asked, "Do you have a copy of the flyer in your bag?"

In response, she reached into the large tote bag she'd dropped on the floorboard next to her feet, then pulled out a file folder. Inside was the flyer. She handed it to him.

After a quick glance, he passed it back, then turned the key in the ignition. "Do you remember seeing the doll in her bedroom after Mandy was kidnapped?" he asked, though he already knew the answer.

Glancing at the photo, she said, "It's the one Mandy's been carrying around since I arrived in town." She hesitated, remembering the moment in Mandy's bedroom when she paused to peruse each of the dolls. "No, I didn't see it, and I looked at every doll when I dropped the box of toys in her room."

As Chad pulled away from the curb, he said, "Why did you ask Kathy to check the bedroom?"

She grimaced before saying, "To be honest, it was something to keep her busy. Do you think the kidnapper switched the dolls?"

"It's a logical assumption," Chad said, careful to keep his tone neutral.

Ashley glanced at his impassive face. Another lie, but why?

As memories he'd buried for months continued to fog his mind, Chad wasn't sure it was the only explanation; however, he wasn't about to change his assertion. It would raise questions he wasn't prepared to answer, even if he could. Ashley's face already had a look of keen curiosity, which spelled trouble. He didn't need her prying into his secrets.

"Before we head to Whitney, I want to make one more stop." He turned onto the side street, where the command center was located.

When they walked into the motorhome, Jim stood behind his deputy seated at the computer monitor. At the sound of the door opening, his head swiveled.

Surprise flashed across his face. "Didn't expect to see the two of you together." He nodded to Ashley.

"Nice to see you again, Sheriff." Ashley managed to keep the smirk off her face as she remembered their last encounter.

Jim looked at Chad. "I thought you were checking the thrift stores."

"Turns out, we were both on the same mission, so it made sense to team up," Chad explained.

A gleam of humor glinted in his friend's eyes. Chad turned his groan into a cough. Jim wouldn't pass up a chance to razz him when he got the opportunity.

"Turn up anything?" Jim asked.

"No. We got sidetracked. The Norton's discovered a doll is missing. It was in the backyard when Mandy was abducted. It's the one in the picture on the flyer."

"What's going on with these damn dolls? We seem to keep tripping over them," Jim muttered, grabbing a flyer from a box.

Chad wasn't about to add to the confusion with any wild and improbable theories.

"The kidnapper probably took it to help keep Mandy quiet and left the other one. I'll add it to the description," Jim told him.

"Any calls on the hotline?"

"A few, but they were duds."

"How about Neville?"

"My deputy still hasn't located him. Where are you headed?"

"Whitney. There are a few more antique and thrift stores in the area."

"Good luck."

Chad glanced at the clock. Mandy had been missing for over twenty-four hours. They needed a break, and they needed it soon. The longer this went on, the less chance they'd find her.

A chill rushed over her. Ashley hadn't missed Chad's glance at the clock or his look of uncertainty. She knew time was working against them.

"I'll be outside," she said, nodding to Jim before she headed out the door. She strode to the sidewalk, taking in deep breaths to control the panic, which threatened to overwhelm her. Where was Mandy? Was she still alive? There had to be something they could do, but what? Nothing in her life had prepared her for this overwhelming sense of helplessness.

Stepping out of the motorhome, Chad watched her shoulders slump. It was his turn to ask if she was okay.

Before turning, she took a deep breath to help push back the churning emotions. "Yes. It's not knowing. I guess it gets to you after a while."

He nodded. "It doesn't matter how many times you handle a case like this, it never gets easier. If it did, then it would be time to turn in my badge."

Even as she stared at him with a new level of respect, an odd yearning swept over her. Yesterday, he'd been impressive in his uniform. He exuded confidence while bordering on arrogance at times.

Today, he was sensual and dangerous. He stood there, legs widespread and sunglasses dangling from one hand. Jeans and a t-shirt molded his lanky body under the light jacket he wore. The sunlight glinted on dark auburn hair that tousled across his forehead. Her hand itched to feel her fingers running through the silky strands. But it was his eyes that drew her in. Enigmatic, they hinted of dark secrets.

"You sure you're all right?" he asked.

"Yes," she said, though uncertainty nipped at her. Her reaction was one she hadn't felt since Lance was killed. It was a hell of a time for her hormones to run amuck, and especially over a cop who wasn't telling all he knew. It's what she needed to focus on. What was he hiding? It was about a thirty-minute drive to Whitney. Plenty of time to ask questions.

Chapter Twelve

*I*n the truck, she pulled the list of locations from her tote bag. "There is one store before we get to the dam, and the rest are in Whitney. Do you need the addresses?"

"No, I know where they are."

She settled in her seat. "For someone who hasn't been here very long, you seem to know your way around."

"After the streets of Atlanta, this part of the country is easy."

"What brought you back to Texas? From everything I've learned, you were a well-respected and highly decorated officer. What made you give up a detective position and move here?"

He glanced her way before steering into the opposite lane and speeding up to pass a farm truck pulling a trailer loaded with large round bales of hay. Damn, she was already prying, checking into his background. She might be Mandy's aunt, but Ashley Logan was also a very astute reporter. *Keep it simple.*

"Even though APD is a good department, I decided it was time to get back to my roots, which was Texas. When the position for the police chief came open, I applied. Simple as that."

She shifted in the seat to look at him. Her unwavering gaze said more than any words. She wasn't buying his answer.

"I understand you and the sheriff have quite a history."

He laughed. "That's putting it mildly. We were roommates at A&M. Been friends ever since. He was the one who recommended I apply for the job."

Ashley persisted. "Still, it's a big change from a major city police department to Meridian PD. I would have thought a small town would be too limiting."

"I suppose it's one way to look at it. I've found it's just a different set of challenges."

Henry said he wasn't forthcoming. Henry was right. "I read about the problems with your last case."

His hands tightened on the wheel. "It was a rough one. What about you? It seems like quite a stretch for a Baltimore Sun reporter to end up at a small-town rag."

Since he wanted to change the subject, she'd play along. It might earn his trust. "Guess we aren't so dissimilar. I wanted a change. Moving back to Texas seemed like a good idea."

"Seemed like … does that mean you regret it?"

Leave it to his detective mind to pick up on the inconsistency. "No, not really. It takes a while to get acclimated."

"What about your family?"

"Kathy and I grew up in Pearland, just south of Houston. Mom died of cancer when we were in high school. Then a couple of years ago, Dad passed away from a heart attack. Other than a few remote cousins, it's just Kathy and me."

"I heard your dad graduated from A&M."

"Where'd you hear that?"

"From Jim."

Ashley chuckled. Yep, there it was, the A&M bond. "What about your family?"

"Oh, they still live in College Station. Dad is the principal of the local high school, and mom is an artist. Some of her paintings have been exhibited at various galleries across Texas."

"That's impressive. I'd love to see some of her work."

"I have several of her paintings in my home. Why don't you come over sometime, I'll show you my etchings?" he quipped.

It was a line from an old movie, and she couldn't resist firing back. "Cowboy, not even in your wildest dreams."

His laughter erupted.

Smiling, she asked, "Any brothers or sisters?"

Still chuckling, he said, "Nope. I'm the only headache of a kid they've got."

Under her breath, she muttered, "I'd believe it."

His lips twitched. "Uh, I didn't hear you."

Looking for the next thrift shop, Ashley had eyed the stores they passed. She straightened. "Hey, isn't that Neville's truck?"

"Where?"

"The bait shop we just passed."

Chad pulled to the shoulder and stopped. As soon as the traffic cleared, he turned around to make another pass by the store.

Pointing her finger, Ashley said, "There. RB's Bait and Tackle." Signs mounted on posts advertised bait, along with other fishing items.

Chad slowed as he cruised by to get a good look at the black truck parked in front of the building.

His voice grim, he said, "You're right, it's Neville's truck. I wonder why he's there. He doesn't strike me as a person into fishing. There are several bait shops along this road and around the lake. Why this one?"

He pulled his phone and tapped the screen. When Jim answered, Chad said, "Jim, did your deputy ever find Neville?"

"No, he hasn't."

"Neville's truck is parked at RB's Bait and Tackle store."

"I'll tell him."

"What about the owners? Got anything on them?"

"I've met Rick and Fran Coleman. I don't know much about them. I'll start digging."

Chad drove a mile or so before turning back. As they passed the store again, the truck was still there.

"Seems like a long time to buy something," Ashley said.

"Yeah. Our first stop is up ahead. We might be able to watch the bait shop from there."

He slowed to turn into a small strip center with a half-dozen stores. He backed into a space in front of Second Chance Gifts.

The bait shop was on the other side of the highway. While it was some distance away, if the truck left, they'd be able to see it from their location.

He picked up the phone from the console. When the call was answered, he said, "Dale, run a search on the owners of RB's Bait and Tackle. Neville's there."

"That's Rick Coleman's place. I'll get started on it. Any idea what's going on?"

"Not yet." Disconnecting, Chad reached for the bag on the backseat. "I'm going inside. Do you mind staying here and keeping an eye on the parking lot? If the truck moves, tap the horn."

"No, go. I'll stand guard."

Inside the store, a young girl was seated on a stool behind a counter. He introduced himself and asked if the owner was there.

"That's my mom. She's unpacking boxes in the back."

"Would you let her know I'm here and would like to speak to her?"

She trotted to the back of the store. In a few minutes, she returned, followed by a woman wearing a full apron.

"I'm Gwen Shelton." She wiped her hand on the apron before

extending it to Chad. "Sorry, unpacking boxes and sacks can be a dirty business. You wouldn't believe the stuff people drop off. Christie says you're the police chief in Meridian. Is something wrong?"

"No. I'm looking for information. Have you ever seen this doll?" He pulled it from the sack.

She reached for it. After studying it for a few seconds, she shook her head no. "I get a lot of used dolls, but I've never seen this one." She handed it back.

"Have you sold any in the last few months?"

She pursed her lips as she thought. "There's only one I remember. I know the woman who bought it. Her daughter was in the hospital."

Chad handed her a business card and asked her to call if she remembered anything else.

"Why are you asking about a doll?"

"Yesterday morning, a girl was kidnapped in Meridian. I'm trying to find out if this doll is connected."

"I saw the Amber Alert. You wouldn't think something like that could happen here. I'll check my receipts to see if I can come up with anything."

"Any help will be appreciated. I see the volunteers haven't dropped off a flyer yet. Would you stick one in the window?"

"Oh, yes, absolutely."

Chad headed back outside and opened the rear door. "Anything?"

"Nope. He hasn't moved."

He dropped the sack and grabbed a flyer from the box on the floorboard. "Be right back."

Gwen was waiting by the door with a roll of tape, and within seconds the flyer was taped to the window.

Back in the truck, he said, "Let's wait here until the tail shows up." He tapped the screen on his phone. When Jim answered, he said, "We're down the road at the Second Chance Gift store keeping an eye on the bait shop. The truck is still there. Tell your deputy to meet us here."

He scooted down in the seat, his eyes glued to the store across the road.

Ashley shifted and leaned against the door to keep from twisting her head to watch the lot. The silence hung heavy in the air. This was too good of an opportunity to pass up. "Why did the attorney for the suspect in the abduction in Atlanta claim the search warrant was defective?"

Christ, the woman wasn't going to let it go. "Know anything about search warrants?"

"Some. I know you have to prove a valid reason exists for the search."

"Close enough," he growled. He hated being reminded of what happened. "In this case, the attorney for the scumbag tried to argue my reasons weren't enough."

"Why? What was wrong with them?"

Chad took a deep breath. "Ashley, it's ancient history. The case is over. End of story. No reason to talk about it now. Why Meridian for you?"

She heard the bitterness in his voice. Okay, she'd back off, but one way or another, she was going to find out.

"When Kathy and I talked about my moving back to Texas, my first thought was Houston. Lots of newspapers in the area. When the editor for the Tribune quit, Kathy called to see if I'd be interested in the job."

"Why move back to Texas?"

Ashley didn't like to talk about Lance's death. Even after a year, the pain could still reach out and grab her. If she answered his questions, turnabout was only fair play. She wanted answers.

"My fiancée was on his way home from work. Lance was also a reporter for the Sun. A drunk driver ran a red light and t-boned the car. He died at the scene." A ripple of grief flashed through her as the memories of that night rushed back.

He shot a glance at her. "Memories. They're hard to escape. How long ago?"

"A little over a year."

A truck backed alongside them. The driver exited and walked to Chad's door. He hit the button to lower the window. "Ken. I didn't know you were the one Jim assigned."

The man laid an arm on the sill as he looked into the truck. "Since I'm the latest hire at the department, Jim figured Neville might not recognize me."

He'd met Ken Larkin several weeks back when he first interviewed for the deputy's job. Jim invited Chad to lunch to meet the man. Ken had worked for the Fort Worth Police Department for twenty-five years. He liked to fish and decided Lake Whitney was a good place to retire. Except, he got bored.

Chad introduced him to Ashley, then said, "He's still inside the bait shop. Been there for some time. Whatever reason he's got, it's not to buy bait."

"I'd like to go inside to see what he's up too, but I don't dare take a chance," Ken said. "I've got it if you want to leave."

"We still have a few stops to make in Whitney."

"Jim said you were tracking down a lead. Anything yet?"

"No, I wish I could say I did."

Ken nodded and walked back to his truck.

Chad pulled onto the highway and headed to Whitney, which was located on the other side of the lake. Three hours later, they'd contacted the stores on their combined list and nothing.

Leaving the last store on their list, Ashley asked, "Did we just waste most of a day?"

"Welcome to a day in the life of a cop, the boring and mundane. More often than not, it's a process of elimination rather than discovery."

Depressed, Ashley sighed and leaned her head against the headrest. "We're not any closer to finding Mandy."

The atmosphere inside the vehicle was glum. *She's right. As leads went, this one went nowhere.*

Reaching into her tote bag, she pulled out a file folder.

Chad flicked a glance at it. "What do you have there?"

"A copy of Peter and Kathy's activity list. I haven't looked at it."

"I didn't spot anything unusual. In a case like this, it's not uncommon."

"Hmm …" she muttered as she scanned the entries. It was all so ordinary, what people did most every day of their life.

Frustrated, she tossed the file on top of the tote bag. "So, now what?"

As Chad drove over the Lake Whitney dam, he looked at the sun, sinking lower and lower in the sky. "Call it a day."

"There's nothing else we can do?" she cried in dismay. "There's got to be something!"

He shot a look of sympathy her way. "Right now, we're at a stalemate. We've done everything we can until something new comes in."

Tears filled her eyes. She turned her head to stare out the window. Soon, it would be dark, and a little girl was out there somewhere. Was Mandy hungry, hurt, or … no, she wouldn't let her thoughts go down that path.

For an instant, his hand gripped her shoulder. She swiped at the tears on her cheekbones before turning her head to glance at Chad. His eyes stared ahead, but his face was taut with determination. How had she ever thought he was arrogant and overbearing? As she was learning, Chad was a man who wore many faces. Fascinated, she wondered about the ones she had yet to discover, then realized where her thoughts were headed. What was wrong with her? She barely knew the man. They were only drawn together because of Mandy. They had no future. Unbidden, the memory of that spark of desire at the deli flicked in her thoughts. Was it possible?

Ahead, a flash of light caught her attention. It came from a water park. The light from the setting sun gleamed off a large slide. She remembered passing it before they drove over the dam on their way to Whitney but hadn't paid any attention to it. Why did the sight of it suddenly seem to mean something to her?

"Chad! The water park. Why does it sound familiar?"

Unknowingly, Chad's thoughts had followed those of Ashley's, about how wrong he had been in his estimation of her character. As a cop, he knew better than to make snap judgments about someone. Instead, he'd let his past memories override his normal good sense. There was no doubt he wanted her in his bed, but Chad refused to believe it was his only reason for thinking he'd misjudged her. Lost in his thoughts, he hadn't been listening. "What?"

"The water park." She grabbed the file folder she'd dropped. "It's on the list." Rifling the pages, she stopped at one. "Yes, here it is. Two weeks ago, they spent the day at this water park."

Chad pulled to the shoulder and stared at the entrance sign ahead of them. "Hmm … I wonder?"

"What are you thinking? Wait a minute, the bait shop. How far is it from the park?"

He wasn't surprised she'd quickly made the same connection. "A mile or two."

"It's got to mean something!"

"It may, then again, it could be a coincidence." He didn't want to encourage her or let her get her hopes up.

Desperate, she was ready to grasp any chance, however slight. "How can you say that? You can't believe it. It's got to be important."

"Ashley, it's a starting point. I won't ignore it, but I don't know if it's a lead or a dead end. We still don't know if Neville is even involved."

She sunk back in the seat. Her eyes gazed up at the ceiling as she thought. "Okay. But I can make a damn good case on the fact your suspicions of Neville were enough to put a tail on him."

He smiled to himself. Ashley wasn't about to stop. He pulled back onto the highway.

"What do you plan to do?" she asked.

"Find out more about the owners. When we get back to town, I'll drop you at your car." He pulled his phone.

When Jim answered, he asked, "Are you still at the command center?"

"Yes."

"I want to talk to you before you leave." He glanced at his watch. "I'll be there in about twenty minutes."

After he disconnected, Ashley asked, "Why the meeting?"

Ever the reporter. "The bait shop is in the county, which makes it Jim's jurisdiction."

His evasion in answering the question didn't go unnoticed. She also hadn't been invited to the meeting, which was okay. Ashley planned on doing some investigating herself. As they passed the bait store, she spotted the closed sign that hung on the front door.

Chapter Thirteen

⸺⸗⸺

 he table and counters had all been cleared when Chad
arrived. Jim was alone.

"Looks like we're on the same page," Chad commented.
"I intended to suggest you shut down."

Jim pulled out a chair. "I hate to say it, but there's not much else
we can accomplish by keeping it here. The volunteers have done all
they can. I'm waiting for one of my deputies to return, then we'll pull
out."

"Any news from Ken?" Chad sat, stretching his long legs under
the table.

"Neville made a couple of stops, grocery store and gas station,
before heading home. He's still there."

"I'd appreciate it if you'd keep an officer on him."

"Already have a rotation schedule set up. How'd your hunt for
information about the doll go?"

"We hit every thrift store at this end of the county. No one
recognized it. Spotting Neville may have made the trip worthwhile.
Plus, I came up with another odd fact. The Norton's spent the day at
the water park a couple of weeks ago."

Jim said, "And the bait shop's only a mile or so away."

"Yep. I told Ashley not to grasp at straws but wonder if I'm doing the same."

"Ah, speaking of which. How'd the day go with the new editor of the Tribune?" A smirky grin crossed Jim's face.

"I can describe her in one word—feisty. She's not giving up. It looks like I'm stuck with her."

"From a purely male standpoint, I can't say it's a bad place to be."

He shot a look of irritation at Jim. "She's a problem I don't need."

"It's about time you got over Ellen dumping you."

Chad snorted in disgust. "She didn't exactly dump me. It was mutual."

Jim threw back his head and laughed. "When your wife changes the locks on the doors, that's being dumped."

"It was a bad deal for everyone. The press was like a pack of wild animals. She couldn't even go to the store without being hounded."

"It wasn't your fault." Angry at the way Ellen bailed when Chad needed the support, Jim wanted to say more. He knew though, Chad wasn't ready to talk about it. Ashley could be just what his friend needed. The town's new editor was irritating enough to break through the shell Chad had built.

Unable to resist stirring the pot, so to speak, just to see if he was right, Jim added in a casual tone. "If you're not interested, I might like to get to know her better. She's an intriguing woman."

The shot of jealousy that surged through him stunned Chad. He didn't want Jim interested in Ashley. From their days in college, he'd learned Jim's rugged good looks were a chick magnet. Nothing had changed in the years since they'd graduated.

Grudgingly, he had to admit his friend still had a certain flair. Jim's pristine uniform hugged a muscular body only two inches shorter and a few pounds lighter than his. Short, black hair augmented Jim's military demeanor. It was the handlebar mustache, that damn mustache he'd heard women rave about during their time at A&M. It seemed to make Jim irresistible by adding a dash of flamboyance to his narrow face and high cheekbones.

Chad growled, "What happened to Amy?" For the last several months, Jim had been dating a schoolteacher in Whitney.

"A mutual parting of the ways. She's moving back to Dallas."

"I hadn't heard."

"It happened a few days ago and hasn't had time to hit the gossip network."

Damn, all he needed was for Jim to be on the loose again with a new prospect in town. "I don't think Ashley's your style," he said, his voice dogged. "What can you tell me about the bait shop?"

Jim's fingers stroked one end of the mustache. His lips twitched upward. *Who did Chad think he was kidding? His buddy was definitely interested.* "Never had a call there or any reports of trouble. At least none since I've been the sheriff. I've met Rick and his wife at some of the county social events, but we're not friends. They've always been standoffish."

"Are they related to Neville?"

"I've never heard anyone comment on it," Jim said. "I sure don't see a connection between the Norton visit to the water park and the bait shop."

"Right now, I can't either." What Chad didn't say was his every instinct screamed there was a link. He just hadn't found it.

Ashley stood by her car in the newspaper parking lot. When Chad dropped her off, she'd intended on going home. The sight of the truck parked near the front door changed her mind. Henry was still inside.

At the sound of the door closing, he looked up. A broad smile spread across his face. "Didn't expect to see you tonight."

"Henry, don't you ever go home?" It hadn't taken long to realize her reporter spent far too many hours at the office.

"Oh, when I get around to it. It always seems like there's something else to do or finish. Fresh coffee in the back. Doc told me to lay off the stuff at night, but it's hard to break old habits."

She grinned. "Want a refill?"

Henry hesitated, looking at the cup on his desk. "Ah, why not. What damage can one more cup do? Besides, I'm too damn old to enjoy much else anymore."

She picked up his cup and returned with two. Setting one beside his keyboard, Ashley settled in the chair next to his desk. As she sipped, she looked at him over the rim of the cup, wondering how to get her information without arousing his suspicions.

"How'd the doll search go?"

She sighed. Would she ever get used to the town's rumor mill? "Who told you?"

"Edith called this afternoon. She's been on my case about an article I wrote. Wants a correction."

"Ah, the peaches."

"She told you?"

Ashley leaned back and laughed. "She had a few pithy remarks about men and canning."

"Humph. I bet she did. The damn woman thinks she knows everything."

"Henry, how long have you known her?"

"Since kindergarten." He grinned. "She was a pain in the ass then and still is. Just don't say I said so." His tone turned serious. "Anything new on the investigation?"

"No. Nothing. Kathy and Peter are going to ask the same question. I dread having to give the same answer."

He nodded. "So, did you find out anything about the doll?"

"Nothing. We've checked thrift shops all the way to Whitney. It seems like it was a waste of time." She lied with a straight face. This wasn't the time to be candid, even with a fellow reporter. "I didn't realize the lake was such a hot spot for fishermen."

"We get a lot of retirees and weekenders. During the summer, the RV parks fill up pretty fast."

"Ah, no wonder there are so many bait shops. I didn't know selling bait could be such a lucrative business."

"They're a mom and pop type operation, not a lot of overhead."

She sipped the coffee. "Most were small stores, though I did see a good-sized one. It was near the Second Chance Gift shop."

"The Coleman place. They're new to the area. It was a bicycle repair shop before they turned it into a bait store. That would be, hmm ..." he hesitated, then said, "A little over a year ago, I'd say."

"Henry, is there *anyone* you don't know?"

He chuckled. "Not bragging, but I expect there aren't too many people in this neck of the woods I don't know something about."

Steering the conversation back to her objective, she said, "It still seems like a tough way to make a living."

A sly look crossed his face. "Coleman seems to have done okay. He and his wife bought the old Miller estate near the lake, which wasn't cheap. I figured he had money, and the bait shop was a hobby."

She hadn't missed seeing the change in his expression, which meant he knew more than he was telling. "Okay, you've got me curious. What's the story?"

"Oh, you know how rumors go. I've been picking up tidbits here and there they may be dealing drugs. Now, it's only a rumor. I don't have any kind of proof, or I'd go to the sheriff."

"Hmm ... drugs. Anything else?"

"No. What's going on here?"

She had more questions but couldn't ask them without arousing his curiosity even more. Instead, she said, "Just an idea for an article. Bait shops would be a good topic sometime down the line. You ready to call it a night?"

"I guess so. You go on, I'll close up."

Rising, she looked down at him. "Henry, go home. There's nothing that can't wait until tomorrow."

A sheepish grin crossed his face. "I will."

Ashley shook her head, knowing he'd stick around. As the door closed, her thoughts shifted to her plan. It was too early to start, but she could use the extra time to put together the gear she'd need.

After his meeting with Jim, Chad stopped at the PD. Lydia had already left, but Dale was still in his office.

A video of the front of a gas station scrolled across Dale's monitor.

"Find anything?"

"Not yet. I've still got about a half-dozen to look at. Since we pulled the tapes for the last thirty days, it's a lot of footage." He reached for a stack of papers and handed them to Chad. "Report on Coleman."

Chad dropped into a chair and flipped through the pages. The couple had moved from Boston over a year ago and bought the store. No record of any arrest, not even a traffic citation. They owned a home on the west side of the lake.

He glanced up at Dale. "Ever meet them or been in their store?"

"Nope. I've seen them around town but never had any direct contact with either one. They keep to themselves."

"Any idea why they moved here?"

"I heard it was health issues. The guy must have money. They bought a large piece of property near the lake, and it didn't sell for chump change. Did you know Jim's shut down the command center?"

"Yes. Makes sense. Not much reason to keep the motorhome there."

"Do Kathy and Peter know?"

A grimace crossed Chad's face. "Not yet. They're my next stop. I know it'll upset them. They will think we've given up."

"I don't envy you the task. What's next?"

"That's my problem. We're almost at a standstill. Jim's keeping a tail on Neville. Unless you come up with something from the tape, we've got nothing. Oh, I picked up the list of the Norton's activities for the last month. They visited the water park near the Lake Whitney dam a couple of weeks ago. I don't like the proximity of the bait shop but have no reason to think there's a connection."

"Hmm … I can't see one either."

"My sitting here is only delaying the inevitable. If you need me, I'll be by the radio."

When he parked in front of the Norton house, he thought, was it just yesterday morning he'd done the same? It seemed like it had been days.

Striding around the front of the truck, he stopped on the sidewalk. Even though it was dark, light from the streetlamp illuminated the gate. The image of the doll in the basket hooked to the tricycle flashed into his mind.

Someone got Mandy to come to the gate. The kidnapper wouldn't have wanted to go into the backyard. Too risky. Kathy might have seen him. No, he had to get the child to the side of the garage where he couldn't be seen by anyone inside the house. Did he use a doll to entice her? Is that where the unknown doll came from?

But if that was the case, how did it get on a chair, and what happened to Mandy's doll? If the kidnapper wanted to swap dolls, he could have used the one on the tricycle. Frustrated by his attempts to find a rational answer for the puzzling details, he sighed. He refused to even consider the irrational explanation as he walked to the door.

Peter opened it. Chad followed him to the family room. Seated on the couch, Kathy's fingers plied a knitting needle, weaving the colored strands. At the sight of him, she dropped the needle and yarn on her lap. Peter picked up the remote and turned off the TV.

"Chad. We hoped you'd stop by." A note of hope was in her voice.

He hated to be the one to destroy it. "I'm sorry, but I don't have any news."

Her face wilted, and she just nodded.

"I wanted to let you know the status of the investigation. Jim is taking the RV we've been using for the command center back to his office. We'll still continue to work every possible lead we can develop." Even to his ears, it sounded weak.

A small cry of despair filled the silence in the room. "You're not going to find her." It wasn't a question. Hands twisted the yarn into a tangled web. Peter eased down next to his wife.

"We aren't even close to such an assumption, and we certainly don't plan on stopping the investigation. I have a question about the day you went to the water park. Did anything unusual happen?"

"No. At least nothing I remember," Peter said, looking at his wife.

She added, "Mandy played in the kiddy pool and went down the small water slide several times. We've been there before. There wasn't anything we did that was different."

His gaze shifted between the two. From their puzzled faces, it was clear he wouldn't find a connection.

"Why are you asking?" Peter said.

"It was on your list, another detail to be checked."

As he headed toward the front door, Chad took a deep breath, which did nothing to ease the grief he felt. He was learning that one of the downsides to a small community was the difficulty in keeping an emotional distance.

When he stepped outside, his steps faltered. A dense, black mist surrounded the house like a thick blanket. Green tinged coils slithered toward his feet. A strange compulsion pulled at his senses, and he felt an overwhelming urge to step deeper into the gloomy fog. *No!* This was nothing but fog … plain … ordinary fog. The eerie green tint was nothing but a coincidence. He wasn't going to let his crazy memories turn it into something it wasn't.

Shivering from the sudden chill in the air, he strode toward his truck, thankful he'd parked in front since it was barely visible. As he opened the door, a faint sound echoed in the distance. Chad didn't hear because he wasn't listening.

On the way to his office, he slowed at the sight of large red letters in a neon sign glowing through the murky haze. Was this a mistake? Only one way to find out. He parked.

Chapter Fourteen

⚬

With her hands braced against the shower wall, the hot water gushed over Ashley's body, soothing the tension in her muscles. It'd been a long day, and it wasn't over yet. On her way home, she'd called Kathy. The agony in her sister's voice had deepened her determination. She had to do something. Since a deputy was watching Neville, he was a dead end. The bait store wasn't.

While she plotted her game plan, she dried off and dressed in black jeans and a long-sleeved, black t-shirt. In the back bedroom, she pulled a small backpack from the closet. There were a few tools in the garage she'd need. Maybe it would be a good idea to make a list. She'd hate to forget something.

She dropped the backpack on the couch and walked into the kitchen. After opening the refrigerator door, she perused the meager contents before reaching for the jar of peanut butter. When the doorbell rang, she jerked, knocking it over. Damn. She had to get a grip on her nerves. Otherwise, she'd be a basket case by the time she got ready to leave.

Annoyed by her reaction, she stomped to the front door and peered through the peephole. Her twitchy nerves rolled into a knot. *He couldn't have picked a worse time to show up.*

Aware of her scrutiny, Chad held up a sack and shook it. "I know you're looking at me. Come on, Ashley, open the door."

Since she couldn't ignore him, she opened it. "What are you doing here?"

He refused to let her somewhat ungracious welcome deter him. Or the fact, he almost swallowed his tongue at the sight of her luscious body molded in black. Grinning like a loon, Chad said, "I come bearing gifts," and held up a sack in each hand.

Puzzled, Ashley studied him. "Okay, what's in the bags?"

"Food and drink."

What *was* she going to do? This would put a kink in her plans. Then again, maybe not. He wouldn't be here all night, and she hadn't planned on leaving until after midnight. Besides, she could pump him for information about the bait shop.

He gave the bags a slight shake. "Are you going to stand there all night debating whether to let me in? The food's getting cold."

The smell of something delectable wafted in the air, tantalizing her taste buds. She laughed and gave in to the temptation. "How can I deny the smell of food."

"Kitchen?"

"Straight ahead, and to the left."

After setting the bags on the table, he pulled out two bottles of wine. "I wasn't sure what you liked, red or white. I got both." He reached inside the second bag and removed several containers, paper plates, and utensils. "There's pasta salad and slices of roast turkey. I even have a cup of the soup you liked today."

A warm feeling floated through her; he'd remembered the soup she'd enjoyed at lunch. "It smells delicious. We can eat here or in the dining room."

Chad looked around at the rich, walnut stained cabinets with lead glass inserts and butter-gold accessories. "I like your kitchen. Let's stay here. Besides, there's no point in carrying everything to another room. Which wine?"

She glanced at the bottles. "You choose, I like them both. The corkscrew's in the drawer to the right of the stove. It looks like all I have to provide are a couple of wine glasses."

He grinned. "A bit more than that. I enjoyed your company today."

A blush crept over her cheeks. "It certainly wasn't a typical day for me."

Pulling out her chair, he waited until she was seated before he sat across from her.

As they dished up the food, she asked, "How'd your meeting go with the sheriff? Anything new?"

"We closed down the command center. Nothing else."

The fork with a piece of turkey dropped to her plate. "So, soon! Why?" Emotion clogged her throat.

His hand reached across the table to touch hers. "Ashley, the command center provided a focal point to coordinate the volunteers and officers assigned to the initial search for Mandy. This phase is over, so there's no point having it sit on the street. The investigation has shifted to a different level, but it doesn't mean we've given up."

"It does make sense, though it seems as if it's over."

"That's because of the visibility factor. It's something people can see and adds to the visual intensity of the investigation. Sometimes it's hard for civilians to envision the long hours' officers invest in the ongoing investigation."

"Do Kathy and Peter know?"

"I stopped at their house earlier and told them."

"I must have talked to them before you got there. Kathy didn't say anything on the phone. How'd they take it?"

"About like you. They had the same concern, what would happen to the investigation. It's my job to make sure they are kept in the loop, and to know everything that can be done … *is* being done."

Over the rim of the wine glass, she studied his face. A lock of hair had fallen across his brow. A hint of a rough stubble covered his chin and cheeks. Then his eyes, dark and disturbing, met hers. Ashley felt the familiar itch of her reporter instincts. What secrets did they hide?

As she stared back, his gaze moved to her lips. Heat coiled and weaved inside her. Stunned by the intensity of a desire she wasn't ready for, she plunked the wine glass down and jabbed her fork at a piece of pasta. "Did you learn anything about the bait shop?"

Did she imagine his sigh of frustration? When she looked up, he'd picked up the wine bottle to refill their glasses, as if the odd interlude hadn't happened.

"The owners are Fran and Rick Coleman. Bought the place a little over a year ago. Nothing on the radar about them."

"I heard rumors they're dealing drugs."

"Who told you?"

She smiled and took another bite of pasta.

He dropped his fork on the plate and leaned forward. "Ashley, I'm serious. Who told you? And don't give me any crap about confidential informants! Such a thing doesn't exist in this town."

She laughed. "You're probably right. It was Henry."

"Henry, as in the reporter who works for you?"

"Yep."

"How would he know?"

"Henry is a walking, talking rumor mill. There's very little that goes on in this town he doesn't know."

"Does he have any facts to back it up?"

"No, which is why he hasn't said anything to the sheriff."

"I'll let Jim know, though I can't see how it would fit into Mandy's abduction."

"Are you done?" she asked as she looked at the near-empty containers.

He motioned to the remaining pasta. Ashley grinned and shook her head no.

Chad grabbed the container. "Too good to waste." He polished off the last few bites.

"Let's finish our wine in the family room," Ashley said, then remembered the backpack. Dang, it was still on the couch. Nothing she could do about it now.

Her nerves fired back up as they walked into the room. When Chad ignored it and sat on the other end of the couch, she dropped into the chair with a sigh of relief. God, she wasn't cut out for all this cloak and dagger business. Curled up, she tucked her feet underneath her and set her glass on the end table.

Chad glanced around the room. His gaze stopped at the pictures on the fireplace mantel. Standing to take a closer look, he picked one up. "Your parents?"

"It was taken just before mom was diagnosed with cancer and has always been one of my favorites."

"You favor her, but Kathy looks like your dad." He set it back down and picked up the one next to it. Ashley leaned against a young man who had his arms wrapped around her. The photographer had captured the look of love as she looked at the man's face.

For the second time, a sharp thrust of jealousy shot through him, followed by self-reproach. This was probably her fiancée. Didn't say much for his sense of fair play to be envious of a dead man. Then he realized it wasn't the man. It was the look on Ashley's face. He wanted to see the same look as she gazed at him. His body stiffened with shock. What was he thinking?

Behind him, Ashley said, "That was Lance, my fiancée."

He heard the slight tremor in her voice. He set the picture back and turned. Careful to keep his tone neutral, he said, "You looked happy." Had she noticed his reaction to the picture? Evidently not, as she casually sipped her wine.

"I was. I heard you'd been married."

"Henry?"

Ashley laughed, glad to get past the moment. "Yep. If you don't mind my asking, what happened?"

"I mentioned the publicity over my last case with Atlanta. It got rough. The news media wanted answers and didn't care who they went after. Ellen got caught in the middle. Every time she left the house or work, reporters hounded her, wanting a statement."

Not wanting to embarrass himself with how the marriage had deteriorated and ended in a bitter divorce, he picked up the glass and took a sip.

"Is that why you got a divorce?"

Chad eased back down on the couch. "Pretty much. It was more than she could handle. Being a cop's wife can be tough, and she'd been unhappy for some time. She wanted me to quit, but I've got to take the blame for what happened. My handling of the case caused the crisis."

Was this the reason for the haunted look she glimpsed in his eyes? As she considered the idea, she twirled the glass. "Hmm. You met her at A&M, right?"

"I really should recruit Henry as an informant. We got engaged our senior year."

"How did you end up in Atlanta?"

"Ellen grew up there. She didn't want to settle in Texas, so we moved."

"Was that when you decided to be a cop?"

"No. I had planned all along to go into law enforcement. My degree's in criminal justice with a minor in psychology." He chuckled. "Figured it was a good way to learn how to read a criminal's mind and actions."

"Did she ever complain about your choice of a profession before you got engaged or married?"

Puzzled, he stared at her. "No, but what difference does it make?"

"All the difference in the world. You're too close to the situation to see it. If she changed her mind after you got married, it's on her, not you. She knew what she was getting into. It's not your fault she had a change of heart."

"I … uh," then paused as the logic of her reasoning sunk in. Was he in denial on this as he was with all the other events which happened? It was something he needed to consider.

"I hadn't thought about it quite in that light. How do you like living in Meridian with its slower pace?"

Even though he changed the subject, she'd caught the brief look of puzzlement. Chad was a smart man. He'd figure it out. "What's the old saying about smelling the roses along the way? I've found it's nice to take my time, though it does occasionally drive me nuts. It's the rush to get a story out I miss."

"Do you think you'll stay, or is this temporary?" The sense of anxiety he felt surprised him.

"I like it here and can't see a reason to make another change."

The relief he felt was even more disturbing.

She chuckled. "Besides, I'm looking forward to seeing Henry play Santa Claus."

His head tipped back as he laughed. "Henry … is the town's Santa Claus?"

"You didn't know?"

"Nope." He grinned. "This Christmas will be my first. I can see why he'd be perfect for the part. Bet the kids love him."

He glanced at his watch. "I'd better go. It's getting late."

When she stood, her foot tingled with numbness, and the leg buckled.

Chad shot off the couch and caught her. Looking down at her face, the supple lips made him want, and he took. With his arms locked around her, he felt her swift intake of breath. Ashley's hands pressed against his chest, then slid around his neck. His lips feathered kisses across her cheeks before claiming her mouth. He pulled her tight against him as he ravaged her lips.

She moaned, giving back with an uncontrolled passion. When Chad lifted his head and looked at her, the heat gleaming in her eyes was nearly his undoing. Desire raged inside him.

His voice deep and husky, he said, "I've wanted you from the first moment you stormed into my office." His head dropped to claim another kiss. When he felt the slight resistance of her hands, he pulled back.

"Chad. I can't deny I feel something, but ..." She stopped, trying to control the emotions stirring inside her.

"I know. This isn't the right time." His fingers whisked the hair from her forehead.

"Thank you for understanding. If this ever happens between us, I don't want it to be tainted with the memory of Mandy."

He nodded and stepped toward the front door. As he stood in the open doorway, his finger brushed her lips. "Ashley, I'm warning you. It's not if, but when." He turned and walked out.

Closing the door, she leaned against it. Her body thrummed with an unfilled hunger she'd never felt, not even with Lance. She'd always believed their sex life had been good, but now ... she had to wonder. As she straightened, she glanced at her watch. Exploring her feelings for Chad would have to wait. She had more important concerns on her agenda, and it was time to get started.

While he'd been inside, the fog hadn't lifted. If anything, it was worse. When he stepped off the porch, the black mist flowed around him, wrapping him in the uncanny silence. He felt the same sensation he experienced earlier. This time it was stronger.

Ignoring the trickle of dread that sent icy chills racing over him, Chad rushed toward his truck. A whisper of wind brushed his face. A faint sound echoed in the distance.

For an instant, terror struck with the speed of a lightning bolt, and he panicked. Was he losing all sense of reality again? Thoughts like this were the path to madness, and Chad had sworn it wouldn't happen again. He'd nearly lost his sanity once before, until he convinced himself it was nothing more than his desperation to locate a missing child.

As logic pushed aside the irrationality in his thoughts, he told himself, there was nothing there, nothing to hear. He started the engine. Tomorrow would be another rough day, and he needed a few hours' sleep. As he pulled onto the road, his phone rang. The surge of adrenaline from his quick glance at the caller ID crushed the emotions the fog provoked and his need for sleep.

Chapter Fifteen

~❧~

It was the awful smell of the pillow bunched around her face that woke her. Why did her pillow smell bad? Then, with a thud of her heart, Mandy knew; she was still in that strange bed. Was the witch waiting for her to wake up? Afraid to even open her eyes, she curled into a ball, sliding deeper under the covers.

Her head and tummy hurt. The same yucky taste was in her mouth. Tears welled in her eyes. Where was her mommy? Was she mad at her, is that why she wasn't here? Mandy hadn't really meant to talk to the stranger; she just wanted to look at the doll.

Unable to stop the sobs that shook her body, she shoved her face into the pillow to bury the sound. It wasn't until she felt the urge to go to the bathroom that the sobs died away. Pushing the blanket away from her eyes, Mandy peered over the edge. It was night, but the light in the room was on, and the witch wasn't there. Reassured by the empty room, she sat up.

After brushing the sleeve of her jacket across her nose, she slid her legs over the edge of the bed, then stared at her feet. Why was she wearing her shoes? Mommy never let her go to bed with her shoes on. One of the pink bows was gone. Then Mandy remembered. The first time she woke, she had them on.

That was when she tried to open the door and couldn't. Crying, she'd run to look out the window, then the scary woman walked in. She looked like the witch in one of Mandy's books. A funny-looking dress hung all the way to the black shoes, and the sleeves covered her arms. Her hair was piled in a knot on top of her head. Behind the glasses, her eyes were big, and her face scrunched with a mean look. The witch told her to shut up, or she'd shove a rag down her throat.

Mandy's legs shook as more tears flowed down her cheek. No one had ever talked to her like that.

After setting a plate with a sandwich and a glass of water on the table near the window, the witch stepped in front of her and leaned over. "Eat that sandwich and drink *all* the water. If you don't, I'll come back, and you will be very … *very* … sorry." The woman grabbed her shoulders and shook her. "Do you understand me?" All Mandy could do was nod her head, yes. With one last shake, the witch walked out.

As the door slammed shut, Mandy ran to the bed and hopped on it. To keep the witch from hearing, she pulled the pillow over her head. As the tears subsided, she sat up and stared at the stuff on the table. Her tummy still felt bad, and she didn't want it, but she was scared of what the witch would do. Sniffling, she climbed off the bed.

On a small plate, purple goo oozed from a folded piece of bread. She hated the purple stuff, and her mommy never made her eat it. Mandy poked at it with her fingertip, then licked off the small chunk. Even though she'd made a bad face at the icky taste, she tore off a small piece and shoved it in her mouth. Chewing fast, she swallowed, then took a sip of water. It tasted funny, but it wasn't as bad as the purple goo.

By taking a smaller bite, she could swallow without chewing if she drank some water. After gulping down the rest, she crawled back in bed but forgot to take off her shoes.

This time, a plate with another folded piece of bread and glass of water was already on the table. It was still the purple stuff.

She'd use the bathroom first. Mandy rinsed her hands in the sink like mommy had taught her, then wiped them on her pants because she didn't want to touch the dirty towel.

With slow steps, she shuffled toward the table. A faint whisper floated in the air. "Pour the water down the sink." Mandy stopped and looked at the door, but it was still shut. How could someone talk to her when there wasn't anyone in the room?

Even though the voice scared her, Mandy eyed the water, remembering the bad taste from before. Once she'd dumped it, she set the glass back on the table, then looked at the sandwich. Picking it up, she tossed it under the bed. A chunk of jelly fell on the floor. She smushed it with her shoe before crawling back on top of the bed. When her small hands pulled the blanket back, Mandy couldn't stop the cry that erupted.

Ashley backed her car near the side of a used bookstore. Hunched behind the wheel, she studied the buildings across the highway. Other than a faint outline, they were invisible in the dense haze. If anyone were there, lights would have shone like a beacon. But at this time of the morning, she didn't expect someone would be inside.

For once, the unnerving fog didn't spark any uneasiness. She could hide in it. Still, her reluctance to leave the warmth and security of the car surprised her. Unless the store had an alarm system, which Ashley doubted, she should be able to get in and out, and no one would be the wiser. Maybe it was the idea of burglarizing a building that set off the roiling in her stomach.

She wasn't making any progress by sitting here. Ashley pulled the black ski mask over her head, positioning it until only her eyes and mouth were visible. It was a last-minute addition to her backpack. When she remembered buying it for a skiing trip with Lance, it had taken some digging in the boxes stored in the closet to find it.

Outside, she paused alongside the car while her hand patted her pockets, making sure she'd stashed what she needed. Dressed in black from head to toe, she was a shadow that drifted into the mist and across the highway. With her back against the wall of the nearest building, her gaze swept over the road.

Reassured by the lack of any approaching vehicles, Ashley darted from building to building until she reached the side of the bait shop, then followed the wall to the back and stepped onto a small back porch. As she paused to catch her breath, she studied the black wall of fog around her. Was it her imagination, or was it getting thicker?

She flashed her light over the lock. Relieved it was a simple one, easy to pick, she tucked the flashlight in her pocket. Her fingers felt for the small opening as she pulled out a lock pick. When she inserted the metal tool, Ashley was surprised at the steadiness of her hands, considering her insides had twisted into a ball of tingling nerves.

A quick toggle of the pick and the lock clicked. Her heart sped up. If she was caught … no point obsessing over it. She'd have to make sure it didn't happen. Ashley turned the knob and slipped inside.

Even through the mesh of the mask, the repellent odor of dead fish clogged her throat. The pick was swapped for the flashlight, and she flashed the beam around the room. Crammed inside were plastic tubs filled with water. The surface of each bubbled and gurgled from the machines pumping air through a tube inserted into the tubs. In the muddy foam, small fish floated. Their dead eyes gleamed when the light hit them. She shuddered and shifted the beam to another part of the room.

Stacked along the wall and on shelves were boxes labeled with pictures of fishing gear. Ashley opened the door to the front of the store. As she strolled around the room, her hand shielded the light to keep someone driving by from noticing it. Fishing gear filled the racks and counters.

At one end, another door led to a combination kitchen and office. Closing it behind her, Ashley started with the file cabinet. Nothing but bills, invoices, receipts, and fishing catalogs. Next was the computer. She tapped the keyboard, and to her surprise, it wasn't passcode protected. Guess Coleman thought no one would ever try to access it. But then, why would he believe someone would break into his store?

Ashley settled into the chair. After scanning different files, it was no wonder he wasn't concerned about security. There was nothing but a few letters to distributors. She tapped the icon to open the web browser, then opened the history file, and found the reason for the computer—the Internet. Damn, as much as she would like to look at all the history files, she had to be satisfied with the last month. She felt she'd already been inside the place too long.

As she scrolled down the list, her innate curiosity kicked in. Why were there so many investment websites from a man who owned a bait shop? He also had a fascination with online newspaper and magazine sites. Still, there was nothing to provide any clue to Mandy's disappearance.

With a sense of desperation, she checked the drawers in the desk. A couple was what she referred to as junk drawers. One had a few folders with more catalogs. With a last glance at the computer, she reached to shut it down. A small icon at the bottom of the screen caught her eye. It was a picture file.

She scrolled through picture after picture. Odd. Coleman must be obsessed with bait shops, she thought. Otherwise, why so many pictures of other stores? Then she stopped. An icy chill raced over her. Her brain locked as she tried to comprehend the significance of what she saw on the screen. A small child stood near a concession stand with a doll in her arms. It was … Mandy! What was a picture of her doing on Coleman's computer?

This was evidence. She had to call Chad and tell him what she'd found. Her fingers fumbled to unzip the pocket with the phone, then paused. What the hell was she thinking? She couldn't call him. She'd broken into the place. He'd have no choice but to arrest her.

A copy. She'd at least get a copy. Then to her horror, she realized she didn't have a USB drive. When Chad showed up at her front door, she'd forgotten all about making a list. "Ashley, you're a frigging idiot," she muttered under her breath.

Okay, if she couldn't download the picture, what else was there? An email was out. She didn't dare take a chance, especially since she didn't know how computer-savvy the man was. The phone. She could take a picture of the screen with her cellphone. Ashley tapped the photo button several times. Better to have too many. Were there any others? After scrolling through the rest of the file, she returned to Mandy's picture. When was it taken? The property page should tell her. She snapped several more pictures.

Elated at what she'd found, Ashley slipped the phone back into her pocket and shut down the screen. Time to get out of the building. When she stepped out of the office, the beam of headlights flashed across the front of the store. Another vehicle was turning into the parking lot.

Damn! Ashley twisted and skidded around counters to get to the back door. Before closing it, she turned the inside lock and twisted the knob to be sure it had locked.

The heavy mist clung to her face and clothes. With visibility practically non-existent, she hugged the wall as she stepped around the corner. The sound of an engine intensified. When her fingers touched the front edge of the building, she peeked around the corner. A truck was backing onto the parking lot.

An arm snaked around her neck, and a hand clamped across her mouth. Terror ripped through her as her body twisted. A husky whisper echoed in her ear.

"It's me."

At the sound of Chad's voice, the scream died in her throat. His hand slipped away from her face and grabbed her hand. He hissed, "Follow me."

Pulling her behind him, Chad moved toward the next building. When he reached it, he turned and headed to the back.

Ashley's panic turned to irritation. Since she couldn't see more than a few inches in front of her, how did he move so easily in this soupy mess? The least he could have done was bump into the damned wall.

With the fog hiding their movements, they moved to the front of the building, then stopped at the sound of a car. Chad stepped back and collided with her.

"What's going on?" she whispered.

"Hush," he muttered, his voice curt.

Annoyed, she pursed her lips and waited.

When the car passed without stopping, he whispered, "Let's go, my truck is across the road."

"So's my car."

"I know."

As he tugged on her hand, she looked back toward the bait shop. From the faint glow inside, she spotted the outline of two trucks. Chills raced down her back at the thought of what might have happened if Coleman had caught her inside his shop. She didn't believe he would have called the police to report a burglary. Would she have disappeared like Mandy? Still, she wasn't in the clear. She had to deal with a pissed-off police chief.

When they reached his truck, she pulled her hand free. "I can follow you in my car."

He opened the door. "Get in. We need to talk."

When she hesitated, he said, "Ashley—get in! You're not going anywhere until I find out what you've been doing. Now, get in the damned truck!"

This wasn't how she envisioned telling him what she'd found. She ripped the mask from her head and slid onto the seat.

Despite his urge to take out his anger on the door, he eased it shut. He walked around to the other side, got in, and twisted to look at her. "You'd better have a good explanation for why I shouldn't throw your ass in jail for breaking into Coleman's store."

She stuck her hands in her coat pockets and glared at him. "What are you doing here?"

"Right now, it doesn't matter why *I'm* here. I want to know why *you're* here."

"Coleman is involved with Mandy's abduction, that's why."

"We don't know that for a fact. And even if we did, have you ever heard of something called a search warrant? Ashley, no matter how well-meaning, I don't need a damn reporter screwing with my investigation! Do you have any idea how close you came to getting caught inside the building when Neville and Coleman arrived?"

Unrepentant, she declared, "Yes, I …" She stopped; her eyes narrowed. "Wait a minute. How do you know it was Neville? You couldn't see them any better than I could."

The woman was like a damn bloodhound in sniffing out a minor detail. "At this moment, it's not important. I want to know what in god's name you hoped to accomplish?"

"Proof he's involved." She paused, and with a note of triumph in her voice, said, "I found it!"

"What could you possibly have found in a bait shop?"

His disbelief stung. "How about *Mandy's* picture ... on *his* computer! If you'll calm down for a few seconds and stop shouting at me, I'll show you."

Speechless, he gaped at her. Then, with a grim look on his face, he said, "Start at the beginning and don't leave anything out."

"If you're still thinking about throwing me in jail, maybe it would be better if I didn't give you any details, just show you the picture. I don't want to incriminate myself."

He groaned in disgust. "As much as I would like too, you know I'm not about to arrest you."

She smirked. "Figured," and began to explain her foray into the store. She pulled her cell phone, brought up the picture on the screen, and handed it to him. "It didn't occur to me to take a USB device. This was the best I could do. I took several pictures, including the page which shows the date and time."

Chad scrolled through them. "I'd have to check your sister's activity log, but I think the date on the picture is the same day they went to the water park. This may be the park's concession stand."

While they talked, she noticed the number of times he glanced across the street. The lights were still on.

"What's going on? Why are you watching the store?"

"After I left your place, Ken called, looking for backup. He said Neville was on the move, driving toward Whitney. I had a hunch he might be headed to the bait shop and got here ahead of him."

"Where is Ken?"

"Down the road."

The lights in the store went out. Chad's phone rang. He listened, then said, "I'll follow Coleman, you stay with Neville," and disconnected.

She reached to open the door.

"You're going with me."

"Why? I can get in my car and go home."

"No. I'm not letting you out of my sight."

As he waited for the trucks to leave, his gut still churned. When he saw Ashley's car, he knew she was inside. With Neville not far behind him, he hauled ass to get to the back of the store. Then Coleman arrived. When Chad didn't see her, the panic ratcheted. The sight of her stepping out the back door was an image engraved on his brain. The overwhelming relief had morphed into anger. Hell, she didn't even have a gun to protect herself. At least, he didn't think so.

"Are you carrying a gun?"

"No. Do I need one?"

"God, no. I wondered if I had to worry about you being armed."

The man was insufferable. Did he really believe she was that incompetent?

"My dad taught me to shoot years ago, and I'm damned good at it. I've got a permit, but I haven't felt the need to carry a gun. Something I'll remedy when I get home."

He groaned. *Why had he brought up the subject?*

The trucks pulled out of the parking lot. Neville headed back to Meridian, and Coleman left in the opposite direction.

Chad waited until Coleman's vehicle disappeared in the thick fog, then pulled out to follow. He sped up until he saw the taillights ahead. When the vehicle turned on a road on the west side of the lake, he said, "I expect he's headed home, but we'll stay with him until we know for sure."

"Since we know a picture of Mandy is on his computer, what are you going to do about it? This is the break we've been needing. Coleman's definitely involved."

"Right now, nothing."

Anger stiffened her back. "What do you mean—*nothing*! The man probably knows where she is. Can't you at least bring him in for questioning?"

"On what grounds? I can't use what you found. If he finds out we know about the picture, we might lose any chance of finding her. For right now, we don't do anything except keep on working the case."

She muttered, "At least admit it's important."

He glanced at her. Dejected, she slumped in the seat.

His voice softened. "You found a link. One we didn't have. It gets us one step closer to finding Mandy. Just don't go breaking into any more buildings."

Ahead, Coleman's vehicle turned into a driveway. His phone rang, it was Ken. After a short discussion, Chad said, "Coleman's home. I'll call you once I get back to town."

He laid the phone in the cupholder. "I'm taking you back to your car. I'll follow you home. I need copies of the pictures, but I don't want them in an email. Do you have a flash drive I can borrow?"

"Yes. Then what are you going to do?"

"Go home and try to get a few hours' sleep."

Chapter Sixteen

⟡

*C*had stopped alongside her car. Once she was on the highway, he pulled behind. With visibility down to feet and her lack of familiarity with the road, the trip back was considerably longer.

She tapped the garage door opener hooked to her visor, drove in and parked. Exiting, she waited for Chad to park in front, then walk inside the garage before closing the overhead door. "My office is down the hall," she said, as they entered the house through the kitchen.

Ashley flipped on the light switch and pulled out her chair. On the corner of the desk, flash drives filled a small woven basket. She grabbed one and inserted it into the computer.

Chad gazed at the basket in awe. "Just how many do you need?" He had one in his desk drawer and didn't remember if he'd ever used it.

"They were on sale, so I loaded up. I do a lot of work at home."

While she downloaded the pictures from her phone to her computer, and then onto the flash drive, he glanced around. A small bookshelf was along one wall; on the other were two file cabinets. Several award certificates for excellence in journalism and a few pictures of Texas scenery were hung on the walls. He studied the selection of books, and it was quite an eclectic assortment; fiction mixed with non-fiction. He spotted another interest they had in common, biographies.

Her voice broke into his perusal. "Got it. You don't need to worry about returning the flash drive."

After another glance at the basket, he quipped, "No, I'd probably better get it back to you. I'd hate for you to run short."

"Humph," she sniffed.

He pocketed it. "I'd better get going." Chad turned and walked to the front door. Opening it, he looked back at her. "About Coleman's store …" then hesitated.

A guarded look crossed her face. She didn't need another ass-chewing session.

He finally added, "Don't say anything about your excursion."

Relieved, she said, "Don't worry. I don't plan on broadcasting it."

He flicked a finger across her cheek. "Get some rest, and I'll talk to you later today."

Before he walked to his truck, Chad waited on the front step until he heard the click of the lock. The ghostly fog still hadn't dissipated. Instead, the heavy mist brushed his face with a light caress. The hair prickled on his arms and neck. With bated breath, he waited, though he didn't expect to hear anything. When he didn't, he knew he was right. There was nothing to hear.

As he slid behind the wheel, Chad remembered he'd told Ken he'd call. When the deputy answered, he asked, "Where are you?"

"Neville's place. Looks like he's in for the night. I'm waiting for my relief to arrive, then I'm headed home. What happened at the bait shop?"

"Nothing we can do anything about tonight." He wasn't ready to broadcast Ashley's nefarious adventure.

Ashley stared out the window and watched Chad back out of her driveway. It seemed she'd been on an emotional roller coaster since learning Mandy had disappeared. The scene earlier in the evening with Chad had added even more turmoil. She wasn't prepared for another relationship, or at least it's what she'd been telling herself for months. But, in a few seconds, Chad had destroyed that belief, and maybe even more.

Damn! What was she going to do? At least, she had enough sense to put it on hold. She hadn't lied when she told Chad she wouldn't consider getting involved until they found Mandy.

She turned away from the window, then walked through the house, shutting off the lights before heading toward her bedroom. After a quick shower, she settled into bed. Even though exhausted, her brain refused to shut down. Her thoughts seesawed between what she found at the bait shop, the kiss, and a desire which had nearly brought her to her knees. As she finally drifted off, Ashley realized her idea of the simpler life in Meridian had become exceedingly complicated.

Neville leaned back in his recliner and took a sip of beer before tapping a number on the burner phone. When the call was answered, he said, "Been thinkin' about the reward."

The voice on the other end said, "It's some serious dough. I've never seen one that high before."

"Makes you wonder how to get it."

The voice said, "You know the plan's in place. It's not going to get changed."

"The reward's a lot more than we're going to get out of this deal."

"Neville, have you been smoking weed again? Because you're not making any sense."

"What if we took the girl and left her somewhere, then called the cops and told them where to find her?"

"If you have even half a brain, try to use it. All that will happen is we'll find ourselves behind bars again. I'm not going back to jail."

"It won't happen; not if we get our story right," Neville persisted. "Tell them we'd been snooping around and heard rumors. Hell, all we're doing is passing them on. When the cops find her, they'll know what we told them was true. Besides, nothing connects us to the kid."

"What if the brat can describe who grabbed her? Did you think about that?"

"The reward doesn't say she has to be found alive—if you get my drift."

"Goddamn, Neville. If you got any dumber, you wouldn't be able to find a chair to plunk your butt on."

"Just saying, it could happen."

"No, it couldn't. You're not screwing this up for the rest of us. Keep your big mouth shut and follow orders. You hear me? We'll get our money, and there's more to come. Another order's been placed."

The phone went dead. Neville tossed it on the table and gulped down another swig of beer. The longer he thought about twenty-five thousand dollars, the more he fumed. It was more money than he'd ever seen.

He lit a joint and sucked the smoke deep into his lungs, holding it to get the full rush, which flooded his senses. His confidence rose. This would be easy pickings once he figured out a way to collect. He didn't need any help.

Then it dawned on him. What about the woman who showed up the other day—the reporter? Even better, he'd found out she was the kid's aunt. What was her name? His thoughts muddled, he fought to remember. Oh, yeah, Logan, Ashley Logan. He'd use her.

After one last drag on the joint, he dropped the butt into the ashtray. Tomorrow, he'd come up with a plan. He wasn't going to lose the biggest pot of money he'd ever come across.

His hair damp from the shower, dressed in a pair of sweatpants, and his feet bare, Chad padded into the kitchen. After grabbing a can of beer from the fridge and popping the top, he walked into his office. When he got home, he'd dropped the flash drive, the sack with the doll, and his briefcase on his desk.

Setting down the beer, he inserted the device into the computer and pulled up the pictures. Behind Mandy, a young man waited on customers at the concession stand. Chad leaned back, his gaze never leaving the screen.

The little girl was adorable. Dressed in a pink and black swimsuit, and some sort of gauzy cover, the sunlight gleamed on the glossy brown curls that tousled around her rosy cheeks. Dark eyes sparkled with mischief as she hugged a doll and grinned.

The doll looked new. The curly hair was similar to Mandy's, except it was blond. The dress was white with pink lace woven with pink hearts around the neck, sleeves, and bottom of the skirt.

Chad opened his briefcase and pulled out a file. Inside was the picture he'd taken from the mantel. It was the same doll in both pictures; Betsy, the one that was missing.

He picked up the parent's activity list and noted the date they visited the water park. Clicking to another picture, Chad blessed Ashley's foresight to include the property page. The picture had been taken the same day the Norton's visited the water park.

How could someone take the picture and not be noticed? Was it possible the kid behind the counter saw something?

Chad returned the list to the folder and picked up the report on Coleman and his wife. He swallowed a swig of beer as he studied it. On the surface, they appeared to be on the up and up. There was nothing to cause someone to suspect they were dealing drugs. Still, their history only went back to a little over a year ago. Chad needed more, and hopefully, he'd get it tomorrow. Nothing he could do tonight. Time to hit the sack.

Tossing the beer can in the trash, he rose and turned to walk out the door. As his hand reached to flip off the light, he felt an odd tingle; a sense he wasn't alone. He looked over his shoulder. What a crazy notion. There wasn't anyone in the room, just him and the old doll.

His gaze, drawn to the sack, had him stepping back to the desk. Chad pulled the doll out of the bag. Disgusted by the trend of his thoughts, he muttered, "Christ, it's only a doll."

The ring of his phone, while unexpected at this time of the morning, was a welcome relief from where his thoughts had been headed. It was Jim.

"Ken sent me a text about the surveillance. A clandestine meeting in the middle of the night definitely moves them up on the suspect list."

"That's not all that happened. Our new editor decided to do a little breaking and entering."

"She *did* what?"

"She broke into the bait shop. After Ken called to let me know Neville was on the move, I suspected he might be headed to Coleman's store. I got there ahead of him and before Coleman arrived. I caught our impudent editor coming out the back door."

"Did anyone see you?"

"No, we got away before they could spot us."

"What was she thinking?"

"What can I say, she's a reporter. To give her credit, she did come across something, a picture of Mandy on Coleman's computer. It might have been taken at the water park. I'm going to check it out tomorrow."

"That's a major development. It doesn't just move them up, they've gone to the top of the heap. Any idea why it was on the computer?"

"None. When I get to the station, I'm going to call a friend of mine at the Atlanta PD. She's as good as they come at getting into someone's background. I want her to check into Neville and the Colemans."

"I'll do some digging myself," Jim said.

"That's a good idea. You've been here longer than I have and know the local sources. Though I'm beginning to learn, Ashley has a path into the pipeline."

"Henry!" Jim exclaimed. "There's not much the man doesn't know. There's only one problem. He's the biggest gossip in town. I hope Ashley doesn't plan on picking his brain about Coleman or Neville. If so, it won't take long for the news to get back to them."

"I'll let her know, though I suspect she's already aware of the problem. And, for right now, I want to keep her escapade between the two of us."

"I guess this means you don't plan to arrest her?" Jim said, and then chuckled.

"The only reason I don't is because I could blow any chance that we've got of finding Mandy."

"Sure, buddy. You keep telling yourself that."

Chad didn't have any trouble envisioning the smirk on his friend's face. A bald-faced, man-to-man lie seemed appropriate. "I'm telling you, whatever you're thinking isn't happening." He wasn't about to admit he might already be in over his head.

"Humph!" Jim snorted. "Like I said, keep telling yourself *you're* not interested." He laughed, and the line went dead.

Chad had to grin at his friend's comments. Jim knew him better than most. He'd forgotten about the doll as he turned off the light and walked out of his office. Behind him, a faint glow filtered into the hallway

Chapter Seventeen

Seated at his desk with his habitual morning cup of coffee, Chad waited for his call to Atlanta PD to be transferred to Detective Vicky Milford. If she weren't at her desk, he'd try her cellphone.

Several clicks echoed before a sensual voice said, "Detective Milford." Vicky was a no-nonsense style of detective, but over the years had been the brunt of many jokes about her sexy voice. Her typical response was, "you should be so lucky." She was right. Her interview techniques were legendary in the PD, and many suspects had spilled their guts to her.

"Lady, you sound as good as ever."

"Chad! You're a lost voice from the past. How's the new job working out?"

"It's a much slower pace, but I'm enjoying it. I've got a tough case going right now, a missing child. I need help and am hoping you can do some digging for me."

"I'd say you were kidding, but knowing you, you're not. Missing kids seemed to always stick to you like glue. It looks like nothing's changed. Tell me what you need."

Chad relayed the names, dates of birth, and driver's license numbers he'd obtained for the suspects.

They talked for a few more minutes as Vicky filled Chad in on some of the latest happenings with his former colleagues. When they disconnected, Chad's mood had improved. If there were any dirt, she'd find it. Vicky promised to have something for him later that day or the next morning.

"Hey boss, you got a few minutes?"

Chad looked up. His detective stood in the doorway.

"Sure. What do you need?"

"I've got something to show you." He turned and headed back to his office.

Chad followed. When he stepped into the room, Dale was seated in front of the computer. On the screen was a picture of a local convenience store. A truck was parked alongside a gas pump.

"I'm not sure what to make of this."

Chad pulled up a chair and leaned forward to study the screen. "It looks like Neville's truck."

"You're right, it is. As the truck leaves, the camera caught the license plate."

"What's the problem?"

"The day and time. Remember when we questioned him about where he was when Mandy was abducted? He said the Red Rooster, and Jim verified it. Look at the clock in the upper corner."

Dale tapped another key to enlarge the image. The date was the day Mandy was abducted; the time—about thirty minutes before she was kidnapped.

"This store is only a few blocks from the Norton residence. How can Neville be at the gas station when he was at the cafe?" Dale asked.

Chad eased back and whistled. "Son of a bitch! Do you have a shot of who was driving?"

"Yes, and it gets even more squirrely." Another tap and the image changed. This time a man stood by the side of the truck, filling the tank. The hood of his jacket had been pulled over his head, and his back was to the camera.

"No picture of his face?"

"Nope. He kept his back to the camera the entire time. When he did slightly turn, the hood obscured his face. But that's not Neville, too short."

"This is enough to justify another visit with Neville," Chad said.

"I may be way out in left field here, but is it possible whoever was driving Neville's truck grabbed Mandy? But why use Neville's truck?"

"Dale, it's a possibility. We've just got to find the reason."

"If you're headed out there, I'd like to come along."

"Grab your gear. Mark and Boomer just came in. They had an early morning accident call on the edge of town. I want Mark to go with us. While we're there, you're going to take a hard look at his truck."

Mark was seated in front of his desk. Boomer had pulled a chair alongside him. Chad stopped in the doorway. Boomer was getting a lesson on the entry procedures to the Texas Department of Transportation's Accident Report System.

"Mark, hate to interrupt, but I need to talk to you in my office."

Mark looked over his shoulder and nodded. "Be there in a minute." He handed Boomer a manual. "This is the state's instructions for entering an accident report. Read it, then I want you to draw the accident scene on a piece of paper. Make sure you include all the required elements. Write down the contributing factors and be prepared to explain why. Be sure to review the Texas Department of Transportation's legal guidelines for assigning a factor."

Boomer stood, glanced at Chad with a curious look, then headed to his desk.

As they walked into Chad's office, Mark chuckled. "That should keep him busy for the next couple of hours."

Chad explained what Dale had found on the tape. "I want you along. While we keep Neville occupied, Dale's going to examine the truck. I don't want Neville to know."

"What about his alibi?"

"We'll stop at the cafe on our way back. We'll get a late breakfast and slip in a few questions about the man."

While he waited for Dale and Mark to get their gear, he called Jim. After bringing him up to speed about Neville's truck, he asked, "Have you heard from your deputy? Is Neville still at home?"

"Yes. Ken's back on him. I'll call him and let him know you're coming his way. In case you need a warrant, I'll stay in my office."

Dale drove while Chad outlined the plan. "If you do spot something, Jim will walk a search warrant and get it to us. I'm not leaving if we get a chance to get our hands on Neville's truck."

Mark said, "You believe Mandy's been inside?"

"I think this is the best lead we've uncovered." Except for the one he couldn't talk about, the picture Ashley found on Coleman's computer.

Neville's truck was parked in front of the mobile home. Dale pulled in behind it. Chad and Mark exited and walked to the front porch. Chad stepped up; his fist pounded the door. He waited for a few seconds, and not hearing anything, he pounded again.

Inside there was a slight rustling sound. A voice shouted, "Hold on. I'm coming."

Jerking the door open, Neville stood in the doorway, weaving as his red-rimmed, watery eyes glared at Chad. An aroma of pot floated out the door.

With both hands, Chad slapped him in the chest, pushing him back. Neville stumbled. Chad stepped into the room and shoved him again. This time the back of Neville's knees hit the edge of the couch opposite the door. His arms flailed as he fell backward. As he pushed himself off the couch, he said, "That's assault. I'll have your damn badge."

"That's weed I smell. If you want to argue, I'll be glad to carry on the discussion at the jail—after I've booked you."

Neville ran his hand across his face. "No call to do that," he grumbled.

"Where was your truck the morning the Norton girl was kidnapped?'

Neville's eyes darted toward Mark, who blocked the door. "I, uh … I don't know what you mean."

"It's not a difficult question. Where was your truck while you were eating at the cafe?"

"In the parking lot, of course. How do you think I got there?"

"It's what I want to know. I have a picture of your truck at the Lakeway convenience store at the same time you said you were eating breakfast."

His eyes darted around the room as his fingers raked through his hair. Flicking another look at Chad and the hand resting on the butt of the gun, his feet shuffled.

Chad widened his stance as he watched Neville with a hard stare. "I asked you a question?"

Neville blurted out, "How the hell do I know. I left it in the parking lot. It was there when I came out. Besides, you checked my alibi. You know I was there."

"Who else has a key?"

He gulped. "No one. Someone must have taken the truck. I left the key in the ignition."

"Who took it? You'd better come up with an answer, or you can be on the hook for abducting the girl."

Neville snarled, "I'm telling you I don't know who took it, and you can't prove otherwise."

Behind him, Dale said, "Need a minute, Chief."

Leaving Mark to keep an eye on Neville, Chad walked outside.

"If there's anything inside the truck, I can't see it," Dale said.

Chad sighed. "It was a long shot at best."

He stepped back inside. "Neville, I think you're in this up to your eyebrows. If I find a way to prove it, you're not going to be able to dance away from a long stretch in jail. And, that's assuming the Norton girl is alive. Otherwise, I'll push for the needle."

Neville glared at him with a mutinous expression. "You can't threaten me. I didn't kidnap the girl, and you know it."

His voice cold and hard, Chad said, "It's not a threat. It's a promise. Think about it. If you cooperate, I'll see your sentence gets reduced."

"I got nothin' to say."

The mood on the way back into town was grim. Mark finally broke the silence. "In my books, the man is guilty as hell. He knows who kidnapped Mandy."

"I can't disagree," Chad responded. "It's why I didn't haul him to jail for the pot. I'm hoping he'll lead us to Mandy."

Dale pulled into the Red Rooster's parking lot.

Inside, they slid into one of the booths. The restaurant was a replica of an old-style eatery with its long counter, stools, and booths along the front windows.

Nancy Sullivan, the owner's daughter, dropped a menu in front of each of the officers. "Wow, it's not often we get three sexy men at the same time."

Dale grinned. He'd gone to school with her. "Fancy words aren't going to get you a bigger tip."

Unrepentant, she laughed. "You might be surprised. Now, what can I get for three … upstanding … gentlemen of the law?"

As they placed their order, she jotted it on a pad and sashayed around the end of the counter.

Mark asked, "Who was working that morning?"

"Nancy," Chad answered.

Dale groaned. "Oh, great. There's only one other person who is a bigger gossip than Nancy, and it's Henry over at the Tribune."

When Nancy walked back with the coffee pot and three cups, Chad said, "It's quiet in here."

"You should have been here an hour ago. There wasn't a seat to be had." After setting down the cups, she glanced at the wall clock. "Won't be long, and the lunch crowd will be trickling in."

She held the pot over a cup. The coffee slowly streamed into it as she eyed Chad with a fervent gleam. "A lot of the customers are talking about the kidnapping."

"I imagine so," Chad said.

"Nobody seems to know anything."

"Nancy, at this stage of the investigation, a lot of details can't be made public."

"Hmm … well, there should be a way to reassure people. Everyone is scared to let their kid out of their sight." She leisurely inched the cup in front of Dale. "Whoever would have thought someone would kidnap a little girl in our small town."

"We're doing everything we can to find Mandy."

With another sideways look at Chad, she tipped the pot. The coffee trickled into the second cup. "Oh, I know you are, Chief Bishop. Don't mean to say otherwise. I feel I have a part in what's happening. You know the sheriff *did* call me. He wanted to know if that awful Doyle Neville had been here. Of course, I had to say he was."

"You didn't have a choice. It was something we had to know." As he shifted in his seat, he caught the smirk on the two men's faces.

"It was the truth. Much as I'd hate to have to say it in court. I, for one, didn't like having to defend him." The coffee dribbled.

"You know him?"

"Everyone knows about that man. You see him around town all the time. Rumor has it he's dealing drugs."

"Does he come in here often?"

She picked up the cup and set it in front of Mark. Her hand hovered above his cup. Fascinated, he waited. Could Nancy possibly make it flow any slower? It dripped.

"He's what I'd call a regular, comes in several times a month."

"What time did he get here?"

"I guess around seven-thirty. Told me he didn't want to sit at the counter, wanted a table instead." She grinned. "I made him wait. It sure ticked him off, which is why I didn't have any trouble at all remembering when Jim asked me."

"Does he normally sit at the counter?"

"Yeah. Come to think about it, it was odd, his wanting a table. Most mornings, he eats, then hauls his butt out of here. Which suits me just fine. I don't like his coming in here, but I can't do anything about it."

"How long was he here?"

"Hmm … he had his usual, pancakes and coffee." She stopped, tilted the pot back as she thought.

His cup was only a little over half full. He suppressed a groan. The drip, drip, drip resumed.

"Too damn long. All he did was ask for refills, and he's never once left a tip. But he had a newspaper and kept flipping the pages. That was a first. I wouldn't have believed he could even read. I know he was here for more than an hour, but I'm not sure when he left. I was cleaning tables, and when I looked up, he was gone."

"Did you see him talking to anyone, or was someone with him?"

"Who would want to be friends with the likes of him unless they're buying dope. But now that you mention it, he kept looking out the window at the parking lot. Like he was expecting to see someone."

Shoving his cup in front of him, she said, "I'll have your orders here in a few minutes. Let me know when you're ready for a refill," and turned to saunter off.

"Nancy," Chad said.

She stopped and turned back toward him.

"What newspaper?"

"Oh, it was the pennysaver. You know, the one where stuff is listed for sale."

Amazed, Chad watched the sway of her hips as she strutted toward the kitchen, then glanced at Mark and Dale. The two were grinning like a couple of idiots. He leaned over the table. "If either one of you even thinks about asking for a refill, you're fired. And get rid of those smug looks."

Still grinning, Dale said, "She's a real trip, Nancy is. Don't get me wrong, she's a super individual. She and her dad provide free meals to the senior center and a couple of other places throughout the year. It's just, well, she has this addiction to gossip."

"Why the question about the newspaper?" Mark asked.

Chad said, "It's a detail, and it doesn't fit. There's a newspaper stand outside the front door. You can pick up the pennysaver for free. I think Neville may have grabbed one knowing he'd need a reason to hang around. Another change in his pattern was the table. Neville knew his truck was gone and why. He was watching for whoever took it to bring it back."

Chapter Eighteen

shley's first stop of the day was at the Tribune. The next edition was due. Seated in front of her computer, she scrapped the editorial she planned to publish on small-town football rivalries. Instead, she typed an appeal from the family for any information on Mandy's abduction.

She'd just finished approving the weekly edition when her phone rang.

"Ashley Logan."

"Ms. Logan, this is Olivia Murray at Past Memories in Whitney. You and Chief Bishop were in yesterday about a doll."

"Yes, I remember you."

"I tried to reach Chief Bishop, but his secretary said he was out of the office and wasn't certain when he'd return."

"Is there something I can help you with?"

"Well, I'm not sure, and it's why I almost didn't call. A high school student works part-time in the store. She came by this morning to drop off a box of donated clothes for her neighbor. I mentioned your visit. Wendy said a man stopped in the store and asked about dolls."

Her heart jumped with anticipation. "Does Wendy know him?"

"I asked her. She said no. She'd never seen him before."

"Would you give me Wendy's last name, address, and phone

number. I'll pass it on to Chief Bishop." Ashley grabbed her notepad and jotted down the information.

"Do you think it's important?"

The eagerness in the woman's voice tempered her excitement. If she didn't downplay her response, this would spread like wildfire.

"Probably not, since we're trying to find who purchased the doll we had with us. It may just be a coincidence. Thank you for calling. I'll get this information to Chief Bishop as soon as I see him."

She tapped the desk with her pen as she stared at the notepad. The urge to pick up the phone and call the girl battled with her common sense. Hating to admit it, in this case, it was better to let Chad handle the contact. Where was he? If he planned on checking out the water park, she wanted to go with him.

She grabbed her tote bag and jacket. On her way out, she said, "Henry, the paper's ready to be released to the printing company. Will you take care of it for me? I have an errand to run."

He eyed her with suspicion. "You're not going to get into any trouble, are you?"

Surprised, she stared at him. Did he know about her breaking into the bait store? "Uh …why would you ask that?"

"This morning at the Red Rooster, I just happened to be talking to Nora and Edith. Nora mentioned the tension she'd noticed between you and our new police chief when you stopped by yesterday morning."

Even though she was relieved, it was a reminder of what it's like to live in a small town. Everyone knows your every move, or at least most of them. Tit-for-tat time then. "I'm glad you reminded me about my visit. Last night, when we talked about the article on the peaches, I forgot to ask what you planned to do about it. Are there errors?"

"Humph," he grunted. "That fool of a woman doesn't know a lid from a ring when it comes to canning." He turned back to his computer. "Errors my foot," he muttered under his breath.

Holding back a laugh, she walked out.

With the police department only a couple of blocks away, the balmy day enticed her to walk. The sun warmed her skin as she strolled past the small shops. The brief moment of humor faded as thoughts of Mandy filled her mind. Her throat clogged as tears formed. It would be so easy to get mired in the depths of anguish and grief of not knowing. She pushed back on the emotions, refusing to give in to them. It wouldn't help Mandy or anyone else. She'd do what she did best, use her investigative skills.

When Ashley opened the door, Lydia looked up from her computer. Her body tensed, and a guarded look crossed her face.

"Ms. Logan, the Chief's not here. Can I help you with something, or give him a message?"

"Please, it's Ashley. Do you know when he'll be back?"

"No."

"Do you know where he is?"

"No."

Mentally, Ashley sighed. This was going nowhere fast. "Tell him someone called from one of the thrift shops we stopped at yesterday."

"I'll let him know."

The two women stared at each other for a few seconds, then Ashley started to turn.

Lydia's voice stopped her. "How are Kathy and Peter doing?"

About to give the stock answer she'd been using, Ashley hesitated when she saw the look of genuine concern on Lydia's face. Instead, she said, "They're devastated. They want answers, and there are none. As each day passes, it gets a little worse as their hope slowly dies."

"Give them my best. Kathy and I are on the special events

committee for the city. I haven't called because I didn't want to intrude."

"Please call her. I'm certain it would help her to talk to you."

Lydia nodded. "As soon as Chad walks in, I'll give him your message."

During the walk back, Ashley pondered her options. Too restless to sit in the office, there had to be something she could do. The thrift shops had all been crossed off the list. The only one left was the water park. Even if she headed out there, she wasn't sure what she could accomplish.

Lost in her thoughts, she didn't pay any attention to the passing car until the driver honked the horn and pulled alongside her. Chad hopped out, then bent over to say something to the two men inside.

The black jeans stretched tight across his impressive backside. When he turned to greet her, the black T-shirt with the Meridian police emblem embossed on the front revealed an equally impressive set of arm and chest muscles. Hooked to his belt, his holstered gun rode high on his hip. If ever a man could be described as eye-candy, it was Chad Bishop. It was impossible to ignore the swell of passion which ripped through her. In a split second, Ashley knew. She was ready for whatever was going to happen between them.

"Hey, you okay?" he asked.

"Yeah, why?"

"You looked a little spaced out."

If only you knew! But right now, her new awareness would stay a secret. She shrugged. "Lost in thought."

"I was going to call as soon as I got to the office. Where are you going?"

"I just left there and was headed to the Tribune."

An eyebrow twitched upward. "Something happen?"

"I got a call from one of the thrift stores in Whitney." She explained, then added, "Why were you going to call?"

"Hmm … to see if you wanted to go with me to the water park. Did you give the woman any indication we were interested?"

"No. I downplayed my answer."

Nodding his head in approval, he grabbed her hand and pulled her along the sidewalk.

"Where are we going?"

"To get my truck. It's at the PD."

As they passed Bits & Pieces, she spotted Nora at the window. *Oh, good!* Here she was holding hands with the police chief, another juicy tidbit for the rumor mill.

When he opened the passenger door, Chad asked, "Anything you need before we leave town?"

She lifted the tote bag she carried everywhere she went. "I'm good to go."

As Chad drove out of town, he glanced over at her. Ashley looked as delicious this morning as she had last night, even though her jeans were worn at the seams, and the boots slightly scuffed. Most women he'd met over the years, including his ex-wife, hated to get dressed in anything which wasn't top-of-the-line designer clothing. Nothing would have induced Ellen to appear in public dressed like Ashley.

The best attire, though, was when he caught her sneaking out of the bait shop. All in black and with a face mask, she looked like the movie image of a cat burglar. Still, it was smart on her part. If there had been cameras, no one would be able to identify her.

"Where are we headed first?"

Her question brought his attention back to the investigation. The musings which sent his blood spiraling downward had to be put on hold. "The water park."

"Anything new this morning?"

For an instant, he hesitated as distrust reared its ugly head. She's a reporter, don't give her any pertinent details. Then logic took over. She needed to know, and he needed to have faith.

He explained what Dale found on the tape, the incident with Neville, and the conversation with Nancy.

"Then, he is involved." It was a statement, not a question.

"I'm convinced he is," Chad said.

"What about Coleman?"

"Still searching. I hope to have more details today."

Chad pulled into the entrance of the water park. Only one car was parked in front of the building.

"Have they closed for the winter?" Ashley asked.

"It's supposed to be open. Let's find out."

The front door was unlocked. "Somebody must be here," Chad said.

Inside the reception area were a small concession stand, a counter, and several chairs. Through an open doorway, several arcade machines were visible.

Chad shouted, "Anybody here?"

A head popped around a door at the back of the room. "We're closed."

"I'm the Meridian police chief. I'd like to ask you a few questions."

A sprightly old man with shaggy white hair covering his ears and bifocals perched on his nose stepped into the room.

"Police chief, huh. Never had any trouble here that needed a cop."

"It's not the reason I'm here."

Reassured, the man stepped closer. "Then what do you want?"

Chad had tucked a copy of Mandy's picture from Coleman's computer in his pocket. He held it up. "I'd like to know if this concession stand is in the park."

His eyes squinted as he studied the picture. "Yep, it's mine."

"How about the little girl? Ever seen her here?"

"No, but she looks familiar. Hmm … where have I seen her?" His fingers stroked his chin. "I know! It's the missing girl. I saw a flyer."

"Who is the person behind the counter?"

"Oh, that's Nick Olsen."

"Is he around? I'd like to talk to him."

"No. He's a high school kid. Works here part-time."

"I need his address."

"He's not in any trouble, is he? Nick's a good kid."

"I just need to ask him a couple of questions about the day this picture was taken."

The man stepped behind the counter and wrote the address on a notepad. Tearing off the sheet, he handed it to Chad, who, in turn, passed him a business card.

As they turned to walk out, the man said, "I sure hope you find the little girl."

With a grim expression, Chad replied, "So do we."

Back in the truck, Chad glanced at the address before sticking the paper in his pocket. "He lives outside of Meridian. We'll stop there on our way back."

"Are you thinking Nick might have seen who took the picture?"

"It's an outside chance at best. Another detail I need to check off my list."

"I'm beginning to understand how you run your investigations." The realization of his attention to the smallest of details raised her level of respect.

"Let's see what Wendy has to say."

Chad plugged her address into the GPS system, and several minutes later was parked in front of the girl's house.

As they walked toward the front porch, the door opened, and a teenage girl rushed out.

When she spotted Chad, she skidded to an abrupt halt. "Oh!" then hollered, "Mom! A cop is here."

Chad asked, "Are you, Wendy Allen?"

"Uh, yeah."

A woman stepped outside. A wary look on her face, she eyed Chad and Ashley. "I'm Mrs. Allen. Can I help you?"

Chad stepped forward and extended his hand. "I'm Chief Bishop with the Meridian Police Department, and this is Ashley Logan. I'd like to ask your daughter a couple of questions."

"Is she in some kind of trouble?"

"No, not at all. This has to do with a man she may have seen in a thrift shop."

With a note of excitement in her voice, Wendy said, "Mom, remember I told you about the police chief who came into the store with a doll."

"Can we talk inside?" Chad asked.

"Forgive my manners. Please come in," Mrs. Allen said. "It was just the surprise of seeing a police officer on my front doorstep."

Seated in the living room, Chad turned to Wendy. "I understand a man came into the store asking about dolls. Do you remember the date?"

"It was Saturday, two weeks ago."

"Are you sure?"

"Oh, yes. I only work there on Saturdays."

"Can you tell me what he said?"

"He wasn't there long. He stopped at the counter and wanted to know if we had any dolls for sale. I told him I didn't remember seeing any, but he might want to check the toy section at the back of the store. He walked back there, looked around, then left."

"Can you describe him?"

"His clothes were pretty scruffy looking, and he hadn't shaved. I really didn't pay too much attention. I was studying for a test on Monday."

Chad pulled his phone and brought up the picture of Neville. "Is this the man?"

"Nope, not him, though he's sure scary looking. Come to think of it, so was the other guy. I was glad I wasn't alone in the store."

Chad switched pictures. "How about him?"

Wendy squealed. "Yes! Oh, my gosh, yes. That's him. What's he done?"

"He's a person of interest we're looking for."

Chad stood and thanked Wendy and her mother for their cooperation. Ashley echoed his comment.

As he backed out of the driveway, Ashley asked, "Who did she identify?"

Chapter Nineteen

C had said, "Lew Walker."

Ashley glanced at him. The bleak expression on his face was chilling. "Any idea why he'd be looking for dolls?" she asked.

A harsh grunt erupted. "Oh, yeah, and I don't like the reason."

"Who is he?"

"The other man we interviewed after Neville. At the time, he didn't appear to be involved."

"But now ... you think he is?"

"Yes." He pulled his phone and tapped a number.

When Dale answered, he said, "Any chance the person on the tape with Neville's truck is Lew Walker?"

"Walker and Neville working together—that's a damn scary thought. But it could be. The build would be about right. What prompted this idea?"

"Walker was in a thrift shop in Whitney a couple of weeks ago looking for dolls. A girl who works in the store identified him."

"I'll take another look at the tape. Maybe I missed something. Are you headed back to the office?"

"Not yet. I have one more stop to make."

Once Chad had disconnected, Ashley asked, "What's going on? Why would two men be involved in Mandy's kidnapping?"

"I don't know. At first, I expected it was a predator. Someone who saw Mandy and decided to grab her. But now, I don't. Walker out looking for dolls on the same day Mandy's picture is taken at the park isn't a coincidence."

"Does this mean you believe Mandy is still alive?" She hadn't wanted to ask the question, but with the hours turning into days, she had to know.

He didn't want to give her false hope, but deep inside, Chad believed she was. "My gut says she is."

"It's good enough for me," she whispered, turning her head to look out the window. She didn't want Chad to see the sudden rush of tears she blinked back.

Within minutes, Chad turned onto the street where Nick lived. In the front yard of a small house, a young man raked leaves. He looked up as Chad pulled to a stop. Leaning on the handle, he watched with interest as they exited and walked toward him.

Chad gestured toward the piles of leaves waiting to be bagged. "Looks like you have a full day's work ahead of you. I'm Chad Bishop, Meridian's Police Chief, and this is Ashley Logan, our new editor for the Tribune. Are you Nick Olsen?"

Nick tipped his head toward Ashley. "Yes. Nice to meet you, ma'am," he said, before looking at Chad. "I know who you are, Chief Bishop. I heard your speech at the high school about a law enforcement career a few weeks ago. Is something wrong?"

"I have a few questions about the water park. I talked to the owner. He gave me your name and said you might be able to help. What do you do there?"

"Oh, most everything, sell tickets, help with the rides, even keep the place clean."

"How about the concession stand?"

"Yeah. Sometimes I help the guy who runs it. Is he in trouble?"

"No, he isn't. Do you remember working the stand on Saturday, two weeks ago?"

He cocked his head with a look of concentration on his face. "Oh yeah. It was the afternoon Barney took off and asked me to cover for him."

Chad pulled the picture of Mandy at the water park from his pocket and handed it to Nick. "Do you remember seeing this girl?"

A grin split his face. "Sure do. She's a sweetheart and made quite an impression dancing around with the doll she's holding. She talked to it, acted like it was a real person." He handed it back to Chad.

"Do you remember seeing someone take her picture?"

He thought for a few seconds before shaking his head. "No, I don't. A lot of people were there. The boss had run an end-of-summer ticket sale."

"Did you see anyone who looked suspicious or out-of-place?"

Again, a thoughtful expression crossed Nick's face. "I'm sorry, but I can't say I did."

"How about either one of these men?" Chad held up his phone and brought up the pictures.

"The first guy, I've seen him in town. If he'd been around, I would have remembered it. Never seen the second one. We get a lot of kids. Walter, the guy who owns the place, tells everyone to be on the lookout for anyone who doesn't fit in."

It confirmed Chad's suspicions. There was someone else involved. Someone … who did fit in!

"Why are you asking?"

"The little girl is Mandy Norton, and she's been kidnapped."

"Oh, man! I hadn't heard about any kidnapping."

Ashley said, "Nick, we've tried to get the word out to everybody about Mandy. Didn't you see any of the flyers?"

He glanced at the house. "My mom … uh … is sick. It's just the two of us, and I've been staying pretty close to home."

"Ah … I understand. Is there anything we can do to help?"

The boy's back stiffened. "No, ma'am, but thank you. I've got it under control."

Chad handed him a business card. "If you remember anything else, please give me a call."

As Ashley buckled her seat belt, she glanced out the window at the teenager wielding the rake. "A lot of pride there, maybe too much. Do you know anything about the family?"

"No, but I bet it won't take much to find out."

"Henry!" They both said, and then laughed.

As Chad drove away, Ashley asked, "Now what? Where do we go from here?"

"I need to get back to the PD. I've shoved most of my work to the side because of the investigation, but there are some administrative items I need to take care of, like approving the payroll."

"Drop me off at the Tribune. I have a couple of ideas I'd like to research."

"Are you going to be around later?"

"Hmm … I suppose so."

"Interested in Tex-Mex? There's a great place on the edge of town."

A look of regret crossed her face. "I'll have to take a rain check. I promised Kathy I'd stop by this evening."

"We'll do it another time then."

A warm feeling settled over her.

Chad swung into the parking lot of the newspaper office and parked. He reached to open his door.

Ashley's hand wrapped around his arm to stop him. "No, you don't need to get out." Her hand on the door handle, she paused. "Thanks for keeping me in the loop today. I felt like I was doing—something."

"I know the feeling. I'll talk to you later."

Henry was sorting file folders when she walked through the door. "How'd the day go?" A sly look crossed his face. "I heard you were with the police chief."

He probably talked to Nora as the image of the woman at the window of her shop flashed in her mind. "It was all connected to Mandy's abduction."

His face turned serious. "Anything new?"

"No, nothing." She sat in the chair next to his desk, her arms wrapped around the tote bag in her lap. "Henry, it's like she's vanished into thin air. The longer this goes on, the more terrified I get."

"Been on this earth a long time, seen a lot, good and bad. One thing I've learned is you can't give up hope, even in the darkest of moments. Sometimes, it's all we have to keep us going."

"I know." She sighed. "Do you know the Olsen family?"

"Grace and her son Nick?"

"I don't know the mother's name, but I met the boy today."

"Good kid. He's on the high school debate team, took honors last year in the regional competition. How'd you meet him?"

Despite the fact he worked for her, she didn't want to tell him they'd questioned the boy about Mandy. Henry would be like a dog on point, wanting to know why. She couldn't explain without mentioning the photograph, and it would lead to how she got it. Instead, she said, "Chad stopped to talk to him. Nick said his mom is sick."

"She's been fighting cancer for several years. Has her ups and downs, though the last I heard she was in remission. I hope she hasn't had a relapse."

"If you find out, let me know." As she stood, her hand squeezed his shoulder. "Thanks for the pep talk. I'll close up today if you want to take off."

"I might do it. Got a few errands to run, and it's bingo night at the senior center."

The idea of playing bingo as her evening entertainment had her shaking her head in amusement as she walked to her office. Seated at her desk, she booted up her computer. An idea had occurred to her on the way back from the water park; were there any other kidnappings in the area? A number of state and national websites maintained databases for missing and exploited children. She began a methodical search of locations, ages, and dates. Ones that matched her search criteria were jotted on a notepad. Engrossed in her research, she didn't hear Henry leave, and the hours crept by. The ring of the office phone broke her concentration. When she looked up, she was surprised to see it was dark outside.

Picking up the receiver, she said, "Ashley Logan."

A muffled voice asked, "Is there still a reward for the missing kid?"

Her heart skipped a beat. "Yes. Who is this? What do you know?"

"You don't need to know my name. How do I collect?"

"If your information leads us to Mandy, you'll get a check."

"Has to be cash."

"If you want cash, I can get it."

A raucous laugh echoed. Though Ashley didn't recognize the voice, the laugh sounded familiar.

"I figured you could. How long will it take?"

"I'm not certain."

"You find out, I'll call back."

"Don't hang …" The line went dead.

She glanced at the screen. The caller ID showed—unknown. Damn, who'd just called? She punched the number for the PD.

When Chad walked into the office, Lydia gave him a stern look.

"Chief, there's a stack of reports on your desk."

"I've gotten behind, haven't I? I promise I'll sign them before I leave."

A look of sympathy crossed Lydia's face. "It's been a rough few days."

Seated at his desk, he worked his way down the documents. It took longer than he expected. He was almost finished when Lydia stepped into his office.

"Anything you need before I leave?"

"That time already? I'll leave all of this stacked on my desk for you tomorrow. Anyone else still here?"

"No. Dale walked out a few minutes ago. Mark and Boomer left earlier. Tania is on a loud music call."

"Okay. Have a good evening."

"Since I thought you'd be here for a while, I made a fresh pot of coffee."

When his phone rang, she wiggled her fingers at him, turned, and left.

It was Ashley, and he could hear the panic in her voice. "Chad! I just got a call about the reward money. He wants cash and said he'd call back. How fast can I get it?"

"Slow down. We're not going to hand out any money until I get more information."

"Damnit! Don't you think I know that, but I want to be prepared. Why didn't I think about this before?"

"Did you get a name?"

"He wouldn't tell me, and I didn't recognize the voice."

"Tell me what he said." As he listened, Chad flipped through the card index on his desk until he found the card for the bank president.

"I've got to find out how long it takes to get the money," she added. "You know the bank president. Can I get it tonight?"

"I'll call Irvin and get back to you. Are you at the office?"

"Yes. I'm not leaving."

After disconnecting, he dialed Irvin's home number.

His wife answered.

"This is Chad Bishop. Is Irvin there?"

"Yes, hold on a moment."

Her voice distant, she said, "It's Chad, wants to talk to you."

"Chad, what's going on?"

"I need to know how fast I can get the reward money, twenty-five thousand in cash?"

"Did you find Mandy?"

"Not yet. I'm following up on a lead. But if I need the money, how long will it take to get it?"

"I can't do anything before nine in the morning. The bank vault is on a timer, and I can't open it."

"All right. As soon as you can get into the vault, get the money in one-hundred-dollar bills. I want a list of all the serial numbers. I'll include a tracking device and will have Dale drop it off."

"I'll start working on it as soon as I can open the vault door. I'll call when it's ready. How solid is this lead?"

"I don't know yet. We can't tell anyone, including Kathy and Peter. All it will do is raise false hopes, so please don't discuss this with anyone, including your personnel."

"I'll handle it myself."

Once the line was clear, he called Ashley.

She answered on the first ring.

"He can't get into the vault until nine in the morning." He added the instructions he'd given to Irvin. "There's nothing we can do tonight. Don't do anything rash."

Since she figured his definition of rash wasn't the same as hers, she ignored the comment, only saying, "As soon as I hear from him, I'll call you."

Time seemed to slow as Ashley stared at the phone, willing it to ring. She glanced at the wall clock. It had been over an hour. Why didn't he call? Her every instinct screamed the man knew where to find Mandy. If he'd just tell her, she'd promise him anything.

Antsy, she shoved her chair back, pacing to the front where she stared out the window. The fog, with that strange eerie glow, was back. How many nights had it appeared, she wondered? Her mind cast back to when it started. How odd, it was the first night after Mandy was abducted.

When the phone rang, every thought fled. She turned and ran. Grabbing the receiver, she said, "Logan."

It was him, the same raspy voice. "Did you get it?"

"I can't until the bank opens in the morning. I've already made the arrangements to pick it up."

"I'll call at ten. You have one chance. If you don't have the dough, all bets are off. Your niece will be history."

"I'll do …" The line went dead. Fear streamed through her. This had to work.

She punched the number for the PD. When Chad answered, she relayed the conversation.

Chad said, "I'll have everything set up. The money will be waiting at the bank. What number is he calling?"

Ashley said, "The office phone."

"I'll have a trace on your phone, ready to record the call." He hesitated, then added, "Don't say anything to Kathy or Peter. Let's not get their hopes up."

"You're right. I won't."

"See you in the morning."

Slowly, she gathered her notes and stuffed them in her tote bag before shutting down her computer. Could she hide her agitation from her sister? But if she didn't show up, Kathy would think something was wrong. She'd have to brazen it out. Ashley sent Kathy a text to let her know she was on her way. After turning out the lights, she set the alarm and locked the door behind her.

An unnerving silence shrouded the parking lot. As she hesitated, staring at the eerie mist, cold chills rippled over her. Was someone there? Watching? Not one to ignore an instinct of danger, she rushed toward her car. Inside, she punched the door lock before breathing a sigh of relief.

As she pulled out of the lot, she began to rationalize her reaction. How could she be in any danger? It was ridiculous. The momentary panic was probably due to the phone call. Besides, what happened in the morning was the only thing that mattered. In all the fear and anxiety, she forgot about her earlier discovery. Eleven children in East and Central Texas had disappeared over the last few months. The ages ranged from two to four. Mandy was number twelve.

Chapter Twenty

⌒◦⌒

Chad's phone rang. It was Vicky in Atlanta. "I didn't expect you to call this late," he told her.

She said, "It's been one of those days from hell. You know how it goes; you never get out on time. Besides, I didn't want to wait until tomorrow."

"What did you find?"

"Nothing on Neville that you wouldn't have come across. His life's an open book, one that's slimy reading. But the Colemans'; there's a mystery there. Did you know he'd been an investment consultant and worked for a Boston firm?"

"I knew he moved here from Boston, but not where he worked. It sure doesn't fit my image of a bait shop owner. No one around here knows it. Believe me, a juicy tidbit like that would have lit up the local grapevine."

"The official story from the investment firm is he retired. The unofficial word is there were irregularities in some of his accounts. The firm hushed it up, and he was fired."

Chad said, "Then he moves to Texas to open a bait shop. It sounds dubious at best."

"I agree. The bait shop is what got my attention. Coleman doesn't just own one, but six across Texas. It's why I dug into his financials.

I found several accounts, including one overseas. Without a warrant, I can't get any details, but the setup fits the profile of someone using the stores to launder money. I just can't prove it."

"I've got the same problem, rumors of dealing, but no proof," Chad said. "Any thoughts on how a kidnapped child ties into this?"

"None."

"How about the wife? Anything on her?"

"She's an accountant and worked for a CPA firm. No criminal history or any suspicious activity."

"This just gets more interesting. An accountant would know how to cook the books."

"I sent you a file on what I've found. I'll keep digging. If I come up with anything else, I'll let you know. How's the case going on the missing child?"

"Not good, though I do have a few leads."

"If anyone can find the girl, it's you. You've got the nose, and everyone here knew it, which is why you always caught the bad cases."

He fought to keep the bitterness from his voice. "Sometimes, it doesn't work out the way you expected."

"You always had the support of everyone in this department."

After a few more comments, he disconnected. He picked up his cup and headed to the breakroom. Leaning against the counter, he took a sip. Was there a pattern he wasn't seeing? Neville, Walker, Coleman, and Mandy, how did they all fit together?

Ashley hugged her sister, thanking her for dinner. On her way over, she wondered if she'd have to cook, but Kathy had a casserole warming in the oven. While she managed to get her sister to eat a few bites, the dark circles under Kathy's eyes bothered her. Peter didn't look much better. She'd never felt so helpless.

When she stepped out the front door, the strange fog closed around her. Ashley shivered as she remembered her earlier reaction. She reminded herself it was just fog. Nothing mysterious about it. Still, the dark haze was unsettling.

As Ashley pulled away from the curb, her thoughts reverted to the phone calls she'd received. Who was the man? What did he know?

A truck passed her going in the opposite direction. When her lights flashed across it, Ashley realized it was Neville. She whipped into a parking lot. Tires squealed as she turned to get back on the street. By that time, his taillights were a faint blur. She wondered if this was a wise move after her encounter with the man. Then it hit her! The laugh. My god, it was Neville who called about the reward.

Determined to stay with him, Ashley floorboarded the accelerator to catch up. Her eyes darted between the roadway and the rearview mirror. Where was the deputy who was supposed to be tailing him? Brake lights flashed, and Neville pulled into a deserted parking lot. By then, she was convinced he was up to no good and had somehow managed to ditch the tail.

Flipping off the headlights, she turned onto a side street before stopping. With a troubling sense of urgency, she shoved her phone and flashlight in her pocket, and scrambled to get out of the car, then hesitated. Reaching back inside, she grabbed the gun from the console, thankful she had the foresight to put it in her car before she left this morning. She dropped it into a pocket, turned, and ran toward the building that butted up against the side of the parking lot.

Reaching it, she crept along the side of the building. Neville's strident voice rang out. Who was he talking too? She hadn't seen another car. A shiver of fear raced over her at the thought of looking around the corner. Would they see her? She took a ragged breath and leaned forward.

In the gloomy fog, the light from the truck's headlights cast a glow around Neville, who stood in front near the passenger side. His back was to her as he raised his fist and gestured toward someone on the other side of the truck.

"Son-of-a-bitch!" he shouted. "Are you willing to pass up twenty-five thousand bucks?"

In a faint voice, the second man answered. Ashley strained to hear the words. He was telling Neville to keep his voice down.

Neville glanced around. "If you're so damn worried about someone overhearing us, why the hell did you want to meet here?"

Unless the other man stepped closer to Neville, she didn't have a chance of getting a look at him. But if she moved around the back of the building to the other side, they could be gone by the time she got there. She was stuck; this was as close as she could get.

Neville said, "Dude, you're the moron, not me. This is a bigger payoff than we'll get out of this deal. I told you before we don't have to return the kid alive. We need to go after the money."

The second voice said, "Your hairbrained scheme is just going to screw this up."

Neville's voice vibrated with anger. "This is cash money! I talked to the woman at the Tribune. She'll have it in the morning. We grab the kid, dump her body somewhere, and split the money."

Ashley leaned back against the wall. Despite the sudden trembling in her legs, shock held her in place. They were talking about killing Mandy. Somehow, she had to stop them. Chad! She had to call Chad. She reached into her pocket to get the phone and felt the gun. Could she stop them from leaving and give Chad time to arrive?

The other man's voice growled. "Dammit! I can't believe you're that stupid. Why in hell would you call a newspaper reporter?"

As she reached into the other pocket for her phone, Ashley looked again.

Neville motioned angrily with his hand. "She's the kid's aunt, that's why."

"For god sakes, tell me you used the burner phone, so she doesn't know who called."

"She doesn't have a clue. I disguised my voice. I'm not *that* stupid, though I don't give a rat's ass what you think. If you don't want part of the action, I'll do it. What are you … no!"

A shot rang out. Neville fell to the ground, and the pounding of footsteps echoed. Her hand shook as she tapped the speed dial for 911. In the distance, she heard an engine, followed by the squeal of tires. The killer had escaped.

When the dispatcher answered, she shouted, "A man's been shot!"

"Where?"

Ashley read off the name of the business painted on the front of the building, then added, "I don't know the address."

The dispatcher asked who was calling, but Ashley disconnected, dropped the phone in her pocket, and ran to Neville. A large dark stain spread across his chest. When she dropped to her knees, his head turned toward her, his eyes glinted with recognition.

With both hands, she pushed down on his chest. Even with the pressure, Ashley couldn't stop the spurts of warm liquid between her fingers and over her hands. "Where's Mandy? Please tell me," she begged.

His lips moved. She leaned over to hear. A wheezing gasp erupted. Then, his chest stopped moving.

She stared into the lifeless eyes. "No! No!" Ashley pushed harder. "You can't be dead." When she realized the flow of blood had stopped, she slowly sat back on her heels. All she could do was stare at the red gore that dripped from her hands.

As he strode along the hall, Chad's mind shifted through everything he'd learned. This was a puzzle, and there were still missing pieces, but he was getting close. He could feel it in his bones.

Back in his office, he swiveled his chair. With his feet propped on the long file cabinet positioned under the window, he sipped his coffee. The fog was back, and the misty haze clouded the glow of the two lights in the parking lot.

The image of Mandy on Coleman's computer occupied his mind. Why would you need a picture? Whoever grabbed Mandy would only need an address and description. So, what other reason?

The squawk of the radio broke his concentration. It was a shots fired call. Tania, his deep night officer, and an ambulance were dispatched. His feet hit the floor, and he raced to the door. The location was only a few blocks away. Before he was even out of the parking lot, he hit the switch for the lights and siren, then grabbed the radio mike to let the dispatcher know he was headed to the scene.

When he turned onto the street, he saw Tania jump out of her car. He slammed on the brakes. One hand hit the switch for the overheads and siren, his other grabbed the door handle. Exiting, he ran.

What he saw would haunt him for many a day. Ashley knelt beside a man. Her hands and clothes were stained with blood. He glanced at the body. Christ, it was Neville.

As he stepped beside her, she stared up at him. "I couldn't save him. He knew where Mandy is, but I couldn't save him."

Tania knelt on the other side of the body and laid her fingers on the side of his neck. When he looked at her, she shook her head. Chad didn't need the confirmation; he already knew Neville was dead.

He'd seen too many bodies during his career.

Behind him, the ambulance screeched to a stop. Two EMTs rushed to his side. He reached to help Ashley stand and move out of their way.

Nodding toward the body, Chad said, "He's dead. Tania, call the morgue. Let them know they've got one coming. Then get Dale out here to process the crime scene."

"Got it, Chief." She trotted back to her car.

One of the medic's knelt beside the body to confirm what Chad had told her. When she stood, she looked at Ashley. "Let's get you to the ambulance. I can get rid of some of the blood."

While this was going on, Ashley had stood by his side, staring at the body. Chad didn't like it. She was too quiet.

"Ashley." He laid a hand on her shoulder and felt the bone-shattering shudder that rocked her.

She looked up, her eyes large and black against the pasty-grey skin. "Chad, he was ..." She choked. "He ...he was going to kill Mandy to get the money. It's what would have happened if *I'd* given it to him. Dear God, I could have killed her."

What did she stumble into? "You don't know for sure what would have happened."

"I heard them arguing. It's what Neville said."

Before he could get it sorted out, he had to make sure none of the blood was hers.

Seated in the ambulance, the medic washed Ashley's hands and wiped the worst of the blood from her clothes. After checking her vital signs, she said, "You can stay here. I'll be back to check on you."

Although she wobbled, Ashley stood and pressed her hand against the side of the ambulance for support. "No. It was a shock, but I'll be all right. Thank you for your help."

"Are you sure? I'd feel a lot better if you'd sit here for a few minutes."

A weak smile crossed Ashley's face. "I can't. I still have a job to do."

"Job?"

"I'm the editor of the Tribune, and that's my lead story out there."

As Ashley climbed out, the medic wondered how the police chief was going to react.

Outside, Chad stood near the body, talking to Dale. As Ashley approached, a look of surprise crossed Dale's face as his eyes shifted toward her.

Chad turned. "What the hell! What are you doing here? You're supposed to be in the ambulance."

"Hmm …" She stared at the body. "There's no reason to stay there. Besides, you need a statement from me."

"I expect it will make interesting reading." The hurt look, which flashed across her face, was a punch to his gut. The sarcasm was unintentional. Nothing he could do about it now, but he was certain an apology was somewhere in his future.

"Ashley, it'll have to wait until we get to the station."

"Good, then you can answer some questions for me. Do you have any idea yet what caliber of gun was used?"

"What do you think you're doing?"

"My job. This is a news story."

A groan erupted, and he ran his hand through his hair as he glared at her. A shift from witness to a reporter was the last thing he needed. "In that case, you need to leave."

"No! I'm not. I'm sticking around to find out what's going on. After all, I'm part of what happened here."

"No, you're not … sticking around. If you don't leave now, I'll hold you as a material witness, and maybe even as a suspect. Dale will take you to the station. You can stay there until I'm ready to talk to you."

Incensed, she fired back. "You can't do that. I have a right to be here. And where in the hell did you get the ridiculous notion, *I'm* a suspect?"

"The gun in your pocket gives me the right. Dale, get it. See if it's been fired." Chad hadn't missed the way her pocket drooped from the weight of the gun.

Dale had watched the fiery exchange in front of him. It was difficult to keep from grinning. A quick glance around, and he realized so was everyone else.

"Uh, right, boss." He stepped behind Ashley, and muttered, "Please don't do anything stupid."

She growled in protest but didn't resist when he slid his hand into her pocket and pulled out the gun. He removed the magazine, locked the slide back, checked to be sure it was empty, then held it up to his nose. After a couple of sniffs, he said, "It hasn't been fired."

"Satisfied, Chief Bishop? My gun." She held out her hand.

Dale looked at his boss.

"I'm keeping it for now," Chad said.

Her body stiffened. "On what grounds?"

"You're still a material witness. You have two choices. Go home, or I'll have you hauled to the station in cuffs."

"Don't you understand?" With an angry gesture toward the body on the ground, she said, "That man knew where to find Mandy. I have to stay to find out what you discover."

The angry blush across her face was at odds with the distress in her eyes. He felt his anger turn to sympathy. "Believe me, I know how important this is. Let me do my job. Go home."

Furious, she turned and marched toward the street. Looking back, she fired a last shot. "This isn't over."

"Chad, you sure know how to stir up a hornet's nest. She's one pissed … off … woman," Dale said as he watched Ashley stomp across the parking lot.

"Yeah, but it got her away from here." What he didn't say was the altercation had pulled Ashley out of the state of shock he'd seen when he arrived. He wasn't, however, looking forward to the confrontation he knew awaited him.

His phone rang. Just when he thought it was as bad as it could get, it got worse.

Chapter Twenty-one

On the other end was Jim. "Neville's in the wind and my deputy is on the way to the hospital. They don't know if he'll live."

Chad said, "I've got Neville. He's dead from a bullet hole in his chest. Who got hurt?"

"Todd Holcomb. Someone bashed him in the head. Left him for dead. I figure it was Neville."

"How'd you find him?"

"He missed his check-in call with the dispatcher. When she couldn't raise him on the radio, she sent a deputy out to Neville's place. Todd was lying alongside his vehicle. What's the deal with Neville? Any idea on the shooter?"

"No. As soon as I'm done with the crime scene, I need to get a statement from Ashley. Then I'm headed to Neville's place to search it. Jim, can you get someone out there until I get there?"

"I'll take care of it. What's Ashley got to do with Neville's getting killed?"

"I found our new editor bent over the body, covered in his blood." His tone was grim. "I'm keeping the pressure on her. Threatened to have her locked up as a material witness if she didn't cooperate."

"You do like to live dangerously, don't you? I'll be at the hospital if you need anything else."

"As soon as I can, I'll come by."

By the time they were finished, Chad's total evidence was a nine-millimeter case and a burner cell phone. Neville's truck was on the way to the wrecking yard, which served as his department's auto pound. Dale was headed there to process it for any clues to Mandy's whereabouts. As Chad helped Tania load up their equipment, his phone chimed. It was Jim.

"Someone torched Neville's place. Ken's on the scene. Says it's a total loss. You know how fast one can burn."

Cursing over another lost lead, Chad jabbed the disconnect button. There must have been something in Neville's mobile home someone didn't want found.

Once he settled behind the wheel, he debated whether to head to the hospital or to Ashley's house. When he pulled onto the street, his car seemed to turn on its own toward her home.

He shook his head in wonderment. Who was he kidding?

Ashley stomped into the house. Never, in her entire career, had she encountered an individual as insufferable as this police chief. His threat to haul her to jail infuriated her. Which she decided was good. The anger pushed back the paralyzing fear she'd felt when Neville was killed. Just thinking about it was enough to set off another panic attack. No doubt, she needed to stay mad.

After tossing the tote bag on the couch, she stripped off her jacket. Ashley shuddered at the sight of the blood smears. *I'm not wearing this again.* It fell to the floor. She'd throw it in the trash later.

A gasp erupted when she stepped in front of the bathroom mirror. Not only were her pants and shirt bloodstained, but globs of the gruesome stuff matted her hair. How the hell did that happen? Like lightning bolts, flashes of memory struck—the shot, feet running, blood squirting, Neville's lifeless eyes.

A wave of dizziness washed over her, and she collapsed onto the edge of the tub, her hands braced on each side to steady her. My god, she'd been within seconds of walking out and confronting the two men. Would she have ended up on the ground and felt her blood spurting out? It was a terrifying and sobering thought.

Her skin suddenly itched. She had to get out of these clothes, get Neville's blood off her. In her haste, her fingers fumbled, and she ripped at the shirt. It didn't matter. The clothes were headed for the trash bin along with the coat.

Turning on the shower, she stepped under the hot spray and let it beat on her body. The water, which cascaded over her head, turned red as it flowed down her body. Ashley poured a handful of shampoo and scrubbed her scalp until it felt raw. Her body was next.

It wasn't until the water turned cold, did she step out and dry off. Between the relaxing effects of the hot water and the soothing lavender-scented lotion she rubbed on her body, the tension began to fade away, though a lingering fear still pulsed in her body.

Dressed in sweatpants and sweatshirt, her damp hair curled around her face. Needing to get her statement typed, she didn't waste time drying it. Ashley wanted to be ready to hand her report to Chad when he arrived. She didn't have any doubt he'd show up at her front door once he finished with the crime scene. With a grim chuckle, she thought, he won't have to step one foot into this house.

With a large glass of wine in her hand, she headed to her office. Because she started with the first phone call, it took longer to type than she expected. All she left out was the gun, and her plan to stop the two men from leaving. Some things were better left unsaid.

When the doorbell rang, her palm thumped the stapler with a sense of satisfaction. The report in one hand, the glass in the other, she sauntered toward the door. The harsh jangle of a double-tap on the doorbell echoed. She smiled and set the glass on the table by the door. Flipping on the porch light, she looked through the peephole. Yep, big as life, there he stood.

She edged the door open and stuck the report through the opening.

"What's this?" he asked as he grabbed the papers.

"The statement you wanted. It should take care of any business we have."

She swung the door shut, but his foot was faster.

He pushed it open and stepped inside.

Backing up, she exclaimed, "You can't come waltzing in here."

With a sardonic snort, he brushed past her and headed to the kitchen. "I need a cold drink?"

What! This wasn't what she planned as she trotted behind him. "Hold on a darn minute. I didn't invite you in."

"We're going to talk." He waved the papers in the air. "I want to know what you haven't put into this report."

"What makes you think it isn't complete?"

He tossed the papers on the table and turned to face her. "Lady, I'm getting to know you. I'd lay odds you left out something. Have a seat."

Defiant, her chin lifted. "You wanted a statement, and you got it. There's nothing more to discuss."

"Don't mess with me. I've had about all I can take tonight. But *we're* going to talk." His eyes gleamed with anger and frustration.

It suddenly struck her that maybe it wasn't all due to her. Something else had happened.

"Mandy! Did you find out something?"

"No, it's not Mandy. At least not directly." He opened the refrigerator door. "Ah …" and grabbed a can of Coke. He popped the top, took a long swig, and dropped down on a chair. "One of Jim's deputies is in the hospital. He's critical, may not make it. He was working the surveillance on Neville."

In an instant, her anger vanished. "Oh, no, Chad. How did it happen?"

"Someone bashed him in the head. I don't have any details yet. From here, I'm headed to the hospital."

"That's why I didn't see anyone following Neville. I wondered about it when I first saw his truck."

He took another swallow. "It's not all. Someone burned down Neville's place before we could search it."

She walked out of the kitchen to retrieve her wine glass, refilled it, then sat across from him.

"This is bigger than a kid being snatched by some predator," he said.

His comment reminded her she hadn't had a chance to tell him about what she'd found.

"Be right back." Earlier, she'd laid the folder on her desk. Ashley pulled out a copy and walked back to the kitchen, dropping it in front of him.

Chad set the can on the table and pulled the papers toward him. "What's this?"

"Locations of kids abducted in the last several months. Twelve counting Mandy. All girls with the same type of appearance. I wrote down their descriptions."

He took another swallow as he studied each page. "When did you come up with this?"

"Earlier this evening. I haven't had a chance to tell you."

A short whistle erupted before he said, "God-a-mighty, why hasn't someone seen the similarities, a pattern in the abductions?"

"Good question. Considering how many kids are reported missing every year, it could be no one was looking for this type of match."

"You might be right. This adds another dimension to the investigation." His fingers tapped the pages as he thought.

"What can you do?"

"Nothing tonight." His hand waved toward the statement on the table. "I don't want to read it. I want you to tell me from start to finish. And, by the way, Neville *was* your caller. I found your number on his burner phone."

"I figured it out when I spotted his truck. It was his laugh. I heard it the day I talked to him and again when he called." It took several minutes to cover what happened. Chad didn't interrupt, but she caught the look of anger which flashed across his face during several of her comments. When she finished, he stared at her as he crushed the can in his hand.

"Do you … have *any* idea how incredibly dangerous it was to follow Neville?" His voice vibrated.

It took a moment before she realized it wasn't anger but fear.

She reached across the table. Her fingers brushed the top of his hand. "Yes, Chad, I do. But when I knew why the caller's laugh sounded familiar, I didn't have a choice. If he could lead me to Mandy, I had to."

His hand rubbed his face while he stared off into space. "You could have been killed."

"I know it now."

"Are you certain there wasn't something that could identify the shooter?"

"No. I've racked my brain, reliving what happened. The entire time he stood on the opposite side of the truck. All I could see was a dark shape. I didn't recognize his voice."

Frustrated, Chad stood. "I've got to get to the hospital."

"If you'll give me a minute to change into a pair of jeans, I'll go with you."

Surprised, he said, "Are you sure? It's not necessary."

"Yes, it is. This is my town."

Walker backed into the driveway of an empty house. Slouched behind the wheel, he watched her front door. What little he'd found out, he knew she lived alone.

When Neville talked to him about getting the reward money, he'd let the boss know the man was up to no good. Livid over Neville's meddling, his boss ordered the hit. Walker set up the meet with Neville, but it wasn't in time. The idiot had already talked to Logan about the reward. After killing Neville, Walker called his boss to let him know the woman was involved. The man didn't like loose ends, and the editor had become one. After torching Neville's mobile home, he headed to Logan's house with orders to stay on her, find out what she was up too.

The arrival of the police chief was unexpected. Uneasy, he wondered why the cop showed up. It wasn't a quick visit. Bishop had been inside for some time. He stiffened when the inside lights were turned off. The porch light, hazy in the heavy fog, came on, and the front door opened. Logan followed the cop outside. They got into his squad car and left. Where were they going at this time of night?

Only one way to find out. He followed them.

Inside the emergency room, a mixture of personnel from the Sheriff's department and his employees gathered in clusters, their voices a low murmur. Jim stood in front of a woman; her hand tightly clasped the hand of a young girl. Chad figured it was Todd's family.

Lydia spotted them and called out. He stepped toward her, and Ashley followed.

Chad asked, "Any news?"

"So far, all we've heard is what Jim told us. Todd's in critical condition. They are operating on him."

Chad nodded toward Jim. "Is that his family?"

"Yes," Lydia told him.

Chad walked toward the group. He spoke to Todd's wife, then pulled Jim aside.

Lydia shivered, saying, "This is awful. How could it have happened? Do you know anything?"

Ashley shook her head as she wondered what the two men were discussing. "I only found out about it a few minutes ago. Chad stopped by the house."

"Oh, that's right. You were involved in the shooting tonight. The man who was killed is the one Todd was following, wasn't it?"

"Yes, but I don't have any details. How long has Todd been in surgery?"

"Hmm ..." Lydia glanced at the clock on the wall. "I've been here for over an hour, and it was going on when I got here."

"What about his family? Anything I can do to help?" Ashley asked.

Tears glinted in Lydia's eyes as she answered, "Maybe. We'll have to see how this goes."

A man in blue scrubs walked in. The chatter died as heads turned.

"Todd is out of surgery. We had to relieve the pressure on his brain. He's still unconscious. The next twenty-four to forty-eight hours are critical. Everyone, except the family, should go home. There's not much you can do now."

Chad stepped back to where Ashley still stood with Lydia.

"Chad, is all this linked to Mandy's abduction?" Lydia asked.

"I can't say with absolute certainty, but I believe it is."

Lydia picked up her purse from a chair behind her. "Well, I'll see you in a few hours."

Chad nodded and looked at Ashley. "Ready to go?"

The ride back was quiet. Ashley stared out the window. The heavy fog formed a barrier around the car, making it difficult to see any of the houses they passed. "What's with this crazy fog? Doesn't it seem strange to you?"

Panic ripped through Chad. His hands tightened around the steering wheel. Did she know?

"I wonder if the green glow has something to do with the weather conditions?" she added.

He bit back a sigh of relief. It was just an idle comment. Nothing for him to be concerned over. After all, it was just fog.

"Hmm ... I'm not sure. I've got a meeting with Jim in the morning. You're welcome to sit in on it."

The distraction worked as her head whipped around to stare at him. "If I remember right, a few hours back, it was tacky remarks and threats because I was trying to do my job."

"I'm sorry about the crack about the report, and all the rest. A murder scene can get a bit squirrely. Seeing you covered with Neville's blood didn't help."

"Humph," she sniffed. "You do recall then—I *am* a reporter?"

"Yes, one who I trust. You have as big a stake in this as anyone."

Her balloon of righteous anger collapsed. His comment was probably the best compliment she'd ever received.

He parked in the driveway and came around to open the car door. His small courtesies still surprised her.

After stepping onto the porch, she turned. Chad's arms folded around her. He laid his forehead against hers. "You scared me. At first, I thought the blood was yours."

"Oh, Chad. It didn't occur to me." A warm glow floated through her, and when his lips touched hers, the glow turned hot. She moaned as desire overtook her senses. Her arms reached and wrapped around his neck. When he leaned back, the gleam of passion in his eyes ramped up her heartbeats until each one thudded against her chest.

"There will be a day when we finish this."

While her hand groped inside the tote bag to find her keys, she said, "Wow, until then, you sure know how to rev the engine."

He chuckled. "That's just for starters."

She unlocked the door and stepped inside. Chad started down the steps, then glanced back over his shoulder. "The meeting is at seven."

When the cop turned into the drive to the hospital, Walker wondered what was going on. Squad cars lined the driveway leading to the emergency room. Stymied as to the reason, he turned and headed back. Parked in the same place as before, he slumped down. Once he knew she was in for the night, he had business of his own to take care of. Lights flashed from an approaching car. Expecting the cop would drop her off, it was a surprise to see him walking her to the door. When Bishop laid one on her, he knew his boss wasn't going to like this new development.

Chapter Twenty-two

❧

*T*he sun had yet to break over the horizon when Chad stepped out of his car. Heavy fog still blanketed the station's parking lot. The sight of tendrils of mist coiling around his feet and legs triggered a sense of trepidation. Unbidden, memories forced their way into his mind. Would he ever be free of them?

His stride lengthened as the anger built. It was done, over, and had nothing to do with Mandy's case. After the deadly events of the night before, he had to concentrate on what would happen today. He couldn't be distracted by the events of a year ago.

Carried by the ghostly haze, the faint voice of a child echoed, "Not dead … not dead." His mind on the upcoming meeting, Chad wasn't listening and didn't hear the desperate sounds.

Lydia was already at her desk when he walked in. "I didn't expect to see you at this time of the morning."

"With everything that's happened, I figured you'd be getting an early start. I might as well too," she said.

"You're right. I'm meeting Jim this morning."

Behind him, the door opened. Mark, followed by Boomer, walked in. One of these days, he had to find out how the kid got the nickname.

Mark said, "Sounds like all hell broke loose last night."

"You must have talked to Tania," Chad said.

"Yeah. She was eating breakfast at the Red Rooster."

"Unless you get an urgent call, stick here at the station for a meeting. Boomer, you're included."

The kid beamed. *God, to be that young again.* With only three hours of sleep, he was feeling the fatigue.

"Lydia, when Dale gets …"

She interrupted him. "He's already here. He beat me in."

Chad nodded and headed to Dale's office. Angry mutters filtered into the hallway. His detective pounded away on the keyboard.

"They do say talking to yourself is the first sign of insanity," Chad quipped.

Dale didn't stop. "Feel free to haul me away to the loony bin anytime you want. Damn, it's what I was afraid would happen." He leaned back in disgust as he stared at the screen.

"What's got you in an uproar?"

"The bullet. Doc Morley sent me a text. The bullet he recovered from Neville's body is too mangled to use. It bounced around inside his body, clipped the aorta, which is why he bled out, nicked a rib, and lodged in the spine. No chance of running any ballistic tests to find the gun."

"Another lead down the tubes. What about the truck?" Chad asked.

"So far, nothing." He nodded toward two large-sized trash bags sitting on the floor. "That's everything from inside the truck. It looked like Neville had been living in it. It's going to take time to sort through all the stuff."

"Any fingerprints?"

"I lifted a few. I haven't had time to run them."

"Call River. Let's see if Rufus hits on the truck. I still have

Mandy's sweater in an evidence bag in my office."

"It's a good idea. What do you want me to do with Ashley's gun?" He motioned toward a box. "I reloaded it."

Chad groaned. "I guess I'd better give it back to her."

"It might help to ease the tensions it created."

"Not likely." He grunted. "The mention of it will probably set her off again."

A sly look crossed Dale's face. "I couldn't help noticing you seemed to have it under control at the hospital. After what happened at the crime scene, I sure didn't expect to see the two of you walk through the door. Is she coming in to make a statement?"

"Already have it."

"When did you get it?"

"Last night."

Despite the growing look of interest on his detective's face, Chad wasn't about to satisfy his curiosity and changed the subject. He told him about the meeting and picked up the box.

"Anything I need to bring?" Dale asked.

"Just your brain."

"Good luck there. Right now, it feels fried." He turned back to his computer.

In the reception area, Jim stood talking to Lydia. When he spotted Chad, he said, "Good news. Todd's going to make it. I stopped at the hospital on my way here."

"It's about the best news we've had around here for the last few days. Have you been able to talk to him yet?"

"He's still unconscious, though the doc's hopeful I can tomorrow."

"Let's go to the conference room. Lydia, when Ashley gets here, send her on back."

Jim cocked an eyebrow at him as they headed down the hallway. "Ashley?"

"I figure she's got as much of a stake in this as we do."

Jim's chuckle bordered on evil.

"Don't even think about it. I'm not up to punching your lights out this morning. There's fresh coffee in the breakroom. I'm going to grab a cup."

Inside the conference room, Chad pulled out a chair. "Anything from the arson investigators?"

Jim set his cup and briefcase on the table. "No, they'll be back on site as soon as it gets light. There's not much left. That sucker went up like fireworks. Just damn lucky it didn't spread to the other mobile homes."

Dale walked in, followed by Mark and Boomer. Steps sounded in the hallway. Ashley hesitated in the doorway as her eyes scanned the room. After greeting everyone, she dropped her tote bag next to a chair and set a small coffee thermos on the table.

"If you need a refill, there's a pot in the next room," Chad told her.

"Thanks, but I'm good." Ashley pulled a notepad and pen from the bag. She looked across the table at Jim. "How's Todd?"

Jim relayed the latest news.

"Can I quote you? Henry is working on an article about the fire."

Chad said, "The man's already at work?"

Ashley grinned. "Sometimes I suspect he sleeps at the office. I swung by there on my way here. He already knew about the fire and Todd. Of course, I had to run his gauntlet of questions regarding Neville's murder."

At the wary look that crossed Chad's face, she hastened to add, "Don't worry. I have the final say on what gets printed."

Chad nodded in relief, then stepped to close the door. As he walked back to his chair, he said, "This meeting is confidential. The details are not to be discussed outside this room. Some locals are involved. I'm beginning to learn how fast word travels in this town." He made a point of looking at Boomer, who nodded his head.

After opening a file folder, he pulled out the picture of Mandy in front of the concession stand. He handed it to Jim. "This picture was on Coleman's computer in the bait shop."

Jim's eyebrows raised as he studied it, though he passed it to Mark without making a comment.

"Who took a picture of his computer screen?" Mark asked.

Ashley saw the sideways glance that Jim cast her way. She wondered if he knew about her excursion, but only stared back with a wide-eyed expression of innocence.

Chad said, "It's not important, but I think everyone can understand why I'm concerned this conversation doesn't get leaked to anyone outside this room."

Jim said, "You're right since there's no way the photo can be used in court. That looked like the concession stand at the water park."

A grim look on his face, Chad nodded. "It is. The picture was taken about two weeks before Mandy was kidnapped."

"Do I want to know how you found out?" Jim asked.

Chad pulled out the second picture of the image's properties and handed it to him.

Jim groaned as his gaze skimmed the picture before passing it on. This time he avoided looking at Ashley.

Chad said, "I contacted a detective I worked with in Atlanta. She's one of the best at background checks. Was anyone aware Rick Coleman was an investment consultant and his wife an accountant?"

Mark said, "We're talking about the guy who owns the bait shop ... right?"

"Yep. One and the same. My Atlanta contact learned Coleman was fired because of issues with some of his accounts, though the company's version is he resigned. Whatever happened, they covered it up. She discovered they own more than one bait shop in Texas."

He handed out the list of locations he'd received. "She also found out Coleman has several bank accounts, including one overseas. Vicky believes the couple fits the profile for money laundering."

As she listened to Chad, a memory sparked in her mind, all those investment sites she'd seen on Coleman's computer. Could they be tied back to a money-laundering scheme? She wanted to say something, but then she'd have to admit she'd broken into the bait shop. It would be better to wait until she was alone with Chad. When she tuned back into the conversation, Jim was talking about drugs.

He said, "I heard some rumblings awhile back, but so far, we've not been able to come up with anything."

"I heard the same rumor from Henry," Ashley added.

Mark said, "I don't understand how this connects to Mandy's abduction."

"I think it does." Chad pulled out another set of papers and passed them out. "We've suspected this was not a random grab from the beginning. This is a list of eleven other abductions, all girls, in the last several months who fit the profile of Mandy's kidnapping."

Dale whistled as he read the list. "Where'd you come up with this? I searched the FBI sites for abductions and didn't find any matches."

"Ashley found them."

Jim shot a look of approval her way. "Good work. We need to get the police reports."

"Do you have someone you can assign to the task?" Chad asked. "Dale has bags of trash from Neville's truck to sort through as well as fingerprints to run down. Mark and Boomer are going to help, but my officers are getting spread a bit thin."

"I'll do one better. I'll assign Ken to work with you." He pulled his phone and tapped in a text. "He's on his way."

"We've got another link—Lew Walker," Chad said.

Jim looked up from the list of abductions. "I thought you cleared him."

"We did. Walker claimed he didn't have transportation, and we couldn't prove otherwise. Now, I think he's got a car stashed somewhere. Walker was in a thrift shop a couple of weeks back, looking for dolls."

Mark laid his list on the table. "That's scary. A sex offender is looking for dolls, and twelve little girls have been kidnapped. It can't be a coincidence."

Chad nodded in agreement. "Dale found a video clip of Neville's truck at the convenience store a few blocks from the Norton residence on the morning of the kidnapping. Neville wasn't driving it. His alibi for that morning is solid. He was at the cafe. Who was driving his truck then? I believe it was Walker."

A knock on the door sounded.

"Come in," Chad said.

The door opened, and Ken stepped inside.

"Have a seat." Chad brought him up to speed before picking up where he'd left off. "I'm certain Neville's truck was used to kidnap Mandy. Since we know it wasn't Neville driving, I suspect it was our shooter, and he may also be the arsonist, which brings us back to Walker."

Jim said, "It makes sense. When Todd ran Neville and Walker's background, he found they were in the state prison at the same time. I wonder if they were buddies?"

"Another lead we need to run down," Chad said.

Jim volunteered to contact the warden.

As Ashley listened to the discussion, she doodled. She drew a box and wrote children in the center. Another box was labeled Coleman. The oddity of an investment consultant owning bait shops prompted a third box titled stores. Then she drew lines to link all three. Her pen lightly tapped the paper as she pondered the connections. Picking up the list of baits shops, her eyes skimmed the locations. She started to lay it down when a similarity struck her. *Was it possible?* Setting the list of abduction locations alongside the list of baits shops, her eyes darted between the two lists. All the abductions occurred in the vicinity of a bait shop.

"I'll be damned!" The discussion stopped as everyone looked at her. "What if Coleman is into something other than selling drugs … like child trafficking?"

When her comment was met with silence, a spark of irritation trickled through her. Maybe she wasn't a cop, but she wasn't off track here. The more she thought about it, the more believable it became. From her experience as a reporter, she knew human trafficking was a high-dollar business, especially when children were for sale.

She picked up a list and waved it in front of her. "Take a look at the location for each bait shop, then compare them to where the kids were kidnapped."

Everyone grabbed their copies and began to examine the two documents.

"My god, you're on to something!" Chad exclaimed. "There's a pattern, which is what we've been looking for."

"How do we prove it?" Ashley asked.

With a grim look, he said, "For starters, pick up Walker. Before we break up this meeting, does anyone have a comment or suggestion?"

When no one said anything, Chad said, "Ken, come with me. Mark and Boomer are going to help Dale process the contents of Neville's truck. Jim, let me know what you find out from the warden at the prison. Somewhere there must be a connection to Coleman, one we can use for a search warrant."

Jim said, "I'll assign another deputy to run down the police reports. It will free up Ken for whatever you need."

As the officers walked out, Chad turned to Ashley. "What are your plans?"

"I want to go with you."

"Not this time. I don't know what problems we might have with Walker, and I don't want you caught in the middle."

She gave him a hard stare.

He threw up his hands. "I know you can handle yourself, but it's not the issue. I have to worry about the impact on getting the case to court. A civilian can be a complication."

Though she didn't like his answer, she understood. Shrugging her shoulders, she said, "I guess I'll head back to the Tribune. I'm putting out a special edition."

Relieved she was going to stay put, he said, "I'll get in touch with you later." He picked up the box he'd set on a table near the door and handed it to her. "Your gun."

"I'd say thank you, but you know darn well all your guff last night could be filed under the heading of police harassment." Satisfied she'd gotten the last word, she strolled out the door.

As she walked to her car, her mind raced over the results of the meeting. Had they just got the break they needed? Fear raged against hope. They had to find Mandy before she disappeared into the dark underbelly of the trafficking network. She refused to consider the possibility they might already be too late.

Damn, she wanted to be part of the Walker interview. She tossed her tote bag on the passenger seat and set the box alongside. She started to put the gun inside the console, then changed her mind, and put it in her bag.

Distracted by her thoughts, she failed to notice the vehicle that pulled away from the curb and followed her.

Chapter Twenty-three

*T*he morning crept by, and her repeated glances at the clock only seemed to slow it down. Ashley dealt with a few salesmen who had called and left a message. Henry sent her the special edition for approval. After adding her editorial with another plea for help, she sent it to the printing company, then to Henry to post on the website.

Now what? Nails tapped the desk as she stared at her phone, lying on the desk. Why hadn't she heard from Chad? She itched to pick it up and call. Not knowing was driving her nuts.

When it rang, her hand darted to grab it. At the sight of the number on the screen, she groaned.

Her sister was in a panic. "Are you all right? Where are you? Why didn't you call? I heard you could have been killed. You should have called, why didn't you?"

"Kathy, slow down. I'm okay. Right now, I'm sitting at my desk at the Tribune." How could she have forgotten about how fast news traveled in this town?

"My god, a man was shot. What were you doing in the parking lot?"

"I'm in the middle of something. In the morning, I'll pick up a bag of muffins and come by for breakfast. I'll explain everything?"

"You're sure you are all right?"

"Yes, absolutely. I'll see you in the morning."

The reports from the meeting stacked on the corner of her desk caught her eye when she laid the phone on the desk. That was something she could do, go back over them. The list of abductions was a good place to begin. Once they were sorted by date, she started with the earliest case and browsed the internet for news articles.

Once she finished with the last one, she leaned back in her chair. Amazed by her results, she stared at the notes she'd made beside each name. The missing children all lived in remote areas. For several, an Amber alert hadn't even been broadcast. She'd only found two blurbs in a TV news report.

My god, no wonder no one had linked up the similarity in the cases. The abductions were under the radar of any attention from law enforcement and the news media. She was surprised they'd even been entered in the national database for missing children.

What a perfect setup for a ring of kidnappers. Ashley could feel the pieces coming together in her mind. Were the buyers looking for a certain type of child? Was that the reason Mandy's picture was on Coleman's computer?

Henry stepped to the door. "Got a wreck outside of town. I'm headed there."

She nodded. If her suppositions were right, Coleman made a huge mistake when he grabbed Mandy. He didn't plan on a savvy police chief or a nosy editor.

The sound of the fire truck racing to the accident echoed in the background. It sparked an idea. She hadn't checked out the fire. Henry had been there and taken a couple of pictures for the article. What about the other residents? She could interview them. Get their take on what happened.

As she passed Henry's desk, she stopped to leave a note before heading out the door.

Chad pointed to the apartment complex up ahead. "Walker lives there."

As Ken pulled into the parking lot, Chad motioned toward the corner of the building. "You circle around back. He might try to run."

Before approaching the front door, Chad waited to let Ken get into place. When his finger punched the doorbell, there wasn't a response. He rang again. He couldn't hear any sounds from inside the apartment. His fist pounded the door. "Police! Walker, open the door."

A man emerged from the office located across the parking lot, then jogged toward Chad, shouting to get his attention. Out of breath, he gulped as he stopped. "I'm the manager. Saw your car pull up and figured you were looking for Walker. He's gone."

"When?"

"I found the door ajar this morning. When I checked the place, Walker had cleared out."

"I'd like to look inside."

The manager pulled out a set of keys and selected one. Opening the door, he stood aside to let Chad enter.

Ken walked up and followed Chad inside. "I saw the manager running across the lot. Figured Walker had hightailed it out of here."

Chad turned to the manager. "When was the last time you saw him?"

The man thought, then said, "Yesterday. He was hauling out a bag of trash."

"Did he say anything about leaving?"

"No. It came as a complete surprise since his rent had been paid for the next month." His gaze skimmed the living room and the stains on the furniture and carpet. "What a mess. It's going to take a while to clean this place up."

"I'll check the bedroom," Ken said.

"How long has he lived here?" Chad asked as he entered the kitchen. Dirty dishes filled the sink. Crusts of dried food coated the countertop, not much different from his earlier visit.

"Hmm ... close to a year."

It coincided with when he got out of jail, he thought. When he opened a cabinet door, a roach scuttled into the corner. He peered inside the other cabinets. Nothing but a few dishes and canned goods. More roaches scurried out of sight as he looked in the drawers. "Did you ever notice any visitors?"

"There was one guy. He drove a black truck and kept parking in the handicap spaces. I finally stopped him one day and told him to park somewhere else."

Chad pulled his phone and brought up the picture of Neville. "Is this the guy?"

"Yeah, he's the one."

Ken walked in. "Nothing in the bedroom. Clothes are gone."

Chad nodded and walked back into the living room. A thoughtful look on his face, his eyes flicked around the room. "Why would he take out a bag of trash? He left this place looking like a dump."

Ken picked up on his train of thought. "Maybe it was something he didn't want anyone to see."

Chad asked, "Where'd he go with the bag?"

"Uh, to the dumpster at the end of the complex," the manager answered.

"Has the trash been picked up?"

"No. Not until tomorrow."

Chad glanced at Ken. "Looks like dumpster diving is in our future."

With one last look at the apartment, Chad followed Ken and the manager outside. After pointing out the dumpster, he headed to his office.

"Got any gloves in your car?"

Ken groaned. "Do you have any idea how I hate digging in the trash?"

"Not near as bad as I do."

Ken popped the trunk and opened a container. He pulled out a set of gloves, handed them to Chad, then grabbed a second pair.

Chad headed toward the large bin near the edge of the lot. He pulled on the gloves and crawled up the side. With his feet braced on the metal rail, he looked inside.

Ken parked nearby, and as he exited asked, "How bad?"

"Thank god, this place doesn't have many apartments. It's not full. Of course, I've got no idea which bag belongs to Walker. I'll toss them down."

He reached in and grabbed the first one. When it landed, Ken pulled it to the side. After a few seconds of struggling to untie the knot, he muttered, "To hell with this," and pulled out his pocketknife. Empty cans, beer bottles, and moldy banana peels spilled out.

Chad looked down. "You do realize we'll have to pick up anything that gets dumped on the ground?"

Footsteps crunched on the gravel. The manager said, "Maybe this will help," and dropped a box of trash bags on the ground. Ken stuffed the open bag inside a new one, along with the strewn garbage. Before opening a second bag, he spread out a couple of the empty bags, then set a full bag in the middle. Inside, he found an envelope. "Not the right one. This is addressed to another tenant."

The manager, who had been watching the activity with an avid gleam of curiosity, asked, "What are you looking for?"

After tossing several bags over the side, Chad climbed down. "This is one of those searches where I'll know it when I see it." He opened a bag. A nauseating odor drifted upward. After glancing inside, he quickly closed it up. "I don't think Walker would be buying diapers."

"Apartment 101. She's the only tenant with a baby," the manager said.

Ken grinned at the disgusted look on Chad's face. "I would have expected that once a person reaches the exalted position of police chief, digging through trash would be beneath them."

"Now, you know. Being a police chief isn't all glamour and fun games. Oh, hell! This one's worse. More diapers."

Ken knelt beside another bag and cut it open. Pulling out newspapers, he said, "Hey, this is it."

Chad quickly stepped to his side. Ken handed him an envelope. It was addressed to Lew Walker.

"Hmm … no return address, which is unusual. Postmarked Waco."

"This isn't really trash. It's all newspapers."

The manager said, "Walker liked to read the pennysavers. One day, I saw him walking back from the store. He had one rolled up and stuck under his arm. He said he liked to see what was for sale. It seemed like an odd remark from someone who didn't even have a car."

"Let's get this bag back to the PD," Chad said.

"Uh-huh," Ken muttered, as he pawed through the contents inside the bag. "There are a few receipts scattered in here." He pulled out a handful and shuffled through them. "Son-of-a-bitch." He handed one to Chad. It was from Amy's thrift shop for the purchase of five dolls.

A look of determination crossed Chad's face. "We're checking every bag to make sure he didn't toss more than one."

Ashley parked in the driveway. No point in pulling into the garage, since she'd only be there long enough to change out of the suit and heels. Tromping around a fire site was dirty work.

Inside, she dropped her tote bag on the bed and shrugged out of the jacket. After hanging it in the closet, she walked to her dresser while her fingers undid the clasp on her necklace. When her hand reached to open the jewelry box, she stopped. The case was always centered on the dresser. Now it was pushed to one side. Not much, but enough to be noticeable.

Had she accidentally moved it when she got the necklace out? Ashley glanced around the room, nothing else seemed out of place. Uneasy, she reached inside the bag, pulling out her gun. This might be paranoia, but she wasn't taking any chances. Walking through the house, she checked every place where someone could hide. The windows and doors were all locked. Inside her office, she glanced at the papers on her desk. Nothing appeared to have been moved. The extra set of notes on the abductions were still where she left them.

Relieved, she laughed. Just what she didn't need, a bit of hysteria. She must have moved the box and didn't remember doing it. It wasn't surprising, considering the stress of the last few days.

She changed into a long-sleeved shirt, pants, and boots, then grabbed a jacket. As she closed the door, she jiggled the knob to be sure it was locked.

Slouched behind the wheel, he watched the house When Walker's phone rang, it was his boss on the other end wanting to know where he was.

"Logan's house."

"Did you find anything?" Coleman asked.

"Our new editor's been busy. She's found some of our previous orders, eleven of them."

There was a short silence, then Coleman asked, "Do you think she's told anyone?"

"I don't know. She was at the PD this morning and came out carrying a box. I heard she found Neville's body."

"Is it possible she saw you?"

"No, or I'd be sitting in jail. I'm not taking any chances. I've already cleared out of my apartment."

"Pick her up."

"I think a bullet would be a lot easier. I can do it when she leaves."

"I don't pay you to think. A shooting gives the cops something to chew on. A disappearance doesn't. Without a body, they can't prove anything. Just follow the damn orders." The line went dead.

Chapter Twenty-four

When Chad walked into the office, followed by Ken, Lydia crinkled her nose in disgust. "What is that disgusting odor?"

"Something I picked up from dumpster diving," Chad said.

"What?" In all the years she'd worked for the PD, this was something new.

"We've been searching through trash bags in a dumpster."

"Good lord! Why?"

"To find out if our suspect tossed out any evidence."

"Oh … I see." From her tone, it was doubtful she did.

When Chad turned toward Dale's office, Lydia stopped him.

"They're not here. Everyone went over to the maintenance garage. Dale said he needed a large floor to spread the stuff out."

"Okay, we're headed there. We've got two more bags of trash to add to the mix."

When he and Ken turned to leave, she said, "You *really* should get cleaned up before you go out in public."

Chad flashed a grin over his shoulder. "That's on my agenda. I just don't know when."

Ken parked behind Dale's squad car. "I'll grab the bags and meet you inside. I may never get the stink out of my car."

As Chad exited, he said, "Occupational hazard, my friend."

"I seriously considered sticking you in the trunk, except there wasn't room," Ken quipped.

Chad strolled through the open garage door. In one corner of the large room, Dale, Mark, and Boomer stood around several trash bags spread across the concrete floor.

Dale looked up when he heard footsteps. "Jeez, what's that god-awful smell?" His eyes raked the stains on Chad's uniform.

"Today, I learned a valuable lesson. When you smell bad, after a while, you get used to it. It may bother other people, but it doesn't bother you." Chad's gaze skimmed the mess of bottles and cans, food containers, sacks, and other trash strewn across the bags.

Behind him, Ken dropped the bags on the floor.

Mark groaned. "I guess we just thought we were done. What did you find?"

"Walker's cleared out. The last time the manager saw him was yesterday. He was hauling a bag of trash out of his apartment. We found it and a second one in the dumpster," Chad said.

"What made you go looking for it?" Dale asked.

"Remember the dump he lived in? There's enough trash left in there to fill multiple bags. Why did he haul out any at all? What was so important he took the time to get rid of it? His mistake was using the dumpster at the apartment complex."

Mark asked, "Just curious, but how'd you acquire the stench?"

"We had to open every bag to make sure we didn't miss one. When I tried to toss one back in the dumpster, it hit the metal edge and split. I got hit by flying diapers."

The men groaned. Mark said, "Okay, entirely too much information."

Ken chuckled. "If you ever play baseball and want to win, make sure your boss is on the other team." A roar of laughter erupted from the other officers.

Ignoring them, Chad motioned toward the mess on the floor. "Find anything?"

With a grim glance at the trash, Dale answered, "Not one damn thing. We didn't miss anything, including scraps of paper. It was Rufus that saved the day. He hit on the truck, so we know Mandy was inside."

"Figured he would. It proves the truck was used in the kidnapping. Now we've got to prove who was driving it, and my money's on Walker. Are you done?" Chad asked.

"Yep. We'll get this picked up and start on your bags," Dale said.

As Mark and Boomer started to fold the bags laid out on the floor around the trash, Chad said, "Wait a minute."

He dropped to one knee and reached for a stained newspaper. He looked up at Ken. "This guy was into the pennysavers too. One of you got a pen and paper?"

"I do," Boomer declared, and whipped out the notepad in his pocket. Flipping it open, he clicked a pen, which had been tucked next to the pad. The tip hovered over the page. "Ready."

Chad bit back a grin. "Write down the date for this one. There's a couple more here."

After all the newspapers had been sorted from the rest of the trash and placed in evidence bags, Chad held out his hand for the list of dates.

"Chief, there are nine." Boomer tore off the page.

Chad glanced at the stains on his shirt and pants. He wasn't sure he had a clean pocket on him. "On second thought, you hang onto it. Drop it on my desk when you get back to the office."

Once the garbage from Neville's truck was bagged, Ken picked up a bag they retrieved from the dumpster. He upended it onto the new bags Dale had spread over the floor. "Walker collected the pennysavers. Another oddity is there's no other trash mixed in with them. It's like he had a stack, picked them up, and dumped them in the bag."

Chad picked up the other bag. "Ken found something else. A receipt for five dolls Walker bought in a thrift shop near Waco."

Mark had begun to sort the papers. "My money is on the theory that we're dealing with more than one kidnapping."

Dumping the newspapers out of the other bag, Chad grunted, then said, "I'd say twelve at least. I want to sort these by dates."

Mark stared at the piles on the floor. "Why did he take the time to throw all these newspapers in the trash?"

Chad said, "I don't know, but we need to find out. Let's get them sorted."

Ashley pulled into the mobile home park. Ahead were the remains of Neville's place. All that was left was the metal framework, and a large pile of rubble and ashes in the middle of a mud pond. The tires of the fire trucks had left deep gouges in the ground. She pulled to the side to avoid getting stuck in the mud.

Exiting the car, she glanced at the other mobile homes. It didn't appear anyone was home, but she'd pound on the doors anyway. She snapped several shots with the camera she always carried, then tossed it back into the car before walking to the first residence. It wasn't until she reached the last one did someone answer the door. A frail, elderly woman peeked around the edge.

"Ma'am, I'm the editor of the Tribune. May I have a few minutes of your time to ask a few questions about the fire?"

The woman's eyes blinked behind the thick lenses of her glasses. "I, uh, guess so. My son's still at work if you wanted to talk to him." She opened the door.

"No. I bet you can answer my questions." Ashley stepped inside and held out her hand. "Ashley Logan and you are …?"

"Hattie Griffin. Please have a seat. Can I get you a cup of tea or a cold drink?"

"No, thank you. I'm fine." She perched on the edge of the couch. Her gaze wandered around the tidy living room and settled on a display of snow globes on a wall-mounted shelf. "What a beautiful collection of globes." She hoped the comment would ease the woman's wary look.

Hattie settled into a rocking chair. "I've been collecting them for several years. I have more packed away. Since I sold my house and moved here, I'm a bit limited on space. But I do rotate them every few months."

"How long have you lived here?"

"It's been about a year now. When my husband died, Vance, he's my son, didn't want me living alone. I heard someone new was at the newspaper. I always enjoy reading Henry's column. I hope you don't plan on replacing him?"

Ashley smiled at the thought. Even if she wanted to, which she didn't, it would take a force of nature to get Henry away from the paper. "No. I'd be lost without his help."

"That's so good to hear. Now, what can I answer for you?"

"I'm following up on the fire." Ashley reached inside her tote bag and pulled out her notebook with the pen clipped to one side.

"It was a frightening sight. When I saw the flames from my bedroom window, I was afraid it would spread."

"The fire department did a good job of containing the blaze. It doesn't appear any of the other homes were affected. Did you know the man who lived there?"

Hattie shuddered. "No, and I didn't want to. If there's one thing I learned in my seventy-two years, it's how to recognize riffraff. I told

Vance the man was up to no good."

She took a deep breath, and before Ashley could say anything, continued, "I heard he'd been killed. Good riddance if you ask me, though I know it's not a Christian thought."

Ashley suppressed a grin. "I fully understand, Mrs. Griffin."

She leaned over and patted Ashley's knee. "My dear, it's Hattie."

"Did he ever have any visitors?"

She leaned back with a thoughtful look on her face. The chair gently rocked. "Neville wasn't a friendly sort. All the time I lived here, I only saw one man. Sometimes he'd show up during the day, but most of the time, it was at night. You see, when someone parked in front of Neville's home, the car lights flashed across my window. Since this is a remote area, everyone tries to watch out for their neighbors. Whenever a car drove in, I'd look out to see who it was."

"Did you know him?"

"No. But he was another one who was up to no good."

Ashley wished she had a picture of Walker. "Can you describe him?"

"Hmm … a heavy build. I'd say well-over two hundred pounds. Short, though, maybe five-nine or ten. Real seedy, like he always needed a bath."

"What about his hair color or any facial hair?"

"He always had on a ballcap. What stuck out over his ears and down his neck was more white than dark. No beard, but he was never what I'd call clean-shaven. A rough-looking man."

Hattie's description matched the picture she'd seen of Walker. "What about a vehicle?"

"An old white clunker, four-door, with lots of dings and scratches. Someone should have written on it—wash me. I think it was a Ford."

Ashley jotted notes as Hattie talked. "Anything else you remember about the man?"

The chair rocked. She thought for a moment before saying, "No."

Ashley started to drop the notebook back into the bag.

"Although, I often wondered why he took Neville's truck. It seemed like an odd arrangement, but I just figured he needed a truck to haul something."

Her hand froze as she looked at Hattie. The woman's eyes sparkled with a gleam of suppressed excitement.

"He took Neville's truck?"

"Yes, several times. I'd see Neville driving his car, then a few days later, the truck was back, and the car was gone. Though there were a few times, they left together in the truck."

"Can you remember any dates when this happened?"

The gleam intensified. "Well, it so happens, *I* can do better than remember."

Hattie stood and walked to a small desk in the corner of the room. She picked up a large notepad. Smiling, she sat back down in the rocker. "I kept notes."

Ashley exclaimed, "You did!" The thought which flashed in her mind was the other abductions. Would the dates coincide?

"My dear, don't look so surprised. I am a retired schoolteacher. Over the years, I found it very helpful to keep track of my student's activities." She opened the book, which was a calendar and journal.

"Let's see, the first one was some time ago." She flipped the pages. "Yes, here it is," and read off a date. "They went together on this trip."

Ashley turned to a clean page and started writing as Hattie read off more dates. Her fingers trembled from the excitement which rushed through her. She'd have to check her research notes, but she was certain many of the abduction dates coincided with Neville and Walker's trips. There was one troubling detail, more trips than abductions. Did it mean there were other cases she hadn't found?

"And," Hattie paused until Ashley looked up from the notepad, "I have a license plate number."

Oh, my god. She had hit the mother lode. "What is it?" She scribbled down the number.

"Since I've answered your questions, I have one of my own. Why do you want to know all of this?"

"Hattie, I can't explain right now. But I promise I'll be back to answer all your questions."

"I think I may know one reason. You're the aunt of the little girl who is missing."

"Now, how did you know?"

Her lips twitched. "It's a small town. I do hope this helps you find your niece. You know, I wouldn't be surprised to find out both men are involved. Had I seen them loitering around a school, I'd have called the cops."

"Hattie, you have very sound instincts. Thank you. If you think of anything else, please call Chief Bishop at the PD. I'll be passing your information to him."

As they stood, Ashley reached for the woman and wrapped her arms around her. For several seconds, the two women clung to each other.

As she stepped back, she said, "I'd better get going."

Walking down the steps, she looked over her shoulder at Hattie, who stood in the doorway. "Thank you again."

Hattie smiled and nodded.

Seated behind the wheel, she couldn't wait. She pulled out the notebook and flipped to the page where she'd written the dates. Then she grabbed the list of abductions from the folder in her tote bag. She was right. The dates matched up. She folded the paper and stuck it inside the notebook, then fastened the clip.

Eager to let Chad know, she picked up her phone. While she

waited for him to answer, she tossed the notebook on the seat but didn't notice it slid off. The call rolled to voice mail. She left a message she had a new lead and was on her way to the PD.

She had forgotten about the mud until she backed. Her rear tires spun when she tried to drive forward. *Damn, of all days to get stuck.* She stopped, then started a rocking motion between reverse and low gear. When she felt the car gain traction, she sighed with relief and drove out of the park.

About a mile down the road, she could feel a vibration building in the steering wheel, making it hard to keep the car from pulling to one side. She slowed and stopped on the shoulder. Exiting, she didn't see a problem until she walked around the front of the car. The right-front tire was flat.

Disgusted, she stared at it. She must have picked up a nail or piece of metal in the damn park, maybe when she got stuck in the mud. She looked around. There was no one in sight nor any houses to get help. It was either call a tow truck or change the dang thing herself.

Opening the trunk, she eyed the toolkit and her emergency stash of equipment. She'd have to move everything to get to the jack mounted under the carpet. As she shoved the metal box to one side, she heard a vehicle stop, and a voice called out. "Can I help you?"

She straightened and started to turn. Out of the corner of her eye, the sight of a dirty white car sparked a sense of danger. Before she could react, something struck her in the head. Her knees buckled, and she sunk into a sea of darkness.

Chapter Twenty-five

~~~

t took longer than Chad expected to sort through the newspapers and examine the receipts. Most were from the grocery store or a convenience store near the apartment complex where Walker lived.

The one solid piece of evidence was the receipt for the dolls. Once the newspapers had been stacked in order of publication, Boomer set them in the boxes Dale had scrounged up.

Chad stood and stretched. He glanced at his watch. "Let's get these back to the PD. I want to start looking through them."

Ken, who also stretched to work the kinks out of his legs, asked, "Any idea what we're looking for?"

"Don't have a clue, but it's another—I hope when I see it, I'll recognize it."

Dale said, "If anyone is interested in pizza, I'll stop and pick up a couple."

When everyone nodded in agreement, he grinned, then stared at Chad. "Eating will be a lot more pleasant if you don't smell like baby poop."

Laughing, Chad said, "Mark, you and Boomer get these boxes back to the station. I'll get cleaned up and meet you there."

Walking out the door, Ken said, "Instead of taking you to get your car, I'll drop you at your house. I live just a few blocks away. After I get a quick shower, I'll pick you up."

Seated in the car, Chad pulled his phone and saw he'd missed a call from Ashley. He listened to the voice mail, then tried to call back. She didn't answer. Instead of a message, he sent a text—pizza at the pd.

"I got a call from Ashley. She sounded excited and said she had a new lead. I'm almost afraid to find out what she's done now. The woman doesn't know when to back off."

Ken glanced at him. "You don't have to answer this, but I suspect Ashley is the source of the pictures from Coleman's computer. What'd she do, break into the place?"

"Yes, and I probably lost ten years of my life span. It was the night we tailed him. I caught her sneaking out the back door of Coleman's store. I thought I'd have a stroke on the spot."

A roar of laughter erupted from Ken. When he finally stopped laughing, he said, "I'd like to have had a picture of your face. The woman has guts, no two ways about it. The picture may be the break we needed."

"Don't remind me. I know it, but for god's sake, don't tell Ashley. All it will do is encourage her."

Ken stopped in front of Chad's house, saying he'd be back in about fifteen minutes. Inside, Chad checked his phone, still no message from Ashley. Her phone was probably in her bag again.

He stripped, stuffed the clothes in the washer, and set it to pre-soak, hoping it might help get rid of the foul odor. After a quick shower, he dressed in jeans, a flannel shirt, and boots. He hooked his holster to his belt and grabbed a canvas jacket from the closet. He was waiting on the sidewalk when Ken pulled to the curb.

At the PD, Lydia was straightening the folders on her desk.

"You're late leaving," Chad said.

"Mark said you were on your way back. I put two letters on your desk for you to sign. Anything new?" she asked as she fiddled with the strap on her purse.

Chad suspected the letters were an excuse. "We're making some progress. That's about all I can say."

"See you in …." The phone rang. "I'll get it." She listened, then handed the phone to Chad. "It's a Vance Griffin. He says it's an emergency."

"Chief Bishop, how may I help you?"

"Chief, this is Vance Griffin. I live in the mobile home park where the man who was shot lived. On my way home, I spotted a car parked on the side of the road. When I mentioned it to my mother, she said Ashley Logan came by to talk to her. She was driving a car which matched the one I saw. Mother felt I should let you know."

A chill crawled down Chad's back. "Was it wrecked? Did you see anyone?"

"No, but then I didn't stop. I didn't see a driver."

"Where was this again?" He motioned to Lydia for a paper and pen. "What is your phone number?"

He bent over and jotted it down. "I'm on my way to check it out."

Vance asked, "Do you want me to meet you there?"

"No. If I need anything, I'll stop at your house." He hung up the receiver.

Ken, who had been listening, asked, "What happened?"

"Ashley may be missing. Her car is on the road leading to the mobile home park." He looked at Lydia. "Tell the others to follow me. Have Dale bring his crime scene equipment."

Panic added speed as he ran to his car.

After turning onto the county road leading to the mobile home park, he slowed. The fog had started to build. A light haze already hovered over the ground. That's all he needed, the damn fog. When his lights picked up a parked vehicle on the shoulder, his worst fear became a reality. It was Ashley's car.

Chad stopped in the middle of the road. Before hopping out, he grabbed the large flashlight mounted under the dash. Running to the driver's side, he opened the door. Empty. He flashed the light across the seat, looking for blood.

Another car pulled to the shoulder. Ken strode across the road. "Is it Ashley's?"

"Yes. I don't see any blood inside." He walked around the car to look for damage. "The tire's flat."

Ken shined his light on the tire, then moved the beam around the trees and brush that bordered the road as he walked to the back of the car. "So, where is she?"

"Her bag's not here." Chad opened the passenger door and shone the light inside. "Maybe she tried to walk to town."

His tone harsh, Ken said, "I don't think so. There are scuff marks back here."

Chad stepped to the back of the car and looked at the deep scrapes in the shoulder. As his gaze followed the beam of the flashlight along the side of the road to where the marks ended, he felt as if he'd been kicked in the gut.

Ken said, "Looks like something or someone was dragged."

Two cars pulled up. Dale hopped out of one, and Mark and Boomer from the other.

Chad pulled out his phone and punched the speed dial. The call rolled to Ashley's voice mail. Stuffing the phone back into his pocket, he said, "Ken, call Jim. I want to get River and her dog out here. Maybe Rufus can pick up the scent. I noticed a jacket in the backseat. Dale, check for prints. Mark, get on the horn and get a tow truck out here."

Mark had walked around to the passenger side and shined his

light inside. "The keys are gone. What's this?" He opened the door and reached down to pick up a notebook on the floor.

He walked over and handed it to Chad.

"It's Ashley's notepad. She usually carries it in her tote bag." When he snapped open the clasp, a paper fluttered to the ground. Chad bent over and picked it up. "It's a list of the abductions." He flipped the pages to the last entry. "There are more dates listed here and a license plate number. Boomer run this. Find out who it's registered to."

"Any idea what she was doing out here?" Dale asked.

"The guy who called lives in the mobile home park. He said Ashley had talked to his mother today. I'm going over there and find out what's going on."

Dale nodded.

As Chad trotted to his car, Boomer hollered at him. "Chief, the car is registered to Lew Walker."

His heart tripped. Every instinct screamed that Walker had grabbed her. "Ken, get an APB out for the vehicle." His face a bleak mask, he slid behind the wheel.

Chad goosed the gas, and a few minutes later slid to a stop in front of Griffin's home. He ran onto the porch, praying he'd find the answers to what happened to Ashley from the woman inside. A middle-aged man wearing wire rim glasses opened the door and greeted him.

"Mr. Griffin, I'm Chief Chad Bishop. I need to talk to your mother."

"Please come in. She's been so concerned since I mentioned seeing the car."

Inside, an elderly woman was seated in a rocking chair. She motioned toward the couch. "Chief, I'm Hattie Griffin. Please have a seat. Is the car Ashley's?"

"Yes, ma'am, it is."

"Do you know where she is?"

"No, we haven't located her yet. I need to know why she was here."

"Oh, dear," Hattie cried, her voice filled with distress. "It was that awful man. I just know it."

"Now, Mother, please don't get excited. You know it's not good for you," her son said.

"Mrs. Griffin, what man?"

"The man who visited Neville. I told Ashley all about it. She even wrote down the dates I'd kept."

Confused, Chad said, "I'm not sure I'm following you. Please start at the beginning."

"I'm sorry. I've been so upset since Vance got home." She stopped, took a deep breath, and began to explain the conversation she'd had with Ashley. At one point, she paused and asked her son to get the calendar from the desk. She handed it to Chad, saying, "The dates are all listed there."

"May I keep this?" he asked.

"Oh, my yes, if you think it will help."

Chad pulled his phone. Punching the keys, he brought up the photo of Walker. Turning the screen toward Mrs. Griffin, he asked, "Is this the man you saw?"

The woman leaned forward and stared at the picture. "Yes, yes! That's him! Did he do something to that lovely young woman?"

"All I know is Ashley's car is on the side of the road with a flat tire. We haven't located her. Hopefully, she hitched a ride into town with someone."

His comment was met with a look of disbelief.

He handed her a business card. "My cellphone number is on the back. If you think of anything else, please call. I don't care what time of day or night."

Vance followed him outside. "I hope you find her. If you don't mind, please let us know. Mother's been so upset. She was quite taken with the woman."

"I will."

Trotting down the steps, the sight of the thickening fog added to his fears. The damn stuff would hamper the search.

When he got back to Ashley's vehicle, more squad cars had arrived. Jim stood on the side of the road, talking to River. Rufus tugged on the leash, and Jim kept moving back to avoid the dog's lunges. Any other time, it would have brought a quick laugh.

As he exited, he asked, "What have you found?"

Ken was the closest, and said, "Her flat tire wasn't an accident. Someone unscrewed the valve stem, letting the air slowly leak out."

Everyone gathered around Chad as he briefly explained what he'd learned from Hattie Griffin.

River said, "Let's get the jacket from the car and see what Rufus can find."

Dale was wearing gloves. He leaned inside the car and grabbed the coat.

"Hold it in front of his nose. Let him get a good whiff," she said. After a few seconds, she said, "Find, Rufus, find."

The dog headed to the back of the car and sniffed the ground. His nose down, he trotted along the edge of the shoulder. Rufus stopped about fifty feet behind Ashley's car and looked at River before throwing back his head and howling.

"Bad news. The track ends there," River said.

Whatever hope Chad had—died. Walker had kidnapped her.

Chapter Twenty-six

Once the tow truck left, everyone headed to the PD. As Chad drove, his thoughts circled in desperation. None of it made any sense. Why would someone kidnap Ashley? And, he had to tell the Norton's.

When he walked into the station, Lydia stared at him. Fear darkened her eyes at the sight of his grim face.

"Oh, no," she cried. "It was Ashley's car."

"Yes. She's disappeared."

"Why? Why is this happening? Mandy, and now Ashley."

In a harsh tone she'd never heard, he said, "I don't know, but I'll do whatever it takes to find them."

The door opened, and the rest of the officers walked in.

He turned and said, "Let's meet in the conference room."

After everyone was seated, he said, "Jim, did you tell dispatch to contact me if they get any hits on the APB?"

"Yeah, I did. You mentioned a journal. What's the deal?"

"I think we can say with certainty we've stumbled on a kidnapping ring." He tossed the journal on the table. "That's Mrs. Griffin's calendar. She kept track of the dates when she saw Neville and Walker leave and when Walker used Neville's truck. There's no doubt they coincide with the dates of the abductions. What still doesn't make sense is why Walker would grab Ashley?"

Ken said, "There might be a reason. Neville called her. Is it possible whoever is behind this thinks she knows more than she does?"

"It's a possibility," Chad said. "We've got to locate Walker. Find him, and we find Ashley and probably Mandy."

Dale stood. "I'm going to contact the places where we pulled the tapes and check the security film for today."

Mark said, "I'll help you. Boomer, you in?"

"You bet!"

Jim said, "Ken and I'll check the bait shop and Coleman's house. It might be a good idea to keep an eye on both tonight. What do you plan to do?"

"Stay here. I want to examine the newspapers and make a few calls. Coleman is the key to this. I've also got to decide whether to tell the Norton's tonight or wait until morning."

Jim said, "For what it's worth, I'd wait. There's nothing they can do tonight except worry. Time enough for that tomorrow."

Chad nodded. "It's sound advice. I think you're right."

As the officers left, Lydia stepped in. "Is there anything I can do to help?"

"No, but thanks for staying. Go home and get some rest."

He glanced at his watch. Even though Atlanta was an hour ahead, there was still time to catch Vicky before she left. He headed to his office. When she answered, he said, "I was hoping you'd still be at your desk."

"Hey, Chad. You must have read my mind. I was planning on calling you. Any new developments on your end?"

He filled her in on the multiple abductions and the missing reporter.

"Have you pulled in the FBI yet?"

"No, I haven't had a chance. We've only started to piece the puzzle together. I didn't want to cry wolf without hard facts to back up what we've found. You know what the feds are like. Did you come up with anything?"

"The Colemans are moving money and using the bait shops to do it. I managed to get access to their tax records."

"How?"

"Don't ask."

"Gotcha. What'd you find?"

"They have a healthy financial portfolio. Who knew that bait shops could be so profitable? On the surface, it all looks on the up and up. The problem I found is the money transfers in and out of the country that doesn't add up. At least, not in my opinion. But I'm not a financial expert. It does make sense if you factor in cash from drugs or trafficking."

"Did you, by chance, find any property they owned other than bait shops?"

"No, but I'll do some more digging."

Chad disconnected and stared at the two journals. He couldn't keep his focus with the images of Ashley popping into his head. When an innocent victim was in harm's way, there'd always been a fear that came with the job. It didn't come close to the terror which crawled up his spine and clawed its way into his mind, numbing his thoughts. How could someone become so vital in his life in such a short period? He remembered telling Lydia he'd do whatever it took. He'd crossed the line once before, and if he had to do it again, he would.

Sitting here in a state of confusion wasn't going to accomplish anything. A phrase popped into his mind from an 'old head' detective in Atlanta. When Chad was a rookie, Arnie Williams took him under his wings and taught him what it meant to investigate.

When all else failed, work the problem and connect the dots was his go-to advice.

A shot of caffeine would help clear the cobwebs in his mind. As he wandered to the breakroom and back to his office, his mind raced over the myriad details they'd uncovered. Coleman had to own a safe house where he could stash the kids. But where? How much time did he have left to find it?

Seated in his chair, he took a sip of the hot brew, then picked up the Griffin journal and flipped to the pages she marked. She'd even entered a notation when the men returned. Thank god for nosy neighbors and a small town. He couldn't imagine this happening in a big city. People tended to ignore their neighbor's activities unless it caused a problem for them.

He compared the dates of travel to the abduction dates on Ashley's list. They lined up. No wonder she sounded excited in the message she'd left. Chad had no doubt Neville and Walker were the kidnappers. The only problem was there were more trips than abductions. He'd bet they'd find more than twelve kids had been kidnapped.

What piqued his interest was how soon they were back in town. All were within a day or two after the abduction. It meant they didn't have to travel any distance to dispose of their victims. Grab the kid, drive back to Meridian, and make the drop. The pattern cemented his belief the stash house was somewhere close.

Another point occurred to him; the call Neville made to Ashley. He wanted to know how long it would take to get the money. How could Neville collect if Mandy wasn't close? Since the money wasn't going to be paid until Mandy was found, the girl had to be nearby. Coleman had to own another piece of property.

The county tax records would have it listed. After accessing the county's website, he entered Rick Coleman. Only one location popped up, Coleman's home near the lake. Chad altered the search and entered the address for the bait shop. He found it was owned by RFC, Inc. He went back to the name search and entered RFC, which had only one property listed—the bait shop.

Damn. The property could be owned any number of ways, another company, or even under a relative's name. Frustrated, he leaned back and took another sip of coffee. His phone rang. It was Dale.

"Nothing on the tapes. If Walker bought gas today, it wasn't at any of our sites. The weather is getting worse. The fog has visibility down to a few feet."

Chad glanced over his shoulder. All he could see was a faint glow from the parking lot lights. Uneasiness added to the mix of emotions churning inside him. "Nothing more we can do tonight. Everyone go home and get some rest. Plan on being back here as soon as it starts getting light."

Since he didn't plan on leaving, what else could he do? His gaze lit on the boxes of newspapers they'd pulled from the dumpster. Why were both men so interested in the same papers? What was so important, out of all the trash in Walker's apartment, this is what he got rid of?

He slid one of the boxes next to his desk, picked up the first paper, and began to scan the ads. The weekly papers were free. The publisher made money from the people who advertised. Most of the ads were to sell something, household goods, farm equipment, property, and numerous other items. There were a few employment ads and some for services. If you wanted a plumber or someone to mow your yard or hayfield, or repair your tractor, there was an ad. Other companies advertised for stuff they wanted to buy, like coins and antiques.

Nothing caught his attention, and he laid it aside and picked up the next. Same thing. Two hours later, he was down to the last one, and still nothing. There had to be something he'd missed.

He went back to the first paper and started over. This time he had a general idea of the layout. Instead of looking at the products listed for sale, he keyed in on names and phone numbers.

Another hour passed as he slowly perused each page. A crick in his neck reminded him he'd been at it far too long. He stood, stretching to work the tension out of his shoulders. Should he call it a night? He didn't want to quit, but so far, he hadn't made any headway. Frustrated, he stared down at the newspaper spread open on his desk. Why were these damn papers so important?

An ad for antiques banded by black lines drew his eye. He hadn't paid much attention to the business ads, focusing instead on the ads by individuals. A small doll was cleverly entwined in an elaborate motif in the corner of the ad.

A sense of disquiet built. Chad eased into the chair as he studied the image. The business was Antiques & More and touted antiques for sale. One of the items listed was dolls. It seemed he'd seen this ad before but didn't remember seeing a doll. He picked up another newspaper, then flipped the pages until he found the ad; no doll in this one. Certain he was on to something, he tingled with a familiar sense of keenness.

Starting with the oldest newspaper, he recorded the date on a pad along with a yes or no for the doll. After rechecking each paper, he had a list of the dates the doll had been printed in the ad. Then he grabbed the list of abductions. Every time a child had been kidnapped, the ad in the next edition of the pennysaver included the doll. And, once again, there were more dolls than abduction dates. It confirmed his earlier suspicion more kids had been kidnapped.

While he was excited over the discovery, it was the doll that had his attention. They'd been part of this from the start. He'd dismissed the connection because he didn't want to remember all the doubts and fears he lived with, or how he'd questioned his sanity.

A whisper, soft and indistinct, drifted around him. His head shot up as his gaze swept the room. A deep, inexplicable uneasiness formed, a sensation someone watched. He swiveled his chair to look at the window. Tension ripped through his muscles.

In the dense, black mist, the lights in the parking lot were invisible. Tentacles of fog, tinged with an eerie green, climbed and swirled against the glass as if they were a living entity. Mesmerized by their movement, he couldn't look away. The memories rose. They pulled at him, compelling him to remember.

Words he'd heard on that strange night exploded in his thoughts. "The past is written. It cannot be altered. It is the future you seek. To find the lost, a gift is given. But … beware! To hear, you must listen."

His mind slipped back in time to another missing child.

Chapter Twenty-seven

One year ago

Assigned to the Atlanta PD Youth Division, Chad had caught the latest missing person call. A five-year-old girl, Susan Eberly, had been abducted from a playground in an apartment complex. Her mother had gone back inside their apartment to get her cellphone. When she got back outside, her daughter was gone.

For three days, they'd tracked leads. Despite the heavy fogs that hampered the search effort, officers canvassed the apartment complex and surrounding homes. Other teams searched the heavily wooded terrain. As the third day wore down, another fog rolled in, and the search was called off.

The command center, SWAT's motorhome, was parked near the apartment building. Chad stayed to answer the hotline. At midnight his relief, Frank Evans, arrived, and he headed home.

His mental condition was on the edge, and he knew it. Driven by desperation and an uncommon sense of urgency, he couldn't back off. Chad didn't know how, but he was certain if he didn't find Susan, and fast, she'd die. What else could he do? Every step the task force had taken replayed in his head in an endless cycle. His instincts told him he'd missed something; a detail he'd seen or heard had been overlooked. The feeling was one a cop didn't ignore.

When he arrived home that night, he'd gone straight to his bedroom. Exhausted, he'd stripped off his clothes, letting them fall to the floor. As he collapsed on the bed, his last thought was of his wife. Since she was at a banking conference, he didn't have to worry about another confrontation concerning his late hours.

Jerked out of a deep sleep by the harsh ring of the doorbell, his glance at the clock told him what his body already knew, two hours was all he got. It rang again. Whoever it was, they weren't going away. Resigned, he pulled on a pair of jeans and a T-shirt, shoved his feet into tennis shoes, and stuck his Glock inside his waistband.

At the front door, he flipped on the porch light and checked the peephole. When he didn't see anyone, irritation flayed his already raw nerves. If this were a gang of neighborhood teenagers, they'd be damn sorry they picked his doorbell to ring.

Chad opened the door and stepped onto the porch that ran along the front of the house. No one was there. The porch steps and rail were barely visible in the black, dense fog that seemed to be gaining in strength. Ghostly, green-tinged tentacles of the murky mist curled and twisted as they drifted across the porch, creeping closer until they coiled around his feet and legs. He shivered, suddenly chilled to his bones.

Certain he was being watched, he cried out, "Anybody there?" Not a sound broke the eerie silence. Still, he couldn't shake the feeling someone waited, hidden within the depths of the thick haze.

He wasn't up to playing games. The kids would just have to find another target. And he wasn't getting any sleep by standing outside, freezing his ass off. As he turned to walk inside, a whisper floated in the air. "Not dead, not dead."

Chad spun. The sound echoed again, louder with a sense of urgency. "Not dead! Not dead!" It was a child's voice. A jolt of alarm pulsed through him before logic kicked in. What would a child be doing out at this time of the night and in this weather? He'd bet the kids were out there laughing their heads off at his reaction.

Then, he realized the joke had become even more bizarre. Chad gaped at a tattered and broken doll propped against the porch rail. He'd have sworn it wasn't there when he stepped outside. Angered by the stupid prank, he walked along the porch, certain some kid was hiding next to the house. When he didn't find anyone, he turned to look at the doll. It was the fog, that was the only explanation. He just didn't see it before.

Still puzzled, Chad stepped back to take a closer look. It was larger than most dolls he'd ever seen, almost the size of a small child. From the neck to the ankles, a ragged, dirty, old-fashioned dress covered the body. Grey hair, tangled and matted, hung to its shoulders. Black streaks ran down the face. One eye was missing. The broken eye socket and the large crack from the hairline to the lips added to a horrifying appearance more suited to Halloween than a child's toy.

Not wanting to leave the damn thing on his porch, he reached down to pick it up. Pain, as piercing as a taser hit, shot up his arms. When he tried to drop it, the doll stuck to his hands like glue. Chad couldn't even move his arms to shake it loose. The pain vanished, replaced by a warm feeling from the doll's body that felt ... human. A fear, unlike anything he'd ever felt, built inside him.

The doll's eye slowly shifted to look at him. A light sparked, and the eye began to glow with an unearthly golden light that shimmered in the fog. Brighter and brighter, it grew. The fear clamped around his chest, and he could barely breathe.

The warmth of the doll's body intensified until a blaze of heat radiated through his hands and arms. Horrified, Chad watched the doll's hand slowly move upward. When the fingers wrapped around his wrist, everything whirled around him. It was as if he was on a carnival ride. The fog turned black and flowed over him. All he could see was the glow of the eye.

Suddenly, he wasn't on his porch. He stood in a cold, decrepit room. Tattered strips of wallpaper clung to the broken-down walls. Tendrils of fog curled and twisted across the grimy floor. As Chad gazed around the morbid room, a sense of hopelessness swept over him.

Dear God, where was he? Was this a step into insanity or the nightmare from hell? Each heartbeat was a hammer strike in his chest as terror clawed at his insides. Looking down, Chad realized his hands were empty. The doll had disappeared.

A sob broke the unsettling silence. His head turned toward the sound. A little girl lay on a bed in the corner of the room. Where did she come from? Was it Susan? Had he conjured her up for this hellish nightmare? But as he looked closer, he knew he'd never seen this child before. Still, the sight of her ripped at his gut.

Strands of tangled dark hair clung to a battered face. Dark bruises encircled an eye that was swollen shut. A filthy nightgown covered her small body. As she sobbed, frail arms, marred with more bruises, clutched a doll against her chest.

The child's voice he'd heard earlier, whispered, "She is dying. All she has left to love is the doll she holds tight in her arms."

Desperate, Chad tried to run to her, but as impossible as it seemed, he couldn't move. Something, an invisible force, held him in place. He cried out, "Let me help her. Please let me go to her."

The voice echoed again. "The past is written. It cannot be altered. It is the future you seek. To find the lost, a gift is given. But … beware! To hear, you must listen."

Helpless, he watched in agony until the heartbreaking cries weakened and stopped. The child's body lay silent and still.

"No!" he screamed. Desolation and anger swept over him. Then, the girl vanished, leaving the doll on the bed.

His hellish nightmare wasn't over. The doll slowly sat up, then climbed off the bed until it stood upright. The head swiveled toward him. Eyes glittered with a frightening light as the doll gradually changed. Black smudges stained the dainty face, hands, and wrists. An eye disappeared. The empty, black socket splintered and broke. A crack crawled up the forehead, then down to the lips. The pretty hair turned into a grey mass of matted and tangled strands. Stains and rips appeared, ruining the dress. The doll had not only become the image of the tortured child, but it was the same doll that appeared on his porch.

The light in the single eye flashed into a living blaze, so bright it nearly blinded him. A cry rang out. "Not dead! Not dead!" Then the doll and bed vanished.

His mind recoiled in denial. This couldn't be real. He was a rational person, and this had to be his imagination. How could he stop it? As the dense fog wrapped around him, he knew he couldn't.

When the haze disappeared, it was daylight, and he stood beside the fence, which separated the apartment complex from a row of houses. The windows on the back of the homes overlooked the playground where Susan had disappeared. In an upstairs window, a light flickered. A man watched through a pair of binoculars.

The black haze flashed, and he stood on the sidewalk across from a row of houses, the same houses that backed up to the apartment complex. A man stood on a doorstep, locking the front door. A doll dangled from one hand.

Another flash of light and he was in a room. This time it was Susan who lay on the bed. Chad tried to step toward her, but as before, he couldn't move. His muscles strained against the strange force as he desperately fought to break free. Was she dead? He couldn't even see her chest rising as she breathed. "No, oh no!" he cried out.

A child's voice echoed. "Not dead, not dead."

Then the fog surrounded him. When his vision cleared, he was back on his porch.

At that moment, he knew, with absolute certainty, where to find Susan, and she was still alive. He didn't bother to question the strange events. The sense of urgency was overpowering—the clock was ticking down on the girl's life.

Chapter Twenty-eight

～❧～

He rushed inside and grabbed his cell phone on his way to the bedroom and called the command center. "Frank, I'm on my way back. Check the interview logbook and get me the addresses and names of the residents for the houses on the street next to the playground. Pull any interviews of the occupants."

Not waiting for an answer, he disconnected, and hurriedly changed into a uniform. Still buckling his gun belt, he ran out of the house.

At that hour of the morning, there was no traffic to slow him down as he raced to the apartment complex. The sight of the doll in the man's hand had triggered a memory … a detail he may have missed. Two dolls were near the swings when he arrived on the scene.

He ran up the stairs to the Eberly apartment. While he waited for someone to answer his knock, he could hear the TV. He'd bet Susan's mother hadn't slept since her daughter disappeared. When it opened, Mrs. Eberly stood in the doorway. The fearful look in her eyes turned to hope. "You found her!"

God, he hated to say the words. "No, I haven't. I need to see Susan's dolls. The ones we found in the playground."

Puzzled, Mrs. Eberly said, "Uh … come in. But one of the doll's doesn't belong to my daughter. I thought it was one someone had forgotten. I'll get it."

How did they miss it, he wondered? Even as he berated himself, he knew everyone assumed the dolls belonged to Susan, and they were unimportant.

She left the room, and when she returned, she held two dolls. Lifting one, she said, "This is Susan's. This one isn't," and handed it to Chad.

Chad barely noticed the first doll. It was the second that had his attention. The doll was old and worn out. The hair was pulled into long pigtails, and the face was marred with stains. An old-fashioned dress, dirty and tattered, covered the soft body. It was the doll he'd seen in his strange vision. Certain the kidnapper had used it to entice Susan, he said, "I'm taking this one with me."

She nodded. "Will it help find my daughter?"

"I hope so."

In his car, he grabbed a large evidence bag and stuffed the doll inside. His next stop was the command center. He dropped into a chair in front of the computer and pulled up a map of the street that bordered the apartments. Studying the location of the houses, he pinpointed the one he believed he'd seen in his dream, nightmare, or whatever the hellish experience was. Chad quickly cross-referenced the house with the resident.

"I need every detail you can find on Harry Bedford."

"Sure, but what's going on? Why this guy?" Frank asked as he started typing on his keyboard.

In his haste, Chad hadn't considered how he was going to explain. If he couldn't answer Frank's question, how could he possibly get a judge to sign a search warrant? His mind raced to come up with an answer as Frank glanced at him with a puzzled look. He couldn't lie, but he could shade the truth.

"An anonymous informant told me I'd find Susan inside Bedford's house."

"What! Man or woman?"

"I couldn't tell, the voice was muffled."

"So, how does the person know?"

"When I started asking questions, the call went dead."

"How certain are you?"

"The informant described the house. Where's the interview, and when was it done?"

Frank picked up a stapled set of papers and handed it to him. "It wasn't until the next day. No one answered the door the day Susan was abducted."

Chad leaned back in his chair to review the notes while he waited for the results of the criminal background request.

Bedford had rented the house about four months ago. He lived alone and worked nights at a local nursing home. The man said he'd been sleeping the day of the abduction and didn't know about the kidnapping until he saw it on the news. Why didn't Bedford answer the door when the officer attempted to contact him? According to his statement, he was home. His house was two-story, and windows on the backside overlooked the playground. He could have watched Susan play from an upstairs window.

When Frank exclaimed, he looked up. The printer was spitting out the returns on the criminal search. Bedford had two prior charges for indecency with a child, but no convictions.

A groan of dismay erupted before Chad said, "How the *hell* did this slip through the crack?"

Frank said, "Probably because whoever ran the background check looked for convictions, not charges filed."

Chad had enough for a search warrant. He typed out the affidavit and handed it to Frank. "Get this to Judge Berry at the jail. He should still be there."

The door opened. His partner, Ray Hart, walked in. Seeing Chad, he exclaimed, "Don't you ever go home? You were here when I left."

"Yeah, I did, but I came back. We've got a suspect." Chad quickly brought him up to speed. "We need a floor plan of the house."

"I can help. I talked to a couple of residents on the street. The houses are all a cookie-cutter style. Except for a different trim, they're basically alike."

Chad handed him a notepad. "Get to drawing."

He pulled his phone and tapped the speed dial for his office. When the detective on night duty answered, he said, "It's Chad. Is the sarge still there?"

"He's about to leave."

"I need to talk to him before he gets out the door."

When Sergeant Anderson came on the line, Chad said, "I've got a suspect in the Eberly kidnapping. I'm walking a warrant. I need a tactical unit."

Knowing his detective, the sergeant's answer was quick. "On it. Where?"

"Command center."

"I'm on my way."

While they waited, Ray said, "Tell me again how you found out about Bedford?"

Chad went back over the details.

Puzzled, Ray said, "It's pretty iffy for a warrant? You've got no idea who it was that called?"

Chad wondered how his partner would react if he said it was a spooky old doll. Since he didn't have a clue how to explain any of it, he just shook his head and picked up the diagram Ray had drawn.

Events moved rapidly once Frank returned with the signed

warrant, and the SWAT team arrived. Chad conducted the briefing.

"I'm going to keep this short. We have a suspect in the kidnapping of Susan Eberly." He indicated the blackboard with the name, address, and diagram Ray had drawn. "Bedford has two prior arrests for indecency with a child, no convictions." He handed a picture to the nearest officer. "Mug shot from when he was arrested. I contacted the nursing home where he works nights. Bedford is on vacation. He's probably in the house. Status of weapons is unknown." He turned the briefing over to Sergeant Hamilton, who was in charge of the SWAT team.

Hamilton, after reviewing the diagram of the interior of the house, called out the lineup of the entry team. "Detective Bishop will follow the team inside."

It was still dark, with only a hint of the coming dawn when the police van pulled into place. The side door opened, and officers dressed in black, wearing helmets and goggles and with rifles slung across their chests exited. The only sound was the faint tinkle of metal on metal. They flowed like water across the grass to the front corner of the suspect's house. The lead officer was carrying a "slammer," a heavy piece of metal used to bust open the door. The rest of the squad lined up behind the officer, and as soon as the door was breached, they ran into the house, shouting, "Police! Police!" Chad was the last to enter and followed the two officers assigned to clear the second floor.

A man wearing a pair of briefs stumbled from a bedroom. It was Bedford. A SWAT officer shoved him against the wall.

Chad looked in the bedroom, then moved to the next. Susan was lying on the bed. It was an unnerving sight. It was just as he'd seen in the ... hell, he didn't know what to call it. Whatever it was, the reality, the proof of what he'd seen, lay on the bed. He keyed his mike to request the medical personnel.

As he knelt, the sickeningly sweet smell of chloroform lingered in the air. It must have been what he used to drug her. She didn't move. Chad pressed his fingers against her neck. He could feel a faint pulse. She was alive. The breath he'd been holding erupted in an almost painful sigh of relief.

He settled back on his heels, and his eyes feasted on the small face, so still, so quiet, but alive. A child's voice murmured, this time with a note of joy. "Not dead, not dead." The sound rose. "Not dead! Not dead!" The emotion in the childish voice resonated inside Chad. The lost had been found.

Footsteps clattered as the EMTs raced up the stairs. Rising, he stepped back to give them room and watched as they began their systematic assessment of her condition. He wasn't leaving until he knew her status.

One of the medics glanced at him. "She's in bad shape. I'm not waiting to get a stretcher up here." He folded the blanket around her body and gently lifted her. Chad followed him down the stairs. Once Susan was loaded in the ambulance, he walked over to talk with the two sergeants who waited on the sidewalk.

Sergeant Anderson said, "Damn good job, Chad. Ray's on the way to get the girl's mother."

"I'd like to get to the hospital. She's in bad shape."

Anderson said, "Take my car, it's parked behind the van." He tossed a set of keys to Chad. "We'll handle the cleanup here. I can catch a ride back with another officer."

In the emergency room, it was heartbreaking to see the tubes connecting her tiny body to the life saving machines. Chad told himself she was alive, so be grateful. He still had one more difficult task—to find out if there were any injuries. Bent over her body, Doc Wilson, a longtime friend, listened to her heart and lungs. When he looked up, he saw Chad waiting.

He removed the stethoscope from his ears, and said, "Chad, the good news is there are no physical injuries. The bad news is Susan's condition is critical. In fact, the first few minutes she was here, I didn't know if I could save her. It's how close it came. I put a rush on the toxicology report. Susan's got enough drugs on board to kill an adult, let alone a small child. Even if she makes it through the next twenty-four hours, she's still got a long hospital stay ahead of her. She's one sick little girl, and it'll take time to get the drugs out of her system. Fortunately, Susan will probably have no memory of what happened to her."

She did survive, and as the doc said, Susan spent several weeks in the hospital. The last time Chad saw her, she was happily playing with her doll while her mother hovered. He expected the memories of Susan's abduction would haunt Mrs. Eberly for the rest of her life.

Unable to reconcile what he'd seen and felt against any logical or rational explanation, he'd been haunted as well. Had any of it been real, the dying girl, the strange room, a doll that was more than a doll? How could a doll's body have felt warm and a hand as real as any small child? Was it all a figment of his imagination, or maybe a tortuous act of insanity? If this was the case, how did he see Susan in the upstairs bedroom? He hadn't been sure he would ever have answers to the troubling questions.

Then, in a desperate attempt to get the case thrown out of court, Bedford's attorney tried to quash the search warrant, and the news media latched onto the controversy. Even though the judge did rule the warrant was valid, his reputation had already been damaged, and his marriage was headed to the divorce court. In the end, he resigned. Hoping to make a fresh start in Texas, he'd crushed the memories, buried them deep in his mind.

Chapter Twenty-nine

Present

The ring of the phone broke through the rush of memories. With a thud, his feet hit the floor, and his chair spun. His hand shot out to grab the cellphone on the desk. It was Jim. "Any news?"

Jim said, "None, and it's a waste of time to stake out the bait shop or Coleman's house. The fog's pushed the visibility down to feet. We'd have to be sitting in front of either place to see a damn thing."

Chad tamped back on a growing sense of urgency as he said, "Then shut it down for tonight. I've already sent my officers home."

They arranged a time to meet the next day before disconnecting the call. Laying the phone down, Chad's thoughts shifted back to the bizarre events in Atlanta.

During the search of Bedford's house, they'd found a receipt for the purchase of the doll. The clerk at the thrift shop picked Bedford out of a lineup. It turned into a vital piece of evidence at the trial. Chad always wondered whether he would have found Susan sooner if he'd known about the doll.

Now, he had a new worry, the one found in Mandy's backyard. The doll had an eerie resemblance to the one in Atlanta, but it couldn't be the same one. That doll was in the evidence locker. It was impossible for it to be on his desk in his house. And why in all the times he'd looked at the dang thing, had he never snapped to the similarities?

Distressed by the turmoil of emotions spinning inside him, his gaze returned to the ad in the newspaper on his desk. The old advice surfaced in his mind—work the problem. Chad studied the list of dates the doll appeared in the ad. Had it been added to communicate a message to a buyer? If this was the case, did another ad start the process?

Chad read the details in the ad again. Then it hit. The phone number! Certain he'd seen it in another ad, he started over with the first newspaper and finally found it. A small ad read, 'Unique, One of a Kind Gifts,' and a phone number. It was the same number for Antiques & More. As Chad worked his way through the rest of the papers, the ad appeared in each one.

He'd bet his last dollar Coleman owned Antiques & More and was using the pennysavers for his trafficking activity. It wouldn't be the first-time criminals' used newspapers to buy and sell anything from drugs to humans.

After a background search failed to turn up any record of the business, he called Vicky and left a message. There was nothing else he could do except go home. Since he planned on starting again at daylight, he needed to get a few hours' sleep, though it was doubtful he could shut down the terror he'd felt since Ashley disappeared.

As he restacked the newspapers, he felt an odd tug in his mind. It was the same sensation he experienced in the Eberly case. Somehow, he'd missed a detail. In the Atlanta case, it was the doll that turned out to be a key piece of evidence.

Good god, could it be the doll again? Chad opened a newspaper to the page he'd marked and studied the ad. It was eye-catching with its elegant script and motifs. Despite the artistic drawing of the small doll, it somehow seemed out of place. He pulled open a drawer and grabbed a magnifying glass. His hand hovered over the paper as he adjusted the focus. Stunned, the glass slipped from his fingers. This time, he couldn't dismiss the similarity as a coincidence. Sure, companies made more than one doll. But what were the odds—the one in Atlanta, the one in Norton's backyard, and the one in the ad—would all look alike?

Vicky would think he'd lost his mind, and she might be right, he thought as he waited for the call to roll to her voice mail. He left another message asking she check the evidence locker for the Bedford case. Was the doll still there?

With a quick glance at his watch, he decided he'd done all he could. He picked up his briefcase and locked up the building. When he stepped outside, he stopped. The fog folded around him. Though he listened, not a single sound broke the eerie silence. Doubts crept into his mind. Maybe, what happened in Atlanta had only been the thoughts of a man on the edge of insanity after all.

A voice buzzed like an annoying mosquito. Floating in a black mist, Ashley ignored it, hoping it would go away.

The voice persisted. Then a jolt of pain pulled her from the depths of oblivion.

The small voice begged, "Auntie Ash, please." A hand tapped her face, then shook her shoulder. Agonizing pricks of sharp needles jabbed deep in her head.

As her mind cleared, she discovered she was lying on her back; the chill from a floor seeped through the thin material of her shirt.

"Please, please, wake up. Auntie Ash, it's me."

Mandy! No, she had to be dreaming. Turning her head toward the sound, she slowly opened her eyes and couldn't believe what she was seeing. The child knelt next to her.

Ashley reached for her only to discover her hands were bound with tape. "Are you hurt?" Her gaze skimmed over the girl. Tangled hair hung around her tear-stained face, and she still wore the same clothes, albeit they were badly wrinkled.

When the child shook her head no, Ashley thought she'd pass out again from the relief which rushed through her.

With a rueful look at her hands, she said, "Sweetie, I can't hug you, but I need a kiss."

"Oh, Auntie Ash, I've been so afraid," Mandy cried, throwing herself across Ashley's chest, and pressing a very wet kiss on her cheek.

Despite the pain that rocked in her head, Ashley didn't believe she'd ever felt anything so good. "I know, sweetie, and it's going to be all right. Your Auntie Ash is going to make sure of that," she said, praying she could make good on the promise.

Mandy leaned back and patted Ashley's head.

"You have to stop patting my head. It hurts." She wondered what Walker used to hit her.

"Your head hit the floor."

Confused, Ashley stared at her. "What?"

"Auntie Ash, two men dropped you on the floor. Your *head* hit the floor."

"Mandy, do you know when that happened?" She didn't hold out much hope the child would have a sense of time.

"It's still dark outside."

"Dark?"

"Yes, dark. It was dark when you got here. The man turned on the light," she said, her tone indignant.

Whatever had happened hadn't destroyed Mandy's spark of sass. If Ashley got it right, she hadn't been here long. Before she moved, she took stock of her physical condition. Other than her head, she couldn't feel any other injuries. Her feet were free, which was a blessing.

"I'm going to sit up."

Jumping to her feet, Mandy declared, "I can help."

Thank god for all those hours at the gym, she thought as she used her stomach muscles, twisting and scooting until her back was against the edge of the bed. Mandy's small hands pulled and tugged. It hadn't done much good, but she wasn't about to discourage the child from helping.

Ashley leaned her head back and closed her eyes. She gulped to keep the bile from rising in her throat from what felt like a needle stuck in the middle of her brain.

A hand patted Ashley's leg. "I knew you were coming."

Startled, Ashley's eyes popped open. Did someone say something she'd overheard? Her mother had warned Ashley about Mandy's habit of listening to conversations. The little girl had moved in front of her and sat cross-legged with a doll cradled in her arms. "How did you know?"

A solemn expression on her face, she glanced down at the doll. "Betsy told me."

"Uh … uh … Betsy?"

"Yes. She knows everything."

Her tone weak, Ashley said, "She does?"

"Uh-huh." Mandy's head bobbed up and down. "She said you were sleeping. But I was still scared when you didn't wake up."

Ashley's gaze shifted to the doll. In disbelief, she stared at it. It was the one that had disappeared. How did it get here?

"Sweetie, did you have Betsy with you when you got here?"

"Oh, no. She came later. She's here to help."

Had she fallen down the rabbit hole and didn't know it? The pain made it difficult to think. Despite the serious look on her niece's face, this had to be her imagination, a way of coping with the trauma of the kidnapping.

"Maybe you dreamed about your doll talking to you," Ashley said.

Mandy bent over, cuddling the doll closer to her chest, and whispered, "No, she talks to me all the time. Betsy said no one would believe me."

Stricken by the crushed look on Mandy's face, Ashley hurriedly said, "Sweetie, it's okay to tell me. I wish I had a doll that could talk to me too."

Her face perked up. "You do? I bet Betsy would talk to you. But … you have to listen."

"Uh, sure." At this point, Ashley would have agreed she was secretly married to Santa Claus if it helped Mandy.

Once the pain had receded, she slowly moved her head from side to side, examining the room. A window was opposite the door to the hallway. The bed was on one side and another door on the other.

"Where does that door go?" she asked, nodding toward it.

Mandy's face scrunched. "Into the bathroom, and it's really, really yucky."

"Do you remember what happened to you?"

"A bad man grabbed me and put a cloth over my face. It smelled funny." Tears built in her eyes, and her arms tightened around the doll.

Ashley hated questioning her. But if she was going to get the two of them out of here, she had to find out what Mandy knew. But first, as much as she hated to move, she had to get on her feet.

"Hop up on the bed. I'm going to stand up, and if I don't make it, I don't want to topple over on you."

With a deep breath, she rolled onto her knees and used the bed to help her stand. For several seconds, the room whirled as she waited for the pain to subside.

Turning, she walked to the door. As her hands reached for the knob, she glanced over her shoulder at the child sitting on the bed. "Mandy, did the man walk into the backyard?"

A look of panic crossed Mandy's face. With her hand, she motioned for Ashley to come back to the bed.

After trying the knob, which only confirmed the door was locked, she stepped back. "Mandy, what's wrong?"

"The witch might hear you."

Wondering what Mandy had dreamed up this time, Ashley eased down onto the edge of the bed. "Tell me about the witch."

Her body trembled. "She's mean. I had to be quiet, or she'd stick a rag in my mouth. And, she grabbed my arms and shook me. It hurt."

Anger ripped through Ashley at the fear on her niece's face. "How many times have you seen her?"

She held up one finger. "She comes back when I'm asleep."

"How do you know that?"

With a wave of her small hand at the table near the window, she said, "She leaves purple goo and water."

Ashley glanced at the sandwich. Evidently, purple goo was grape jelly. Her fingers brushed the girl's cheek. "I'm here now. I won't let her hurt you again. Tell me about the man. Where did you see him?"

"At the gate." She sniffed. "Mommy is really going to be mad at me. I'm not supposed to talk to anyone I don't know."

"Sweetie, I don't think she'll be mad. Your mommy just wants to know you're all right. Why did you walk to the gate?"

"A doll. It was dirty, but I just wanted to hold it. Then he put a cloth over my face."

So, he did use the doll, but it still didn't solve the mystery of how it got on a chair in the backyard. "Where did you wake up?"

Mandy looked around. "Here. I was sick and cried a lot."

Ashley ached to hold her, to wipe away the fear on her face. She leaned over. "Give me another kiss." The warmth of Mandy's lips threatened to start a round of tears. Ashley swallowed before saying, "Oh, that made me feel so much better. See if you can pull on the edge of the tape."

Her small fingers plucked at the edge, but after several tries, Ashley said, "It's okay, we'll try later." She looked at the doll lying in Mandy's lap. "When did you get Betsy?"

"She was under the covers."

It didn't make sense. "You mean she was already here when you woke up?"

She shook her head and sighed. "No, Auntie Ash, later. The second time I woke up."

"Mandy, I don't understand. How could she have come later?"

"I already told you. She came to help. Betsy told me to pour the water down the sink."

"What water?" Her brain felt fuzzy from trying to make sense of her niece's answers.

"The *water* in the glass. It tasted funny. I didn't like it."

Were they trying to keep her drugged? "You didn't drink it then?"

"Auntie Ash." Annoyed, she huffed. "Betsy *told* me to pour it into the sink, and I did."

Frustrated, Ashley decided to let it go. There was something she was missing, and Mandy was getting upset. "How many people have you seen?"

Mandy held up three fingers.

"Two men and the uh … witch," Ashley said.

"Uh-huh. I want to go home. This is a bad place."

"I know, sweetie. I'm going to see if I can make it happen." Ashley shivered. The temperature in the room was dropping. "Get under the covers. It's getting cold."

With Betsy snuggled against her chest, Mandy watched Ashley explore the room. When she opened the door to the bathroom, a noxious odor drifted out, and Mandy hissed, "Told you it was yucky."

Ashley had to agree. Grime crusted the sink and floor. The toilet was worse. Stripped bare, including the mirror, there wasn't anything she could use to cut the tape. Quickly shutting the door, she stepped to the table. The plate held a dried-out sandwich oozing with jelly. A small glass was filled with a cloudy liquid. Another surge of anger shot through her at the thought of Mandy being drugged.

She turned her gaze toward the window. It was the only way out. Though it was nailed shut, one of the nails was loose. Ashley's fingers tugged on it, then rocked the nail until she could pull it out.

"Betsy said the policeman is coming."

The nail fell as she twisted to look at her niece. "Tell me that again?"

With a roll of her eyes, Mandy said, "Betsy said to tell you the policeman is coming."

To hide her disbelief, she bent to pick up the nail, then laid it on the table. "What policeman?" She surely could not mean Chad.

"Auntie Ash, I don't know. She just said the policeman."

Dealing with Mandy's delusions would have to wait. "I hope he gets here soon then. Are you getting warm?"

"Uh, huh. Betsy keeps me warm." Her eyes closed as she drifted to sleep.

Ashley's gaze lingered for several seconds on the child. An overwhelming relief that Mandy wasn't hurt swept over her before she turned back to the window.

When voices echoed in the hallway, she panicked. What should she do? Since it might be best to let them think she was still unconscious, she dropped to the floor and rolled onto her back.

The voices grew louder as two men argued. One had a deep tone, the other a rasp.

The man with the deep voice said, "After what you found in her house, it has to be done tonight."

She'd been right. There had been an intruder. What did they find? Then she remembered the notes she'd left on her desk. Was that it, the list of abductions?

The raspy voice said, "What happens to the money that's been paid? I didn't get my share."

"I'll find a way to fill the order. Stop complaining. You'll get your money."

"I don't understand why you can't use the girl."

"It's getting too dangerous. We've got to get rid of both of them. If I'd had any idea the brat's aunt was a damn reporter. Well, too late now."

"I still don't like it."

"Walker, I don't pay you to like or not like." The menacing tone had deepened. "I pay you to do a job. If you know what's good for you, it's something you'd better remember."

Walker! Chad was right on his suspicions. Was the other man Coleman?

His tone mutinous, Walker said, "All right. I'll take care of it."

"Make sure you get to the middle of the lake. I don't want to take a chance on their bodies washing up somewhere."

A mocking laugh erupted before Walker said, "Don't worry. With what I tie to their feet, they won't be going anywhere."

Raw terror pulsated in her. They were planning on killing her and Mandy. Dear, god, how much time did she have?

The door opened. "Good, the woman's still out. Get the boat ready.

Call when you've got everything in place. I'll help get them to the dock."

The door closed, followed by the click of the lock. Ashley rolled onto her knees and pushed herself upright. How was she going to get them out of the room? If she couldn't get her hands free, they didn't have a chance.

Chapter Thirty

~∾~

She turned toward the window. Her eyes lit on the glass of water. *That might just be the solution.* Hampered by the limited range of movement in her fingers, Ashley carefully carried the glass into the bathroom, where she poured the murky liquid down the sink. She grabbed the towel draped over the edge of the tub. Rolling the glass in the corner of the cloth, she slapped it against the sink and heard a satisfying tinkle of breaking glass.

She laid the towel on the bedroom floor and spread it open. Not only was there a large piece of broken glass, but it was still attached to the base.

Dropping to the floor, she braced her back against the wall, then brought her knees up and set the glass in between her feet. Once the base was securely gripped by her shoes, she scraped the tape on the underside of her wrists along the jagged edge of the glass. A small slit appeared, but the pressure pushed the base out of position, and she had to stop to move it back. She tried again with the same results. Unnerved by the amount of time it took, she forced herself not to rush. If the glass spear broke, it would take even longer.

When the last section split, a gleeful, high-five shot through her mind. Rolling her wrists outward, she repeated the slicing motion on the tape that covered the top of her wrists. This time it was easier and only took a few cuts. Once she had a piece she could grab with her teeth, she tugged, and the tape ripped. With her hands free, she jumped up and headed to the window.

As she stared at the other nail solidly in place, a groan erupted. Cripes, she didn't have anything except a piece of glass to pry it out. Or did she?

Reaching down, Ashley picked up the other nail lying on the table. She dug into the wood around the nail until she could get the tip under the head, then pried upward. The nail moved. A couple more thrusts and she yanked it out. With a few tugs, the window slid open. Her hands pushed against the thin screen, and it tumbled to the ground. *We're out of here.*

"Mandy, wake up." Ashley gently shook the child's shoulder. "Come on, sweetie, wake up."

Mandy lifted her head.

"We're going to crawl out the window," Ashley whispered.

When a noise sounded in the hallway, she didn't waste any time. She picked up the girl and headed for the window.

"Betsy," Mandy cried.

"Shh … I'm going to drop you to the ground. It'll be okay, and I'll be right behind you."

"Please, Auntie Ash. Don't leave Betsy."

After thrusting Mandy's legs through the window, Ashley leaned forward, holding the girl under the arms. Thankful it was a short drop to the ground, she let go.

She darted back to the bed, grabbed the doll, and promptly juggled it in the air. *What the hell? How could it be hot?* Now wasn't the time to figure it out. Ashley tossed it out the window, then crawled out and fell to the ground.

The dense fog was back. How the hell was she going to see anything? "Mandy," she whispered as she got to her feet.

"I'm here."

She turned toward the sound. Her shape faint in the thick haze, Mandy stood near the corner of the house, her arms wrapped tight around the doll.

Ashley ran to her, picked her up, then raced away from the house toward the trees barely visible in the heavy mist.

"Where are we going?" Her voice trembled as she bounced against Ashley's chest.

"I don't know, but anywhere is better than where we've been."

Behind her, someone shouted, "They're gone. Get outside. Find them."

As she worked her way deeper into the woods, it struck her the fog had tapered off. Light from the moon filtered through the mist. She had to find a place to hide. Even though she considered herself to be in excellent physical condition, Ashley's arms felt the strain from carrying Mandy. Dodging trees wasn't easy, and she'd had to slow her pace. Ahead, a dense thicket around a cluster of trees emerged. If they could get underneath it, no one should see them.

She set Mandy on the ground and whispered, "Slide under the branches."

Mandy shoved the doll toward Ashley, then dropped to her knees. While Ashley pulled the small limbs aside, Mandy crawled under them and was soon out of sight.

The shouts behind her grew louder. Ashley glanced over her shoulder, but all she could see was a wall of black fog. The odd difference in the visibility registered, but she didn't have time to consider the reason. She fell to the ground. Holding the doll in one hand and trying to ignore it was definitely generating heat, she snaked her way inside until she was next to Mandy. She rolled on her side and pulled the child against her.

Mandy grabbed the doll and clutched it against her chest. She whispered, "Auntie Ash. It's going to be okay."

Despite the terror surging through her, Ashley had to smile at the almost adult reassurance in Mandy's voice … until she added, "Betsy told me."

Even as he fought the urge to wake, an awareness crept into his thoughts—the doorbell. The urgency in the harsh clangs resonated deep inside him, sparking a sense of *déjà vu*. Good lord, was it possible? The thought sent him tumbling out of bed. With quick movements, he pulled on jeans and a shirt and jammed his feet into his duty boots.

The cellphone went in a shirt pocket, and the gun was shoved in his waistband. The cold metal against his palm brushed away the lingering fatigue but did nothing to alleviate the growing sense of anxiety.

As he rushed toward the front door, it opened. Green-tinted tentacles of a ghostly fog curled and twisted as the murky haze slithered into the room. The icy mist coated his face and arms, chilling his blood. From the depths of the mysterious fog, a sibilant whisper floated. "Not dead! Not dead!"

He knew what waited … his destiny. If it would save Ashley and Mandy, Chad had no choice but to embrace it. He stepped through the doorway.

On the wooden step, the doll waited. Tattered and broken, it seemed more fragile than before. The cracks around the blackened eye socket were larger, more defined. A wave of grief flooded his senses as he recalled how the doll had absorbed the injuries to the little girl who died.

The glow from the remaining eye set off an uncanny heat, which pulsated in his blood. The doll's arm raised. When Chad extended his hand, the doll's fingers wrapped around his wrist and with a tug, pulled him deeper into the dense mist. When it cleared, he stood on the shore of a lake. Waves splashed against the rocks, and a boat rocked at the end of a dock. A man stood at the helm. As he turned to step out of the boat, Chad recognized him. It was Lew Walker.

Another man approached. "Is everything set?"

Walker answered, "Yeah, but I'm not heading out until this fog clears."

"Don't wait too long, I told you this had to be done tonight."

He turned and walked away. Chad's eyes followed. The man headed toward the faint glow of lights from a nearby house.

Walker muttered as he turned back to the boat. "Don't wait. Right. You're not the one who has to find the middle of the lake, dump two bodies, and then find your way back to the dock."

A chill of terror shot through Chad. Was he referring to Ashley and Mandy? Were they dead? He spun, trying to find a point of reference. Where the hell was this dock?

The darkness overtook him, and when it vanished, he stood on a driveway. In front of him was an old, rundown bungalow. Was this where Ashley and Mandy were being kept? But how could he find the house? He didn't recognize anything. Desperate, his eyes scanned the front looking for an address, then turned to look at the road behind him. On the corner was a mailbox with a number on the side—1821.

As the dense vapor churned, he cried, "No! No! I need to get inside the house." Instead, he was back on his porch. The doll had vanished.

Panic-stricken, he tore open the front door, pulling the cellphone from his pocket as he raced to his office. When the dispatcher answered, he said, "This is Chief Bishop. I need an address."

Within seconds, the dispatcher matched the box number with a county road, and Chad entered the address into his computer. A red arrow marked the location of the house on a map of the west side of the lake. After memorizing the roads leading to it, he headed for the front door, grabbing extra magazines and his heavy canvas jacket on his way out.

As he turned the key in the ignition, he considered whether he should call for backup, then decided it was too risky. He didn't need the lights and sounds of the cavalry coming over the hill, at least not until he had Mandy and Ashley out of harm's way. He refused to consider he might already be too late.

When he reached the roadside park that was about a half-mile from the house, he parked. Hopping out, he ran. The fog had diminished, making it easier to stay on the road.

Up ahead, shouts rang out. The faint glow from the house intensified as lights were turned on.

Chad couldn't take a chance that a car would leave. He headed into the brush, then turned, moving alongside the road. He slowly picked his way forward. A bush rustled. He stepped behind a tree. Despite the urgency that raged inside him, he stood motionless and waited. Whatever made the sound was ahead. Chad caught a glimpse of movement. A man glided from tree to tree. His shape looked familiar.

He gave a short whistle, then whispered, "Ken."

When Ken reached him, he asked in the same hushed tone, "What are you doing here?"

Chad said, "Mandy and Ashley may be in the house."

"Coleman's there. I followed him," Ken told him.

"We need to get to them and fast. Coleman's planning on killing them, then dumping their bodies in the lake."

Ken sucked in a deep breath. "How do …"

Chad interrupted. "No time for explanations. Are you familiar with the house?"

"No."

"It backs onto the lake. There's a boat dock. I need you there in case they get by me."

"Got it." He turned and vanished into the deep haze.

Chad rushed toward the sound of the voices.

Chapter Thirty-one

The crunch of leaves grew louder. With her lips next to Mandy's ear, she whispered, "Don't move or make any noise." She felt Mandy's head bob up and down.

"Damn fog! I can't see a foot in front of me. How the hell are we going to find them in this soupy mess?" More curses erupted.

Walker's raspy voice rang out. "Rick, since they can't see any better than we can, they won't get far."

Ashley tightened her grip around Mandy. She was right, the other man was Coleman.

"You'd better hope they don't escape, or all our heads are in the noose. Get to the dock. Maybe they went in that direction," Coleman told him.

Leaves crackled, then the sound died away. Ashley was almost afraid to breathe. Where was Coleman?

"Auntie Ash. I'm going ..." Mandy sneezed.

Oh, hell, that did it. They couldn't stay here. She scooted out. When she turned to reach for Mandy, an arm snaked around her chest and tossed her to the ground. Coleman stood over her with a gun pointed at her face.

"Okay, little girl, come out from under there if you don't want your precious aunt to get hurt."

Mandy crawled out, dragging Betsy with one hand. Coleman motioned toward her. "Come here."

Mandy stood but looked at Ashley. Coleman took a step sideways and grabbed her arm. She screamed in pain as he jerked her in front of him.

Fury overrode Ashley's paralyzing fear, and she started to rise until Coleman pointed the gun at Mandy's head. "You try anything, and she gets a bullet."

Sobbing, Mandy huddled in front of him, clutching the doll with a death grip.

Coleman snarled and shook her. "Shut up. I don't want to hear you squawking," then looked down at Ashley. "Get up, real slow. You don't want to do anything stupid."

"Let her go. She can't hurt you. She's a child, and no one's going to pay any attention to her."

"Do you think I'm that dumb? She'll lead the cops right to my door. And even if she didn't, I'm not taking a chance it could happen."

Ashley slowly stood. As long as he had the gun pointed at Mandy, she was helpless.

He motioned with his head. "Start walking. Remember ... one false move and she's dead. The next bullet will be yours."

Ashley's body tensed. She wanted to lash out and strike the gun from his hand, but she didn't dare. Instead, she turned.

"That's it, keep walking ... straight ahead," Coleman told her.

When a ghastly shriek ripped the night air, followed by a second, Ashley pivoted. The inhuman sounds came from Coleman. Wild-eyed, he stared at the doll's hand clamped on top of his wrist. In the shadowy mist, the doll's eyes blazed with a sinister light.

Another high-pitched shriek erupted. "Goddamn. It's burning me!" Coleman tried to shake it loose. Even though the doll jumped and swayed from the violent swing of his arm, he couldn't dislodge it.

Ashley darted forward, but Mandy was already running to her. She screamed, "Run, Mandy! Run!"

The child turned and dashed away, disappearing behind a clump of trees.

Ashley raced after her. Coleman shouted. "You nosy bitch! You're dead, the kid's next." A shot rang out. Ashley flinched, waiting for the pain to hit. Instead, she heard a gasp. She whipped around.

Blood stained the front of Coleman's shirt. He dropped to his knees, then collapsed facedown. Splashes of blood dotted the dried leaves that littered the ground.

Stupefied, she stared at the man sprawled in front of her. Ashley's mind couldn't grasp what just happened. She thought she was going to die. Her eyes shifted to the doll on the ground. How could it look … so normal?

"Ashley!" Chad materialized in the fog.

His voice shattered her mind-numbing bewilderment. The gun in his hand barely registered in her thoughts as she shouted, "Mandy, where are you?"

The child stepped from behind a tree. Ashley ran to her and picked her up. Holding her tight against her chest to keep Mandy from seeing Coleman, she fought back the tears.

Even though he was certain the man was dead, Chad dropped to one knee and felt for a pulse. He stood, gazing down at the body for a few seconds, then looked at the doll. Shaking his head in amazement, he walked to Ashley and wrapped his arms around her and Mandy.

"Are you both all right?"

The trembling in her legs eased. "Yes, we are now."

A shot echoed in the distance, followed by a second.

"Chad, what's happening?"

"I'm not certain." He stepped back, pulled out his phone, and tapped the speed dial. Tense, he waited for Ken to answer. "Everything okay?"

"For me, yes," Ken said. "Walker, not so much. He popped off a round. I shot back. He's bleeding like a gutted pig. I've got him trussed up nice and tight with a rope I found on the boat. How about on your end? I heard a shot."

"Coleman's out of the picture. I've got Ashley and Mandy with me. Call dispatch and get the cavalry started, then get back over here. We'll need to check the house. There may still be someone there."

Hearing the roar of an engine as a car raced down the road from the house, he added, "Scratch that. I guess whoever was there has cleared out. Still, we need to make certain."

"I'll handle it," Ken said.

He disconnected, then motioned with his hand. "Ashley, head to the road."

Once the body was out of sight, she set Mandy down. Feeling a tug on her shirt as they walked, she looked at the child. Her face was pale, too pale. What happened was a lot for an adult to handle, let alone a four-year-old. "What sweetie?"

"Betsy?" Mandy whispered.

God, for a moment, she'd forgotten about the doll. How could she ever explain what happened—and who would believe her? "Don't worry. He's the police chief, and he'll take good care of her."

Mandy nodded. "I know. Don't you remember, Auntie Ash? Betsy said the policeman was coming."

Solving the mystery of the doll was more than Ashley could handle at the moment, so she let the comment pass.

Shivering in the cold night air, they waited on the edge of the road. The fog had lifted, and she could see the house in the distance.

Despite the chill, she wasn't taking Mandy back inside it.

Chad emerged from the trees with the doll under his arm. When he reached the little girl, he knelt and said, "I'm Chad, and I'm so glad to meet you." He held out his hand, and Mandy slid hers on top of his fingers.

With a solemn tone in her voice, she said, "You're the policeman."

Chad smiled. "And how do you know that? Did your aunt tell you?"

"Oh, no."

Ashley cleared her voice. When Chad looked up, she just shook her head in resignation.

Mandy leaned toward him and whispered, "Betsy told me."

"Ah … I've heard about Betsy. But who is this?" he asked, handing the doll to her.

Mandy frowned at him. "Don't you know?" She held it up with both hands to face Chad. "This *is* Betsy,"

In the dark, he hadn't looked closely at the doll. Even though he wanted to examine it, he'd have to wait. Now, a shock of recognition rippled through him. How was it possible there was another bizarre piece to the puzzle of the dolls?

At the look of expectation on the little girl's face, he said, "Hello, Betsy. It's nice to meet you too."

Mandy giggled. "She likes you."

"Well, I like her too." His hand brushed over Mandy's hair as he stood.

With the doll cradled in her arms, she leaned against Ashley's leg. "I'm hungry. Can we go home now?"

Chad laughed. "Your magic carriage is on the way."

He laid a hand on Ashley's shoulder and squeezed. "How are you doing?"

"I have a lot to tell you, but it'll have to wait." She glanced down at the little girl who was entirely too interested in their conversation.

"Ken went to get my car. This should be him coming now."

The squad car pulled to a halt. In the distance, the sound of sirens echoed. As Ken jumped out, Chad called to him. "Have dispatch broadcast an order to squelch the sirens. They'll wake everybody up. I don't want to have to deal with nosy neighbors."

Ken grinned, then said, "I already did." The whine of the sirens died as the sound of the engines drew closer.

He greeted Ashley, then knelt to say hello to Mandy. After she hugged him, he rose, his eyes suspiciously wet. He told Chad he'd check the house and hurried away.

Chad held out his hand. "Mandy, would you like to sit in a police car?"

Her eyes gleamed with excitement as her fingers gripped his. "Can I make it sound loud?"

"I bet you can. Come on, let's get you warm."

Chad opened the passenger door and lifted Mandy onto the seat. Once Betsy was settled in her lap, Chad pointed to a switch. "If you press there, the siren will go off."

Mandy leaned over; her fingers jabbed the switch. The whine of the siren echoed.

Giggling, she covered her ears.

Chad let it wail for a few seconds before flipping the switch. "You sit here while I talk to your aunt."

As a row of squad cars, an ambulance and fire truck streamed down the road, Chad motioned for Ashley to step away from the vehicle. "Let me see your hands." He pulled off the remaining bits of tape. "We need to get her to the hospital."

Rubbing each wrist, she glanced at the girl huddled on the seat. "What's going to happen here?"

"I have to stay. We've got a large crime scene. I'll have the ambulance take you back. One of my officers will pick up her parents and get them to the hospital."

"What about Walker?"

"He'll have to wait." He suddenly realized the fog had disappeared. "It won't take the ambulance long to make the round trip. I'll alert the EMTs."

"Let me borrow your phone. I don't know what happened to mine."

Ashley stepped close to the car and tapped in Kathy's number. It took several minutes for anyone to answer. Peter's voice was groggy and tinged with fear. "Chad, has something happened?"

"Peter, it's Ashley. Where is Kathy?"

"Next to me. What's going on? Why are you calling on Chad's phone?"

"Long story but put me on the speakerphone. I have someone who wants to talk to you."

She leaned over, holding the phone. Mandy's hands reached for it. "Your daddy and mommy are waiting for you to say hello."

Kathy's squeal was a loud cry of joy. "Mandy!"

"Mommy?"

"Yes, baby, it is. Daddy's here too."

Tears rolled over Ashley's cheeks as she walked away. Giving herself a few seconds to recover, she swiped away the tears with the sleeve of her shirt, before stepping back. "Let me talk to them for a minute."

"Ashley, is she all right? How did this happen? Where'd you find her?" In her excitement, Kathy's questions tumbled over each other.

"Yes, she seems to be okay, but just to make sure she's headed to the hospital. Chad is sending one of his officers to pick you up. As for what happened, I'll explain later." Seeing Chad walking toward her, followed by a medic, she added, "I have to go."

The medic leaned inside the car to talk to Mandy.

Ashley handed Chad the phone. "Her parents know."

His fingers brushed away a few lingering tears on her cheek. At the look of promise in his eyes, an unexpected buzz of excitement trickled through her.

Chad's hand reached for hers. "Let's get both of you out of here."

With Mandy snuggled in his arms, the EMT headed toward the ambulance. After Ashley climbed in the back, Chad told her he'd see her in a few hours, then disappeared into the woods.

Inside, the medic had gently laid Mandy on the cot, then tucked a blanket around her. Ashley dropped down on the opposite bench and watched while he checked the girl's vital signs.

She suddenly realized the doll wasn't there. Ashley remembered Chad setting it in Mandy's lap, but it wasn't there when the EMT picked her up. Was it still in the squad car? "Mandy, where's Betsy?"

"She's gone."

"Gone. Gone where?"

"She had to leave. Another little girl needed her help." A sly smile crossed her face. "I'm supposed to tell you she said goodbye, and she really likes the policeman." Her eyes closed, and she drifted off to sleep.

The medic glanced over his shoulder. "Is there a problem? Is someone missing?"

"Uh ... no. It's okay." How could she explain they were talking about a doll?

The man nodded and turned back to write on the clipboard.

As the ambulance pulled onto the roadway, Ashley's thoughts raced. She'd felt the heat of the doll's body. Surely, she hadn't imagined it. And, she couldn't get past the image of the doll hanging onto Coleman's wrist. While the ambulance raced along the highway, with the siren wailing and lights flashing, Ashley mulled over the improbability of what she'd felt and seen. One thing she knew for sure, it wasn't something she'd forget any time soon.

Chapter Thirty-two

Unlocking the door, Chad stepped inside and headed to the bedroom. He eyed the bed, wanting nothing more than to drop face first and let himself slide into a welcoming stupor. The aftermath of the adrenaline dump had played havoc with his body. Instead, he walked into the bathroom and turned on the jets in the shower. He stripped, dropped his clothes in a pile, and stepped under the streaming cold water. The shock wiped some of the cobwebs from his mind. After a few seconds of the punishing cold, he pushed the handle to the hot water side

All that was left was the cleanup. The inevitable reports, along with a multitude of phone calls, waited. It would take days, maybe even weeks, but it was over, and life, as he'd come to know it in Meridian, would return to normal. What Chad couldn't escape was the images of the last several hours. This time he knew he wouldn't be able to bury the memories. He'd live with them for the rest of his life. The worst was seeing Coleman's gun pointed at Mandy's head. It still sent a horrifying shudder rippling through him. Sighing, Chad turned off the faucet.

Attired in a clean uniform, he stopped in his office to get the doll Ashley had found in the backyard. He wanted to compare it to the picture in the newspaper ad.

Though the sun had peeked over the horizon, the room was still dark. Walking in, he switched on the light, then stopped and stared at the desk. The sack was there, but the doll wasn't. He didn't remember putting it anywhere else. It must have fallen on the floor. After stepping around the desk, he had to admit the doll had vanished. Somehow, he wasn't surprised.

If he was going to cope with any more mysteries, he needed a strong jolt of caffeine, and he desperately wanted to see Ashley. A stop at the café would get the coffee, but since he figured Ashley had already crashed, he'd have to wait to satisfy that itch. Tania had called earlier to tell him she'd dropped Ashley off after Mandy was released from the hospital.

When he backed out of his driveway, he turned toward her house, just on the off chance she was still up.

Ashley had showered and changed into sweatpants and a sweatshirt. Despite her exhaustion, her system still raced. She'd heard about the potency of adrenaline, but this was the first time she'd ever felt its full impact. She should be writing her news article, but she was wired and too restless to concentrate. She jumped when the doorbell rang. With a sense of caution, since she wasn't expecting anyone, she looked through the peephole. A surge of happiness wiped away the lingering agitation.

Swinging the door open, she said, "I'm so glad to see you."

"Not half as glad as I am." He stepped inside and dropped her tote bag on the floor before he pulled her into his arms and kicked the door closed with his foot. With a groan of pleasure, his lips smothered hers.

As the kiss deepened, her body throbbed with longing as she felt his rising need. Despite her overwhelming desire to crawl under his skin, her hands pushed back.

When he lifted his head, she asked, "Is it really over?"

He sighed. Once again, duty intervened, though he made himself a promise; this was the last time.

"For you, Mandy and her parents—yes. What's left will take a few weeks to wrap up. Which is why, as bad as I want to finish this, I've got to go to the office," Chad said.

"So, do I. I have one hell of a story to write, though I bet Henry's already there, pounding away on his keyboard."

"Tonight?" His fingertips brushed her cheek.

"What time?"

"I'm not sure, but how about I pick up dinner at the deli?"

Ashley smiled. "This time, I'll provide the wine. Or would you prefer beer?"

"Uh, now that you ask …"

She chuckled, then said, "I'll get both."

"When you get a chance, I need you to come by and give me a statement." Stepping back, he tripped over her bag.

Ashley glanced down. "Oh, my god, my bag! Where'd you find it?"

"It was inside the house."

She picked it up and rummaged through it. "Thank goodness, here's my phone. I dreaded having to replace it."

After one more quick kiss, he reluctantly walked out the door.

As Ashley closed it, the fatigue vanished, replaced with an intense wave of euphoria. She'd change clothes and head to the office. Would she be able to get there ahead of Henry, she wondered? Her laughter rang out.

Walking into the station, Mike, Dale, and Boomer were grouped around Lydia's desk. Lydia said, "I was just getting the story from everyone. You had one hell of a night. Tania just left. She said Mandy had been released from the hospital."

You don't know the half of it, he thought. "Let's put it this way, I hope to god, we never get another case like this one." He looked at his officers. "As soon as Jim gets here, we're having a meeting, so stick close."

As he stepped toward his office, Lydia said, "There's a fresh pot of coffee."

Oh, yes, there is a god. He turned and headed to the breakroom.

His first call was to the FBI. It took less than an hour, and two agents were seated in the conference room surrounded by his officers, Jim and Ken. He touched on the highlights of the abductions, the ads in the newspaper, and turned over a notebook he'd found in the house. It listed dates and locations. Chad was certain the details would lead to the missing children. Once they had exhausted all their questions, the agents left.

While he'd been in the meeting, Ashley arrived and handed Lydia a typed statement. Chad closed his door and read it. Even knowing everyone was safe, it was still frightening to know how close they'd come to being killed. If it hadn't been for Ashley's ingenuity, he might not have gotten there in time.

By the end of the day, search warrants had been executed for all of Coleman's properties. Coleman's wife and two cousins were in the county jail. The FBI was on the trail of the missing children. They had identified a lawyer in East Texas they believed was involved in a scheme to sell children to couples who couldn't adopt. Walker still clung to life, though the outlook wasn't favorable.

Chad also had a strange call from Vicky in Atlanta. The doll in the Eberly case was missing from the evidence locker. No one had any idea how or when it disappeared, which didn't surprise him at all.

He'd even managed to squeeze in a trip to visit Mandy and her parents. He didn't stay. Their gratitude overwhelmed him to the point of embarrassment. Ashley was there and wasn't one iota of help. All she did was sit with a smirky grin on her face. Mandy had insisted on sitting next to him with her hand clutched around his fingers. Against her, on the other side, was the inevitable doll. Though he was surprised it wasn't Betsy, he didn't want to ask. Chad still hadn't decided how to handle that issue.

He'd picked up another report when Lydia stepped into his office.

A fire-engine red fingernail tapped her watch. "Boss … go home. Get out of here."

"I will just as soon as I finish these last two reports."

She marched to his desk and snatched the file out of his hand. "We both know it can wait until tomorrow. I have a hunch someone is waiting for you."

He eyed her with suspicion.

"Henry called, wanting additional information for his article. He mentioned he'd kicked Ashley out of the office, told her to go home."

A roar of laughter erupted as he pushed back his chair. Why did he feel he was the center of a conspiracy? On his way out the door, Lydia hollered at him. "He also said to tell you the florist got in a shipment of roses."

Would he ever get used to the town's grapevine seeming to be one step ahead of him?

Since he promised to bring dinner, he stopped at the deli. Fielding questions about the abduction, Chad watched Peggy box up a side of salads, and her take-out-tray of lasagna.

"You're sure you know how to reheat this?" she asked.

"Yeah, I guess so. Just stick it in the oven, right?"

Peggy grinned, then said, "Don't worry. Ashley will know."

God, did everyone in town know where he was headed?

As he walked out the door, he eyed the small floral shop. Why not. It was a night to celebrate. He dropped the food in the truck, then sauntered across the street. When he left, a long white box with a dozen roses was tucked under one arm. A voice called out.

"Hello, Chief."

Nora stood in front of the thrift shop. Behind her, Edith locked the door. The two women eyed the box as they stepped toward him.

"Looks like someone is getting a nice surprise," Nora said. Her lips twitched upward before she added, "You know, everyone in town is sure proud of what you did." With a sideways look at her cousin, she jabbed her in the ribs with her elbow.

"Humph," Edith snorted as her hand swatted Nora's arm. "No need to punch me. I'll say what I got to say."

She looked at Chad. "Wasn't sure you were the right man for the job when the council hired you. Big city cop, coming in, changing everything. It's what I told them. After this kidnapping, well, I've changed my mind."

She shot a look of irritation at Nora. "And, it's *all* I've got to say on the matter. When you give those flowers to Ashley, you tell her Henry still hasn't corrected that article. Anybody trying to preserve a batch of peaches his way is going to have a mess on their hands."

"Yes, ma'am, I will." Chad wasn't a coward, but he fled toward his truck.

Chapter Thirty-three

When he pulled into the driveway, Ashley stepped onto the porch. Exiting, he said, "I could use some help here."

As she approached, he picked up the box of roses from the back seat and handed them to her.

Ashley's eyes widened with delight. "Flowers. Oh, my, god, you brought flowers."

His sense of well-being intensified. Whatever lingering doubts Chad had over another relationship vanished.

"What is the delicious aroma?"

He picked up the two sacks of food. "Peggy's lasagna. She said you'd know how to reheat it."

Chad followed her into the kitchen and set the sacks on the table next to the box of roses. Ashley was already rummaging in a cabinet for a vase.

"I know I unpacked one when I moved in," she mumbled to herself. Bent over to look in the bottom cupboard, her leggings pulled tight across her small, tight butt. The thrust of desire he'd felt when he saw her standing on the porch blazed as it raced to his groin. He groaned.

She straightened and turned. "Are you all right?"

"No, I'm not." Chad reached for her, pulling her into his arms. His hands cupped her face as lips danced across her cheeks. His eyes gleamed, and before he crushed down on her lips, he said, "Now, I am."

Several hours later, Ashley lay sprawled across his bare chest, her head tucked under his chin. Satiated, he nuzzled her hair.

"I'm hungry," she murmured.

"Hmm ... give me a few minutes, and I'll be happy to oblige."

Lifting her head, she chuckled at the foolish grin on his face and rolled over. "I *meant* food."

"Uh, oh well, I can do that too. The only problem, I need you to tell me how to reheat the tray."

Her laughter rang out as Ashley stood, her body a statue of alabaster in the moonlight which streamed through the window.

As he gazed at her, he said, "Ah, maybe a few minutes was an exaggeration," and reached for her.

She danced away. "Food. I need food." Ashley picked up the clothes strewn across the floor. "I'll be in the kitchen."

Groaning, Chad gave in.

The oven door was open, and Ashley was sliding the container inside when he walked in. "There's a bottle of wine on the counter, and the beer is in the fridge," she told him.

Filled with the deep red roses, the vase stood in the center of the table. The heady aroma overrode the smell of garlic and Italian spices.

Opening a bottle of wine, he filled the two glasses sitting next to it. Handing one to her, Chad said, "Happy endings ... and new beginnings," and clinked his glass against hers. He pulled out a chair and sat.

She took a sip and leaned against the counter. "What happened today? When I stopped by, Lydia said you were in a meeting with FBI agents."

After listening to the details, with a sigh of relief, she exclaimed, "Oh, god, that is such good news. Even though we found Mandy, I have been so afraid about what happened to the other children. When can I write an article?"

He chuckled. Her reporter's mind never seemed to stop. "As soon as I get the all-clear from the FBI. They're still running down leads, but hopefully, it'll be in the next few days."

"That's one story I'm going to enjoy writing." She hesitated, swirling the deep-red liquid in her glass. "Chad, I'd like to know what happened in Atlanta."

Fear raced through him. Would she think he was crazy? Did he dare risk the future he wanted with this woman? Logic pushed back. It was a matter of trust. What kind of life could be built on secrets?

With his arms resting on the table, he leaned forward and began, starting with Susan's kidnapping. As he talked, he watched her face, waiting for the look of disbelief or rejection. Instead, he saw acceptance tinged with thoughtfulness.

When he finished, he said, "I saw the doll again last night. She led me to the house where you and Mandy were held."

She picked up the bottle and refilled his glass, then hers. Absorbed in his story, he didn't realize he'd drunk the first one.

"An unbelievable experience." She motioned with her glass. "You know what I think?"

Chad held his breath; fear nudged its way back into his mind.

"You've been given an exceptional gift."

An intense wave of relief flashed over him. Ashley didn't think he was nuts.

Unaware of his turmoil, she added, "Dolls have been involved in this from the beginning."

"More than you know." Chad explained about the ads he'd found in the pennysavers. "What caught my attention was the doll in the ad. It turned out, it's the same doll we trotted around to the thrift stores."

Ashley added, "It led us to Walker. If we hadn't stopped by the store in Whitney, we never would have interviewed Wendy."

"The doll's disappeared … for a second time."

"What! I don't understand."

"It was in my office, and it's gone. I can't find it."

"But you said, a second time."

"I contacted a detective with Atlanta PD and asked her to check the evidence locker in the Eberly kidnapping. The doll used by the kidnapper is gone, and no one knows how or when it disappeared. I'm the one that put the doll in an evidence bag and logged it in."

After a quick glance over her shoulder at the timer, she said, "I'm still not making a connection."

"The doll in the ad, the doll from the backyard, and the doll in the Atlanta kidnapping are one and the same. I know someone could argue it's nothing but a fluke; manufacturers make more than one doll. I know different. Though I sure wouldn't want to admit it on a witness stand."

"Umm … too many twists and turns to believe otherwise. Even that eerie fog was part of it. It slowed Coleman's search for us, which let you get there."

"It also slowed down their plans on the boat trip," Chad said, with a grim look on his face as the memory of Walker at the dock flashed into his mind.

"Just the thought of what they planned sends chills down my back." Ashley shuddered. "Something else was strange about the fog, though I'm not sure how to describe it. As I ran, it wasn't as thick in front of me. But when I looked back, all I could see was a wall of heavy black fog."

She set her glass on the counter. "Is it possible *your* doll could have controlled the fog?"

Stunned, Chad leaned back in the chair. "Hell, why not? Considering the fog didn't appear until Mandy disappeared, it's possible. Though, when I stop to think about it, as I was trying to get to you, it wasn't as thick. Cripes, just how many mysteries can there be?"

"Here's another one. Another doll's vanished … Betsy."

"Well, hell. That's why she had a different doll today. I was hoping to get a closer look at it. How do you think she's doing?"

"Surprisingly, she doesn't seem to have any trauma. To be on the safe side, Kathy and Peter are taking her to a psychologist. Henry stopped by and just happened to know one. Seems Dr. Porter was born and raised in Meridian, went off to college, got her doctorate, and now has a practice in Waco."

A wide grin crossed his face. "Oh, the joys of living in a small town. By the way, do you know how Betsy ended up with Mandy? I didn't want to question her about the doll."

"All I know is Mandy found her under the covers and said Betsy came to help. She believes the doll talked to her. I wonder … you're going to think this is crazy. But could Betsy's presence have helped Mandy? Like I said, she doesn't seem to have any adverse effects. It was a lot for me, let alone a four-year-old."

His head tilted back, and he roared with laughter. "Why would I think that's crazy after what I just told you? It's an interesting theory, and one I would say is highly likely. Any idea what happened to it?"

"Mandy told me in the ambulance the doll had to leave; another little girl needed help." She hesitated, then asked, "Did you notice anything strange about the doll when you picked it up?"

"Other than seeing it attached to Coleman's hand. No, why?"

"Uh …I wondered if you saw what happened. You never said anything."

"It was hard to miss when he was screaming like a banshee. Until that happened, I didn't have a shot. And I have two more odd details to add to this mystery. I got a call from the medical examiner, wanting to know about the burns on Coleman's wrist. He mentioned they had a strange pattern, almost hand-like, and did I have any idea how it happened?"

"Oh, my, god, what did you tell him?"

A smirky grin crossed his face. "Said I didn't have a clue."

Tickled by his comment, she laughed. When she caught her breath, she said, "That's a detail that won't be seen in print. I guess what I experienced is another piece to add to the puzzle. When I touched Betsy, the dang thing was warm. As warm as you or I. Just like the way you described the doll in the fog. So, what's the second?"

Chad said, "Betsy was Susan Eberly's doll. When I went back to the apartment to check the dolls left at the scene, her mother brought out two dolls. One was Susan's, the other was left by the kidnapper."

Dumbfounded, Ashley stared at him. "Jeez, I really do feel as if I've stepped into another dimension." She picked up her glass and swallowed what was left.

With a mocking chuckle, he said, "I've had that same feeling many, many times. I didn't remember about Betsy until I saw Mandy hold it up. That's when it finally pinged in my mind; I'd seen it in Atlanta. I don't understand why I didn't recognize either doll."

Setting her empty glass on the table, Ashley mused, "There are so many unanswered questions. I asked Mandy about Walker. She said he was at the gate and didn't go into the backyard. So, how did the doll get onto the chair?"

"Somehow, they have a way appearing and disappearing and don't ask me to even attempt an explanation. That old doll became a key piece of evidence that helped convict Bedford. And in this case, the same doll led us to Mandy. Without it, we'd never have taken a trip to Whitney, or seen Neville's truck at the bait shop." Chad pushed back the chair and rose. He walked toward her and pulled her into his arms.

Ashley laid her head against his chest. "I don't expect we'll ever fully understand. It's one of those things you don't question, just accept."

His grip tightened around her. "Ashley, I know we haven't known each other that long, and we did get off to a rough start."

She lifted her head and shot him a wry look. "As I recall, you *did* threaten to throw me in jail on more than one occasion."

With a twinkle in his eyes, he looked down at her. "Hmm ... well, yes, I did. But you must admit, there was ample provocation. And, don't forget, you accused me of incompetence."

"I did, didn't I?" She chortled.

The tension in his body worked its way into his throat. Would she believe him? "Ah ... what I'm trying to say here is that I sure didn't expect to fall in love, but I did. I don't want this to end here. I want a future with you, and maybe one day, a little girl like Mandy."

Tears of joy welled in her eyes. "Oh, Chad. I feel the same way. I didn't believe I'd ever find someone I loved more than Lance. But I have."

The timer dinged.

Later, when the food had been consumed, and Ashley was washing the wine glasses, Chad grabbed a beer. He walked onto her porch and leaned a hip on the railing. Along with the dolls, the fog had also disappeared. The night air was crisp and cold. Moonlight flowed across the landscape. He swallowed a swig, then set the bottle on the wood rail.

In his mind, the incredible events replayed. Could the soul of a tormented child remain to save other children from torture and death? At first, he'd thought the strange words, "not dead, not dead," meant Susan and Mandy. Now, he knew there was a deeper meaning. It was the unknown little girl who wasn't dead, who lived on through her love of a doll. And, somewhere, in a dimension beyond his comprehension, other dolls had joined in. He wondered how many children they'd saved.

Ashley stood in the doorway and watched as he stared into the distance. She sensed he was reliving memories. Already she felt an uncanny link with this kind and caring man.

At the sound of her footsteps, his head turned toward her. "I can still feel the desperation I felt when I saw the little girl in that room. The doll said, 'The past is written and cannot be altered. It is the future you seek. To find the lost, a gift is given. But, beware. To hear, you must listen.' She was there, but I wasn't listening. And because I didn't, I almost lost you and Mandy."

"Maybe that's why you didn't recognize the doll from the backyard or Betsy. You had to believe. In the end, you did, and that's all that matters," Ashley told him. His arm circled around her as she leaned into him.

He looked out at the shadows, shifting in the light of the moon and mused. "I've often wondered … why me?"

"I can't say with any certainty, but I can hazard a guess. You were chosen because you would listen. And you may not be alone. There could be others."

For a brief instant, Chad saw the doll, standing as if on guard, alone and desolate in a barren room of lost hope. The doll's head slowly turned to look at him, the eye started to glow. Once more, he heard the faint echo of a child's whisper. "Not dead, not dead."

He felt Ashley jerk.

When his head turned to look at her, Ashley's eyes were wide with astonishment. "You heard her?"

"Yes."

Another faint cry, this time filled with joy. "Not Dead! Not Dead!"

Epilogue

Two Weeks Later

*S*quished between a used coffee pot and a stack of books on a shelf in a dusty and cluttered thrift store, a small doll sat, propped against the wall. It was old and had seen better days. A stained and tattered dress covered the soft body from its neck to its ankles. Long pigtails framed a dirty face.

Dressed in bib overalls and mud-spattered boots, a tall, lanky man stomped along the aisle. Startled by a sudden chill, he stopped. As he looked around, he spotted the doll. For a few seconds, his blood-shot eyes studied it before he muttered, "You might be just what I need."

His hand, hardened with heavy calluses, grabbed it. He flipped the tag over and grunted. *Damn thing's only a quarter.* As he carried it by one arm to the checkout counter, a flash of light sparked in the doll's eyes.

In a town, several miles away, a birthday party was underway in a small house on the edge of town. A group of children sat around a table with a large cake and a pile of wrapped gifts.

Chloe leaned forward, huffed and puffed until she had blown out all four candles on the cake. Her mother sang Happy Birthday. The other little girls giggled.

"Which package do you want first?" her mother asked.

Jumping up from her chair, she said, "The one with the pink bow," and pointed to the large box on the end of the table.

Her mother set it on the floor, and Chloe fell to her knees. Strips of paper flew as she ripped and tugged. The other girls clustered around her. When she lifted the lid, they oohed and aahed.

Her hands picked up the doll. "Oh, momma, she's so pretty." Fingers stroked the blond ringlets, then smoothed the wrinkles from the white dress with pink lace woven with pink hearts around the neck, sleeves, and bottom of the skirt.

"She needs a name," her mother told her.

Cuddled in her arms, Chloe stared at the doll for several seconds. Her head cocked to one side as if she was listening. "I know. It's Betsy."

"What a nice name." She wondered where Chloe had heard it. "Do you have a friend at school named Betsy?"

Chloe looked at the doll. "Oh, no. She just told me."

Her daughter's imagination brought a smile to her face.

Outside, a fog slowly built. In the far distance, a child's voice echoed, "Not dead! Not dead!"

Was anyone listening?
Not Yet!

The Story Behind the Fiction

The Doll

The doll that takes Chad on his unearthly journey does exist and is sold by companies for use in Halloween houses. I came across the doll on a website for a short story contest. In 2013, I'd just finished my first book, *JFK Assassination Eyewitness: Rush to Conspiracy.* The book, non-fiction, detailed my research and findings into the death of Lee Bowers Jr., who was a key witness to the assassination. He was inside the railroad tower overlooking Dealey Plaza. In 1966, Bowers was killed in an automobile crash just south of Midlothian, Texas. Conspiracy theorists had always claimed Bowers had been murdered.

After completing the Bowers book, I decided to try my hand at fiction. I found an online contest for short stories. Each month a new picture was posted. The entries had to be about the picture, and the word count was limited to 500.

A short story contest seemed a good way to get started. What caught my attention, though, was the picture. I was intrigued by a broken and tattered doll standing in a decrepit room with skulls on the floor. As it turned out, the picture was an advertisement for the doll.

I wrote a story, *Not Dead, Not Dead,* and submitted it. Much to my surprise, I won third place. That's all it took, and I was hooked.

Even though I've gone on to write other books, I've always wanted to turn that first story into a full-length novel. It is now titled, *Not Dead*. The doll is still center stage, in the plot, and on the cover.

Meridian, Texas

Situated 70 miles southwest of Fort Worth and 130 miles north of Austin, Meridian is *A Hidden Gem at the Top of the Hill Country*. The seat of Bosque County, the town hugs the cliffs and canyons of the scenic Bosque River valley.

The National Championship Barbecue Cookoff, the Award-Winning Red Caboose Winery & Vineyard, Murder at the Flint Creek Manor, historic landmarks and buildings, nearby lakes, the rustic setting, and Main Street storefronts offer a unique experience to visitors.

Since my plot for *Not Dead* included a lake, I visited Lake Whitney and the surrounding towns. When I stopped in Meridian, I knew I had found the perfect fit for the small-town atmosphere and characters I wanted to create. Lake Whitney provided the inspiration for the bait shop and water park.

To learn more about Meridian, please visit the following websites:

https://www.meridiantexas.us/visit

https://texaslakestrail.com/plan-your-adventure/historic-sites-and-cities/cities/meridian

http://www.redcaboosewinery.com

http://flintcreekcountryestate.com/murder-mystery-dinner

I hope you enjoyed *Not Dead*.

For more information, please visit my website.
www.anitadickason.com

Best Wishes

Anita Dickason

❧

About the Author

Anita Dickason is a retired police officer with a total of twenty-seven years of law enforcement experience, twenty-two with the Dallas Police Department. She served as a patrol officer, undercover narcotics officer, advanced accident investigator, tactical officer, and the first female sniper on the Dallas SWAT team.

She uses her extensive law enforcement knowledge and experience to create her plots and characters. Anita continues to reside in Texas.

www.ingramcontent.com/pod-product-compliance
Lightning Source LLC
Chambersburg PA
CBHW060954120726
47910CB00002B/628